Xenos

A Romantic Novel of Travel & Self-Discovery in the Grecian Isles

David A. Ross

Published by Open Books 2012

ISBN: 0615698360
ISBN-13: 978-0615698366

PROLOGUE

FEW CONDITIONS OR CIRCUMSTANCES determine our sense of identity more profoundly than our nationality. Other than our own bodies, our families, or in some cases our religion, national heritage plays a primary role in our definition of who we are and what we believe. Each society imparts cultural messages to its offspring at an early age, and those messages are usually repeated often enough and with such conviction that they begin to ring with unequivocal truth long before an individual develops the capacity for critical analysis. This is true in every culture: indeed, such a set of shared values and behaviors is the very definition of culture itself.

No doubt, this practice of cultural assimilation is an ancient one, and given the universality of the process, it is difficult to imagine an alternative. Yet, for those who develop and embrace a more analytical perspective, such ideals and practices, often unquestioned by the culture-at-large, are sometimes the seeds of dire personal conflict.

CHAPTER 1
MISSING PERSONS

ASIDE FROM THE FACT THAT IT WAS ALL FOOL'S DAY, and also aside from the fact that the pilot's advisement of a turbulent approach into Denver was looking more and more likely, Doran Seeger remained reluctant to trust any conclusions he might presently draw concerning his past *or* his future. At thirty-nine, his personal history seemed all too pedestrian. His best efforts to date came to little more than a series of complex, but ultimately meaningless, hoop-jumping exercises. Regarding authority, he was excessively obedient and far too willing to be led. He'd never formed, nor followed, his own vision. He felt constantly distracted.

Knowing for some time that he desperately needed time to cultivate a new attitude, he had decided to afford himself the luxury of a prolonged sabbatical. He had never owned a house, but he sold his car and stored his belongings. His career was placed on hold—indefinitely. Maybe it was not too late to change things.

As the plane neared the Continental Divide, he felt the first indication of turbulence, and a sudden loss of altitude

2

stole away his breath. Closing his eyes to wait, he heard only the sound of air rushing through jet engines. "I've come through rough air dozens of times," he said to himself. "This is nothing to worry about."

The passenger seated next to him shared his insights regarding the flight plan: "They have to fly high enough to clear the peaks because the air aloft is less stable," he explained "Then they have to bring it down fast. Pilots call landings at Denver a 'controlled crash'!"

Looking out the window, he could no longer see the snow-covered peaks of the Rockies; the clouds were too thick. Without any visual sense of depth upon which to rely, he employed less specific senses in determining relative position. He could feel the continuing descent—at times predictable, at other times surprising. Suddenly the plane lurched violently. With his sense of balance left in question, a loop of unwanted recollections paraded before his mind's eye.

While fulfilling a long-term contract as an engineering consultant for Lockheed-Martin Corporation, he had met Xanthe Travers at the Chitaqua Nightclub in Boulder, Colorado. This tensile girl with black hair, raven's eyes, and a florid complexion had captivated him in a way quite unfamiliar to him. The slight tilt of her head, or the way she leaned forward in expectation, or the humor she expressed over her inability to convey a suspected connection: these attributes, as well as the fact that she was a bona fide member of Mensa and held two graduate degrees (a Ph.D. in Astrophysics from Stanford and a Master of Arts in Philosophy from New College in Sarasota, Florida) had encouraged him to pursue a relationship with a girl whose approach to life seemed at times inverse to his own.

"When an inner situation is not made conscious," Xanthe had told him, "it happens outside, as fate. The world is constantly dividing itself into hemispheres."

Always empirical in nature, he was hardly prepared to

3

see the world in such Jungian terms. Still, even at thirty-one thousand feet, he was able to visualize her face at will, and he could not keep from smiling at the hologram. His memories of Xanthe were bittersweet.

He recalled how she had wanted to have three-mile-long mylar dolphins manufactured to her exact specifications (she seemed to be aware of a company on the west coast that was up to such a project) and then have them shuttled into space. Once in orbit, a hundred miles out, they would be silhouetted each evening against the setting sun. Indeed, she already had made the calculations: the angle of the visual arc; atmospheric distortion; prismatic irregularities—the curvature of the earth itself! On a cloudless evening at twilight, Xanthe maintained, these playful oceanic mammals gone celestial would be visible with the naked eye from any place on Earth. The point, she explained to Doran, was to move people's attention off the planet and out into the cosmos.

Which was where he—or more specifically Lockheed-Martin—was supposed to come in. Whether her idea was a manifestation of her inspiration or her madness, Xanthe was going to need a rocket, not to mention a formula for rocket fuel!

"I want to know," she demanded, "are you willing to commit industrial espionage for the sake of art?"

"No," he answered plainly. Although lately images of dolphins seemed to be popping up in the most unlikely places: dangling from the left earlobe of a waitress; printed on a marker wedged into the latest book he was reading; or staring up at him from a computer printout left anonymously on top of his desk at work. A symbol of freedom, peace, and intelligence, these dolphins were perhaps trying to draw him out of practiced rigidity and into the warm waters of some anomalous experiment.

Xanthe's gaze remained serious and intent. "What about stealing for love?"

"Are you crazy? I could get into a lot of trouble. You

realize we're talking about Defense Department secrets."

"You always avoid taking risks, Doran."

"We're talking about classified documents, Xanthe!"

Solutions to the mysteries of propulsion and guidance passed through his hands every day, and though the government was paying him handsomely to help them become even more proficient than they already were at implementing 'controlled' destruction, he had to admit that he felt a far greater affinity with Xanthe's celestial mammals. Most of the engineers at Lockheed-Martin who were working on Defense Department contracts were even younger than he was. Many had been recruited directly out of the best engineering schools, while others (those with either talent or a record of accomplishment) were plucked out of go-nowhere jobs and seduced with handsome compensation packages. He had traveled a different road. A top-notch mechanical engineer, he had spent time working at Underwriters Laboratories in Pyrotechnics before signing on as a consultant with Lockheed-Martin. So he'd never really been part of the gang, per se. He rationalized time and again that if somebody absolutely had to do this sort of work, then someone that was competent might as well be in charge. Though that fact did not change his ever-evolving perception that the very obsession with designing and manufacturing such hideous weapons was, in the end, wholly self-destructive. In other words, bullshit!

Xanthe Traverse was another story altogether. She was a visionary. Furthermore, he was certain he loved her. So with a nagging sense of reluctance, but also with minimal guilt, he handed over two pounds of computer-generated printouts.

With the necessary specification now in hand, Xanthe sequestered herself in her basement laboratory, firmly intent on the belief that a butterfly twitching its wings in Kansas (or Boulder) could actually set off a monsoon in India; and just as their relationship had begun to blossom,

Xanthe's single-minded dedication to her quasi-scientific space-art project all but stripped the petals from their romantic flower. He, too, lost himself in his work, until one day he received a fax from his only sister, Kenya. The desperate message was scrawled in her own handwriting:

"Dad has taken a turn for the worse.
Meet me in Houston, ASAP."

Immediately, he took a night flight bound for Texas. Kenya met him at the airport in Houston.

"What's this all about?" he asked his sister as they moved up the concourse toward the baggage claim.

"He's disappeared without a trace," Kenya blurted. "He hasn't been seen in three weeks, and his house is in a horrible state. Last week a man from the Health Department phoned me and said that if it wasn't cleaned up by the beginning of next month, the house would be condemned. And apparently, back taxes due!"

"Calm down," he reassured his sister. "We'll find him. And we'll take care of the house, too."

Over the next three weeks he and his sister made every effort to find their father. Help from the police was minimal. Neither friends nor neighbors had seen him. No record of air travel existed, and his car was parked in the garage. He was not registered as a patient at any of the local hospitals. He was not at the morgue.

Having no idea where else to look, he and Kenya spent three weeks reclaiming the house and waiting for Hank Seeger to show up. Several times Doran tried to reach Xanthe by phone, but each time he was unsuccessful. For some reason the answering machine had been turned off. When Hank Seeger did not turn up after twenty-three days, Kenya volunteered to remain in Texas to wait. Doran returned to Boulder, concerned for the well being of his father and wondering why he'd been unable to reach Xanthe by phone.

Back in Colorado, he found their rented house now abandoned. Apparently, Xanthe had moved out, laboratory and all. In desperation he questioned her friends, but nobody seemed willing to give out information as to her whereabouts. Missing persons were becoming a recurrent theme in his life.

Ten days later, Hank Seeger turned up, brought by paramedics to a hospital emergency room in Houston.

"We received a call from one of the homeless shelters," the administrator explained to Kenya.

"Can I see him?" she asked.

"The doctors are with him now; perhaps it's best to wait" she was told.

Feeling utterly baffled, she called Doran immediately. "He's turned up," she told him. "I'm at the hospital now."

"How bad is it?" he asked.

"I haven't seen him yet, but I think it's bad."

Now staying at the house of a fellow Lockheed-Martin employee, Doran packed his bags again and took the first flight back to Texas.

Entering the white environment of the hospital room, he was shocked by the sight of his father in such a devastated condition. With his body invaded by tubes, and his vital signs displayed on overhead monitors, Hank Seeger seemed only to want to let go. But apparently he could not let go. Coming to from each lapse of consciousness, he seemed frustrated to re-emerge within a world he was bound to exit. Until he saw his son's face not six inches from his own.

"Where have you been, Dad? Kenya and I have looked everywhere."

The dying man seemed to want to say something. What was it?

"I think he's delirious," said Kenya.

Hank Seeger motioned for his son to come closer, and when Doran's ear was only and inch or two away from his lips, he uttered the words: "Move quickly, son, before it's too late."

At the cemetery, he and Kenya approached their father's casket and each laid a rose at its head as a final acknowledgment of feeling—and of the man's influence. Together, they spent a number of days attending to thier father's affairs, and then they drove together from Texas to Kenya's house in Las Vegas.

"I don't understand why you've decided to quit *another* job and leave Colorado," she said as they passed through Tucson. "Your life seems to have no permanence."

"Who has permanence these days?" he asked. "Nobody of our generation."

"You just can't bum around indefinitely, Doran," she said.

"Why not?"

"It's just not responsible, that's why not!"

"Screw that!" he said. "Besides, there are things you don't understand."

"What things?"

"A lot of things. For one, I can't work for the government anymore."

"Why not? I thought you were making good money."

"Yeah, I make great money," he huffed.

"Then what's the problem?"

"You just don't realize… Nobody outside the loop does."

"Realize what?"

"The really sinister shit that goes on. How the government hides the real application of the work by diversifying projects. Most of the time it's not recognizable for what it is. If it were, nobody with a conscience would ever sign on."

"That's just your paranoia, Doran," she countered.

"A mercenary is a mercenary," he said in self-castigation. "Working for the government, I can attest to the notion that your worst fears are all true."

"So your answer is to run away?"

8

"Look, we've lost Dad. I don't know where Xanthe's gone. I can't sleep nights because of my job. Besides, I've compromised my security clearance."

"What?"

"Don't worry. Nobody knows," he said.

"What have you done, Doran?"

"I guess you could say that I *shared* certain information."

"With whom"

"Nobody important."

"Not with the Russians? Or the Chinese?"

"Nobody like that."

"Who then?"

"The less you know, the better, Kenya."

"So, the truth is not that you *want* to go away; the truth is that you *must* go away."

"It's not that serious, believe me."

"It certainly sounds serious," she said. "It sounds like espionage."

"It's not like that," he said.

"What am I suppose to say if somebody from the Government comes around asking where you are?"

Doran shrugged. "Tell them you don't know where I went. It won't be a lie."

"That's just great," said Kenya, now truly worried not only about her brother but about her own standing as well. "I don't want to be involved in whatever it is you're involved in," she said.

"Don't worry," he reiterated. "Nobody's going to come around asking questions. And if they do... Like I said, just tell them you don't know where I went."

"I really don't understand you, Doran. Time and again you involve yourself in sensitive work for the Government, but the truth is that you've never been a team player. You've never been able to play by the rules. Whatever it is you've done, I hope you're ready for the consequences."

9

"There aren't going to be any consequences," he said. "At least not the kind you imagine. I've saved some money. I just want to get away and explore other possibilities."

"What sort of possibilities?"

"Shit! I don't know. Other possibilities."

"You're not going to Russia, are you?"

"No. I'm just going on a little sabbatical to Europe. People do it all the time. What's the big deal?"

"Most people who leave the country haven't just compromised their security clearance. That's the big deal, Doran!"

He shook his head. "If you only knew just how trivial, how utterly insignificant what we're talking about really is…"

"I just hope for your sake that you've got this under control," Kenya said.

Staying at Kenya's house in Las Vegas, he prepared to leave for Europe. He read guidebooks and consolidated his affairs in Colorado. He bought an expensive leather backpack and a good pair of walking shoes. He arranged a flight through a travel agent.

Now on approach to Denver, he saw only white oblivion as he looked out the window of the plane. Crosswinds buffeted the aircraft from side to side as it began its descent. The cabin lights flickered, and he could see ice on the wings. Three hundred feet off the runway there was still no sight of solid ground. Certainly the pilot was maneuvering the plane by his instruments; he was flying by the seat of his pants.

At last the plane touched down, and the scenery outside the window took off in fast motion. The gale was driving the snow down horizontally, and there were massive drifts everywhere he looked. Once the aircraft reached the gate, he gathered his bag from the overhead compartment, took a place in the crowded aisle, and waited for the doors to open. At the end of the telescopic causeway an airline agent waited to direct off-loading passengers to their connecting flights. He handed over his ticket.

"I'm sorry, Mr. Seeger," said the agent in a voice that was at once apologetic but not personally responsible, "your flight to Boston is delayed."

"How long?" he asked.

"I'm afraid nobody knows," she said. "The storm caught us off-guard, and traffic is backed up in both directions."

He explained further: "I'm supposed to fly out of Boston to Amsterdam at 6:45 tonight. Any chance?"

"I have no information about international flights," she told him. "You'll have to see an agent in the main terminal." She pointed the way.

The agent at the Northwest Airlines podium told him that due to the storm there was no chance he would reach Boston in time to make his connection. He was re-booked on a KLM flight leaving Logan Airport for Amsterdam at one-forty in the morning. This unfortunate change of itinerary added seven hours to his travel time, but apparently there was no alternative.

Standing before a wall-length mirror inside the men's room, he could see that he looked profoundly tired. Still, no wrinkle yet furrowed his forehead, cheeks or neck. Only recently had tiny crow's feet appeared on the soft skin near his temples, punctuating his somewhat sad, blue-gray eyes. His nose was unassuming, and his mouth was slightly understated. His cheeks remained in a state of perpetual blush, lending him the pageant of false innocence. His brows were thick, and his hair was still boyishly blond. All in all, he thought, his face resembled the rather sentimental image of a Valentine's Day heart.

Coming out of the restroom, he walked the length of the concourse, mostly killing time. He bought a single rose, drank an Irish coffee, and talked to a wine importer who was on his way to Chile. He looked over a copy of *Sports*

Illustrated, and then studied the stock quotations in the financial page of the *Wall Street Journal*. He reread the *Berlitz Pocket Guide To Amsterdam* and tried to imagine himself walking the picturesque streets of the Dutch city. The waiting went on and on.

Like shattered glass, his attention spread out in every direction. His inability to focus his thoughts concerned him, even scared him. Unmanageable stress, detachment from nature, addictions, ruptures, nightmares, compartmentalized living: he suspected all these features of the modern world were responsible for the onset and perpetuation of his fussy attention span. All these and more...

It was nearly eleven o'clock when his second flight landed in fog at Logan Airport in Boston. Coming off the plane, he found the inside of the international terminal gloomy and confining this late at night. He felt famished, but the only concession stand open sold only nuts and dried fruits. He walked round and round the terminal to stretch his legs, but the arduous day of travel began to take its toll. Dark, cyanotic crescents appeared underneath his usually placid eyes, and finally he collapsed onto an uncomfortable chair near the gate from which his next flight was to depart in two hours.

Feeling ruined, and barely still functioning, he finally boarded the KLM jet just after one o'clock a.m. Still, an eight-hour flight across six time zones awaited him.

The pilot took off over black water and dimmed the cabin lights once the plane was airborne and headed up the coast of Nova Scotia. The usual sense of cheer shown at embarkation was decidedly missing due to the lateness of the hour. Once away from the eastern seaboard the skies cleared, making it possible to see the light of the full moon reflected off the icy waters below. The view was surreal and hypnotic. Usually unable to sleep on airplanes, he dozed off from sheer exhaustion.

After only three hours of in-flight darkness, the six

hundred-mile-per-hour blind rush of oblivion gave way to the emerging light of the European day, now visible on the eastern horizon. Hot towels came round, and the flight attendants served coffee, croissants, and cheese. Over the intercom the navigator said good-morning in Dutch and informed everyone that they would be on the ground in Amsterdam by noon.

He set his watch to European time. Yet the time adjustment seemed to make little sense. Everything, it seemed, was out of kilter. All the angles that defined the various aspects of his life now seemed misaligned. He desperately needed to take a breather, to reassess everything he'd once thought to be right and true. Just how to stop the world long enough to regain his balance: that was his challenge.

CHAPTER 2
CAFÉ OUDE HAVEN

AT FIVE-THIRTY ON FRIDAY EVENING, cars and bikes and pedestrians crowded the streets of Rotterdam as its citizens made their way home after work or shopping. In this city of *Stijl* architecture and shipping magnates, the Delftshaven Quarter was a welcome return to the charms of old-time Holland. There, eighteenth and nineteenth century buildings had been spared during the Nazi bombardment of nineteen-forty, and the Quarter remained more pleasing to the eye than the city's newer, cubist divisions. Even the mentality of the people seemed to shift away from characteristic Dutch efficiency toward a more serene outlook.

Alarice Van Zyl did not stop to window shop this evening, nor buy flowers from the street vendors. She was late for her regular Friday evening rendezvous at Café Oude Haven, where she was to meet her mother for coffee and cake.

At twenty-nine, Alarice had lately begun to feel ancient and socially ineffective. She knew she was spending far too much time working. Her once healthy social life had all but ceased. When she met old friends from her days at the *gymnasium*, by chance on the street near her home in the *cubiswoning* at the Blaak, or in the Delftshaven, they seemed to look at her curiously, as if they had once known her but now barely recognized her. In more reflective moods she found herself wondering where the time had gone since her graduation from the university at Leiden.

Arriving at the café near the old harbor, she noticed that only one table remained unoccupied in the outdoor seating area. Since this was one of the season's first warm days, she claimed the table and sat down to wait for her mother.

Actually, she was happy to have a few private moments. Lately it seemed as though she had far too little time for reflection. With each year she spent working at her father's import/export business, the demands on her time grew exponentially. Methodically reassessing the ever-so-convenient lifestyle that she'd once slipped on like an old friendly sweater, she was coming to understand that her professional place in her father's business had been pre-determined for her from an early age, without her knowledge or consent. Perhaps she had been slow to equate this subtly enforced structure with a growing sense of dissatisfaction, and her realization tended to evoke some disdain—at least as far as she was openly capable of negativity, recrimination, and bitterness. Her inclination was to repel by degrees, as outright rebellion was not her nature. Also, she felt concern and sympathy for her younger sister, Gisela, as she envisioned the same fate awaiting her.

Within minutes her mother came riding up on her heavy-framed, black bicycle with its fat tires and coaster brakes. It was the same venerable bike on which she had transported herself around Rotterdam for thirty-five years. She parked and locked the bike at the rack near the café's entrance.

To Alarice, her mother's habits and characteristics were

decidedly familiar, though lately she had become aware of an aspect that was new and different. Something undeniable, yet foreign—encroaching, not wholly anticipated. Maude's hair was nearly gray now, and even though she tried to keep herself fit, she now stood with a little stoop in her shoulders. This was the result of too many years bent over her pre-pubescent dental patients. Maude's walk was noticeably heavier now, and she often sighed tired, breathy sighs when she finally sat down after a long day at her practice.

"Mama, I'm over here!" Alarice waved.

Wearing her raincoat over a dark gray dress and cardigan sweater, and carrying her favorite umbrella with the extra large canopy, Maude Van Zyl made her way between the crowded café tables and the planters filled with blooming tulips. Reaching the table where the lovelier, if less evocative, of her two daughters sat, she laid down her belongings one by one and kissed Alarice on each cheek. "Hello, my love," she said. "Sorry I'm late."

"Don't worry. I arrived only a moment ago." Alarice brushed her light brown bangs away from her eyes, revealing more of her softly rounded, clear face.

Maude Van Zyl always found herself pleased by her elder daughter's appearance. Alarice had beautiful skin, and her balanced features flowed together with a grace of which Alarice, herself, was not yet aware. Her new haircut—short above the ears and a little wild and thick on top and at the back of her neck and temples—looked especially smart on her. Light always seemed to fall upon her at just the right curve or prominence, accenting some unexpected aspect of her appearance. The highlights on her cheeks, the dimple at the cleft of her chin, her delicate ears: these features conveyed much about the sentimental side of her personality. Then there were other, more submerged characteristics: a tentative smile that often hid behind a more pensive expression; and fathomless blue eyes that suggested a vibrant being, so alive yet still

16

uncertain, and trapped within an untenable situation not of her making.

"I didn't want you to have to wait alone," said Maude.

"It's nothing," Alarice shrugged.

"Is Papa still at the office?"

"Of course."

"I suppose he won't be home until late again tonight. So there's no need for us to hurry, is there? Unless you're going out later..."

"I have nothing planned," she said. The look on her face was one of boredom and distraction.

Seeing her daughter's discomfiture, Maude came without hesitation to her rescue. "What's the matter?" she asked sympathetically.

"It's nothing, really" was Alarice's unspecific answer. Not that she was trying to be purposely evasive, but she was simply not altogether in touch with the forces that determined her present mood. "Another hard day at work. That's all."

"Well, you're certainly not alone in feeling the monotony of your labor," said Maude. "My days are becoming more tedious all the time. I wonder how much longer I'll have the stamina to continue my practice."

"I may be feeling a bit lonely, too," Alarice confided to her mother. "I don't know why, but I always envisioned myself married at this age. Lately, I've begun to consider the prospect that there is no singular, profound relationship in store for me. At least it hasn't come along yet."

Maude patted her daughter's hand as the waiter came to take their order. As they had come to this particular café many times before, they had no difficulty choosing their favorite desserts.

The six o'clock bells rang out from the bell tower at the Catholic cathedral, and the glorious daylight was fading all too soon. Once clear images went fuzzy and out of focus in the deepening shadows near the canal boats and shop doorways. Out of the corner of her eye Alarice watched a rag-tag fellow with a bit of stage make-up on his face make his way from table to table selling flowers.

"Mama, what would you do if you retired?" she asked, never believing for a minute that Maude was serious about giving up her dental practice.

"Maybe I would go on holiday in the Alps," she said. "Or perhaps see Spain or Italy."

She gave her mother a subtle, yet familiar look—a distinguishable family expression somewhere between tolerated exasperation and realization. "You know Papa would never go."

Just then the waiter brought their coffee and desserts. Maude had her usual torte with kiwis, strawberries, bananas and whipped cream, but since childhood Alarice had been crazy for double chocolate.

"That's the sad truth," said Maude referring to her husband's less than adventurous nature. "But he tells me you have been talking about a holiday for the entire summer. Now what's this? Is it true?"

"I'm feeling bored, Mama," she said as she took a big bite of her chocolate torte. "I work too much. I never seem to have fun anymore. For me, there's little challenge in exporting. I don't mean to be disrespectful, and you know I love both you and Papa dearly, but I'm thinking that perhaps my life is too safe. I'm afraid I will stop growing and become a dull person."

Maude looked at her daughter thoughtfully. "So where do you want to go?" she asked.

"I thought I might spend the summer in Greece," she answered.

"I've not been there myself," said Maude without judgment.

"When I was at Leiden, so many of the students would go traveling—to Paris and Madrid and Rome and Stockholm. But I never went along. I stayed behind and studied business. I can speak French and German and

English fluently. But I talk only with businessmen. Of course business is important, but I'm still young. I'm afraid I'm missing too much!"

"Sounds to me as if you've already planned your holiday."

"Well," she said, "I thought I might start by taking the train through Germany or France. Maybe stop in Munich or Nice. After a couple of days I could continue through Switzerland or Italy. At the Port of Brindisi there is a ferryboat to Corfu. I might stay there all summer long, tanning myself on the beach and swimming in the sea. Or perhaps I'd set out to see Athens and the Oracle at Delphi. Or some of the other Greek islands—Zakinthos or Mykonos or Crete... A few weeks ago I bought a travel book. It's not difficult; people do it all the time. Maybe just once in my life I might do something to shake myself out of this funk. Something extraordinary, really different!"

"You know that Papa does not want you to go," said Maude.

Alarice laughed smugly. "Of course he doesn't want me to go..." She took a sip of her coffee and stared directly into her mother's eyes. It was a habitual expression she had developed and employed since childhood to let Maude know when she was altogether serious about something. "What do you think, Mama?"

"Actually, I think it's a wonderful idea," said Maude.

Alarice smiled. The last glint of sunlight colored her cheeks, and her full lips declared a charming bashfulness that sometimes compelled others to favor her point of view. Certainly she did not need the approval of either parent to go on holiday, but she *was* glad to have her mother's understanding concerning this less than specific need she felt.

"I'm only wondering," said Maude, "whether you might consider taking your sister along with you?"

"Gisela?" Alarice was truly surprised. "She's only nineteen. And she's wild!"

Smiling, Maude nodded.

"I must admit, Mama, that Gisela was not part of my original vision. And I'm not certain I could control her."

Over the rim of her coffee cup Maude declared, "I don't expect you to control her. Gisela is a little wild, but so was I at her age."

Alarice smiled her naughty smile. What could she say?

"I'm sure it's hard for you to imagine it," Maude said.

"Papa will never allow Gisela to go," Alarice said.

"I can take care of Frederick," said Maude.

"I feel as though we're plotting some grand betrayal."

"Hardly. You're telling me you need some time to think about your life, to make a new friend, or find a new direction. Gisela needs a sense of direction, too. A long holiday might be just the right medicine for both of you. Besides, you are ten years apart in age. You've never been close. To me, that seems a tragedy. But perhaps it's an opportunity as well. I've given this serious thought. But that must be obvious."

"I'll consider it, Mama. I promise."

Alarice ordered each of them another coffee as the lights in the commercial center began to glow yellow and white, and conversations grew more intimate.

"Just remember," Maude continued, "distant shores can be seductive, but when all is said and done, heart and soul define one's temperament."

Indeed, Greece seemed seductive, if far away. But this plan of hers, so recently contrived from feelings of emptiness and detachment, was taking on an unexpected, albeit capricious, new dimension. Of course she had made plans in the past, but she was often ineffective when it came to arranging all the variables in the most propitious way. Balanced at this curious fulcrum, Alarice was eager to learn which way the pendulum might swing.

CHAPTER 3
THE GRAY LIGHT OF A NEW DAWN

THE GRAY LIGHT OF A NEW DAWN was just beginning at Puthena Village, but the dreams of Aphrodite Thromos were not yet complete. In her bed she lay underneath her heavy quilt, still and flat on her back. Her mouth was wide open and her eyes darted back and forth beneath closed lids. Though her heart was now weak, the ageless child within remained ready to frolic through fields of heather. Sadly, Hellenic meadows and boundless Ionian horizons were no longer reachable for her now frail and decrepit body.

These dreams were the remembrances of a lifetime spent on the Island of Corfu, or as the Greeks called it, Kerkyra. Such visions were but wicked contrivances when cast in the chromium light of the present tense. Aphrodite was too old to wish for miracles; she was cheating death every day through no effort of her own. But in sleep, the ravages of time held no sinister power over her declining influence. It was almost as if the unremitting years had actually been dreams, and the reality was that she was still a young girl in her father's simple house.

Yet even as she lay enfolded by charitable delusions, an alarm sounded inside her head. The moment was unstable, turbulent, filled with impending catastrophe. Somebody was trying to beat down the door to her private convictions and treasured recollections. Until now, that portal had always remained blocked, a world within, wholly unknowable.

"Open up! Let me in!" cried the voice.

The intruder continued to yell and clap his fist upon her locked door, and even in fitful sleep she realized the untimely nature of this summons.

"Go away!" she called.

Her life had been one of well-defined connections. Church, family, and friends were the foundation upon which Greek traditions rested. These customs offered comfort, safety, and a sense of familiarity. Well into her ninth decade, she had little capacity to absorb the changes taking place in Greek culture, and even less influence to hold them back.

Recalling her happy life as a girl in Puthena Village—long before money had come pouring into the economy from Northern Europe—the progression of seasons had determined the rhythms of their lives. In summertime, gleeful games of hide-and-seek took place between the houses, shops, and cafés in Puthena Village. In autumn, when it was time to slaughter the largest of their pigs, her father cut out the bladder, dried it in the warm September sunshine, scored it, and then sewed it into a durable though imperfect ball for the children's play. When the rains came in winter, her older brothers went off to school in Corfu Town, but the girls stayed home to help with chores.

As an adolescent, Aphrodite cultivated the charms in keeping with her namesake. So demurely she flirted with village boys, but when the time came for her to marry, it was her father who chose her husband, Constantine Thromos, a cosmopolitan man from Corfu Town. He was twelve years older than she, and on the day of their wedding they still had not so much as held hands. But her dowry was made, and she graciously accepted the union which tradition ordained.

In the beginning their life together was a happy one, as they absorbed themselves in the tasks of homemaking. Eighteen months after their marriage their first child, Kostas, was born. Tassoula followed shortly, and then came Modestos. But soon after the birth of their third child the romance unaccountably went out of their relationship. Absorbed in business, Constantine spent many hours away from home, and as the weight of childbearing reformed his wife's figure in mid-life, he'd made her sleep in a separate room. Even into old age she carried anger and spite for his cruel omission, and later his absence.

Still another great issue remained without closure in her life. She had never been able to free herself from the torment of her firstborn son's death. Still a boy, Kostas had been a hero during the resistance effort against the Axis Powers, but the Nazis had learned of his undercover activities and killed him.

Her grief was silent and suffocating. It burrowed into her intestine like a worm for a long stay. Conversely, Constantine wept for a solid month, and then he cried no more. Over time he grew dour and became withdrawn. Finally, he was unable to maintain the life they had made together in Puthena Village, and in absolute despair he abandoned not only his family, but his homeland as well, and she was left to raise her thirteen-year-old daughter Tassoula, and her ten-year-old son Modestos, alone.

At first money and promises arrived from Italy, and then all communication from her expatriate husband abruptly ceased. She never knew what had become of him. Where he'd gone, if he were alive or dead; and she had spent half her eighty-seven years wearing the widow's black dress and veil.

Now, as the light of day broke with candor upon Puthena Village, her eyes flew open. The images of her dream glowed like morning embers, though her body shivered at the remembrance of the intrusive voice at her door. She sniffed at the musty air that had gathered slowly in her rooms during forty years of mourning. Her evening candle had *not* gone out; it burned still in front of her altar, seven saintly icons facing east. In the weak light of her salon, she could barely distinguish the photographs of her family, but even as the meddlesome knocking grew more urgent, she recalled the day Kostas had left home for the war.

"Open the door now! Let me in!" Again the terrible summons.

Struggling to stand on her arthritic feet, she pulled on her shawl over rumpled, colorless bedclothes and dutifully placed her sheer black veil on top of her thin, disheveled, gray hair, then found her cane and moved stiffly and slowly toward the door. Her hips always ached now, and she wanted to curse her feebleness, but not in front of Jesus.

Reaching the threshold of her sanctuary, she walked onto her balcony. The intense light blinded her for a moment. Searching door to door for the mischief-maker, she saw only the familiar sights of the *dhomatia's* patio garden: the stairway; the vines and flowers; the garden wall. As her weakened eyes reluctantly adjusted to the light of a new day, she caught a fleeting glimpse of the presumptuous visitor retreating down the alleyway that led toward the church. His shadow grew shorter and shorter as it moved away on the cobblestones.

Probably a drunk or a derelict, lost and floundering out of control, she thought. Since he's headed in the direction of the church, let the priest deal with him. Redemption is Father Dimitri's mysterious domain.

She went back inside her apartment to wash her face. Her *toilette* was a once-a-day affair at most. With the same

24

comb and silver-handled brush she had been using for twenty-five years, she arranged her hair as best she could, though nowadays her efforts usually fell flat, along with the many loose strands she could not keep pinned up. No use hovering over a ruin, she thought. Besides, her mirror had clouded. Or was it her vision that was dark?

In her kitchen, she lit a propane burner with one practiced movement and made herself strong black coffee. She sweetened the thick brew with a generous portion of sugar then cut a slice of bread from the loaf on her board. She dipped the entire piece in olive oil but ate only half. Most of her life she'd eaten eggs for breakfast, but lately her appetite had waned.

"Hearty food is for younger people," she declared. "Those with purpose and a strong will!" She decided to cook *stifada* for her son Modestos, who would soon be coming to visit her.

LADIES AND GENTLEMEN, PATRIOTS AND HONORED VISITORS," the ship's loudspeaker crackled, "we will be arriving shortly at the port of Kerkyra. All passengers traveling to Kerkyra: please prepare to disembark!"

Standing on the deck of the *Poseidon*, Modestos Thromos felt profoundly absorbed in the overtones of the Ionian twilight. He surveyed the familiar landmarks of his homeland as the ship made its way slowly into Corfu Harbor, and for a single moment he had to hold back a copious rush of emotion.

Normally, springtime did not come to Greece until the beginning of May, but this year the sciroccos were blowing early, and the balmy African air mantled not only the islands of the Aegean and the villages of the Peloponnese, but Ionian shores as well. Tonight not a single cloud gathered over the vast Adriatic. As the sun dipped below the aquatic horizon, the sky was awash with a characteristic golden tincture. Such an Apollonian value surely conveyed power and drama; yet it also revealed a softness of hue that was irrepressible and beguiling. This inspired light was capable of moving strident men of the sea almost to tears.

With one hand on the deck railing, and the breeze blowing through his fine hair, Modestos stood with his robust chest held out. He had the thick, convergent eyebrows of a native Greek, and his fine, aquiline nose—the same nose seen time and again on the classical statuary that depicted the most favored Olympians—lent his face an air of confidence and self-assurance. The light accented the features of his softly contoured, earnest face, and the lines and furrows, which for most men were characteristic of endured tragedy, disappointment, hardship or emptiness, were noticeably absent from his smooth, olive-colored skin. At fifty, he had weathered the vicissitudes of his life with patience and grace.

He put his hand to his lips, as if to seal off some errant expression, then ran his well-formed, nimble fingers through thinning hair. He stared longingly at the coastline with warm, sienna-colored eyes. The lights of Corfu Town were visible now; and in the distance he could make out the twin fortresses that had welcomed sailors to this port for more than three centuries. He felt relieved to be returning to Kerkyra. But perhaps a weeklong stay in foul and frantic Athens, with its pollution and its congestion, its high prices and constant noise, was enough to make any Corfiot long for home. Besides, he was eager to see his wife, Sophia.

The mental image of Sophia's face never failed to bring a smile to his lips. Her eyes conveyed warmth and spirit, as well as a spurious sense of humor. He knew he was a fortunate man.

Somewhat reluctantly, he had made the journey to Athens to meet with an official in the Greek army. General Stratiotis had vicariously learned of his specialized skills with radar and thought it necessary that they confer at once. After twenty-four years of civilian employment, he was understandably surprised, though the meeting was certainly preliminary.

Prior to the trip, Sophia had speculated endlessly about the purpose of this summons. Certainly the politics of their country and its surrounding regions were very complex. But when had that not been true? Recent Greek history was overflowing with various intrigues and insurrections—from the 1821 War of Independence to the Nazi occupation; from the military junta in the seventies to Papandreou. Sophia was skeptical of benefits from the start. "Military men are not likely to offer gains without sacrifice," she warned him. "You are fifty years old, a family man. You are no soldier. Not anymore. What could they possibly want from you now?"

Aboard ship, he could not help replaying in his mind some of the defining moments of the recently completed trip to Athens.

It was a bright morning in the city as he headed for Omonia Square. Decidedly unaccustomed to such commotion, he felt invigorated by the intensity of the city. Athens was bursting at the seams, yet its personality remained decidedly friendly. Locating the building where the meeting was to take place, an aid escorted him into General Stratiotis's office.

The general was a fit man with a square face, big ears, and short-cropped black hair. Everything about him seemed to suggest economy. Extending greetings, he offered Modestos a seat and took a place behind his desk.

"I trust you had good sailing, Thromos," Stratiotis said.

"*Poli kala!*" he said. Outside the third floor window he could see the Parthenon on top of Acropolis Hill.

"The city has changed a great deal since the war," the general surmised. "Not for the better, I'm afraid," he added. "The air is lousy and traffic is impossible."

"Corfu has changed as well," he said. "Though it is still far removed from Athens."

There was a far-away look in the general's eyes.

27

"Kerkyra is a beautiful island," he acknowledged. "A beautiful island indeed!"

"I have lived on Corfu all my life," he told the general.

Stratiotis lit a cigarette, took a single puff, and then extinguished it in an ashtray. "After all these years away from military service, you must be wondering why I've asked you to come here, Thromos," he said.

Modestos raised one eyebrow. "I *am* curious, General Stratiotis."

"Your skills are unique, Thromos," said the general. "We need a man with your ability at Cyprus."

Cyprus? He's never expected Cyprus to be the focus of the meeting.

The general continued: "This job—this *position*—comes with an honorary rank of captain, Thromos. And there is money, too!"

"I assumed you wanted me in Macedonia. I did not expect Cyprus, General."

Stratiotis nodded thoughtfully. "Macedonia is another problem altogether," he said. He cleared his throat as if he meant to say something more, but in recompense he remained silent.

Modestos watched the general's expression for any clue that might reveal hidden difficulties of this assignment, but the clever tactician was giving away nothing. Modestos's posture stiffened as he spoke. "Naturally, I want to perform my duty to my country," he said. "But I am no longer young. I am fifty years old. Life is not as simple as it was when I was twenty." Stratiotis managed a knowing smile as Modestos constructed his case for doubt. "I have a family on Kerkyra," he continued. "My son is about to enter the university at Bari, Italy. My mother is eighty-seven years old!" Concerning Aphrodite, his smile was made as much of irony as it was of love. "And I have an auxiliary business, too—a five room *dhomatia* at Puthena Village—as well as a rental apartment at Glyfada Beach. Do not misunderstand me, General; I'm not necessarily turning down your offer."

Trying to read his recruit, Stratiotis stared without embarrassment at Modestos. "Of course this assignment is *not* mandatory," he said. "And I understand such decisions are never easy, Modestos."

"If I decide to accept, I will need time to prepare," he postured.

"The work does not begin until October," said Stratiotis.

Modestos was filled with consternation as he prepared to leave.

"There is just one more thing," said Stratiotis as he lit another cigarette. Modestos turned to face him. "How is your game of darts?" the general asked him.

"Darts?"

"Yes. It seems an Austrian sergeant in the UN Peacekeeping Force, along with a Turk named Mustafa Bolkaner, has arranged for forty Turkish Cypriots to cross the *Green Line* for a friendly competition with an equal number of Greek challengers at the Nicosia Hilton."

Modestos remembered smiling as he'd left Stratiotis's office.

At journey's end, the ship's crew now hurried about the business of preparing for the docking. On deck, the practiced hands of career sailors tied off ropes, while the purser closed his office. Repeatedly the ship's horn sounded a rheumatic announcement of arrival.

Impatient to be off the ship and about their business at Corfu, passengers gathered their luggage and began moving toward the stairways. Not yet inclined to go below, Modestos perused the attractive harbor.

At last the captain turned the *Poseidon* one hundred eighty degrees in the harbor and backed into the designated berth. Once the anchor was cast, the door to the hold was lowered with an almost deafening, steel-on-steel cacophony, and the ship's disembarking passengers poured onto the pier like an Ionian wave washing ashore.

NEARLY THE LAST PASSENGER TO DISEMBARK, Modestos searched the crowd on the pier for his wife. Not finding her at first, he crossed Zavitsianou Street. Then he heard her calling to him. Wearing a pink dress and a colorful scarf on her head, Sophia waved to him from the other side of the busy portside boulevard. Reunited after an uncharacteristic separation, they kissed cheek to cheek. He tossed his case into the trunk of the car then slid behind the wheel. Through a bevy of dust-raising, diesel-spewing trucks and a hornet's nest of gear-grinding motorcycles and scooters, he inched his way up Veilissariou Street. Repeatedly he sounded the horn at loose dogs that ran at will in front of his car.

While the traffic and commotion of Corfu Town always tested one's patience, it was nothing in comparison with the density he had confronted in Athens. Finally reaching one of the main thoroughfares leading away from the port, he headed west on the National Highway.

Away from the superfluity of Corfu Town, he savored the fecund scent of the olive groves and the tall grasses, the aroma of the flowering Judas trees, the lavender, gorse, thyme and heather. These were like an anodyne to his body and spirit. The trees that covered the mountains cast shadows in the fading light, and now and then he caught a fleeting glimpse of the sea at the end of a long vista.

Sophia was chirping like a bird that had found her long-lost mate: "Was the sea rough? How was it in Athens? Did you eat well? What did the general say?"

"So many questions," he said. "Tell me, how is Yanni?"

The rush of emotion Sophia felt when she thought of their only son always seemed to take her by surprise. "He's driving me crazy, of course," she said.

"What new catastrophe?" he asked.

"Nothing since you left," Sophia reassured him. "I told him we would be staying overnight at Glyfada. I begged him to stay out of trouble."

"Small chance of that, eh?" he said.

"Never mind Yanni right now," said Sophia. "You must be hungry after twelve hours aboard ship. After you shower and change, let's walk down the beach to Taverna Loyiza Hara-Theou. It's Friday, and that means roast lamb."

Over Corfu's winding, one-lane mountain roads, beneath the canopy of trees, he drove. Bouzouki music from the car radio whirled round his head like an insistent swarm of bees. He barely took notice of the simple homes of those still living the old way. Made of stone and various natural materials, these one-room houses usually had neither running water nor electricity. Just as often, they had only a dirt floor hardened by the feet of two or three generations. Perhaps a mule or some goats or sheep—always a flock of laying hens and a cock—might languor near a crudely constructed shelter on an adjacent hillside.

In contrast, his apartment at Glyfada Beach was part of a small, upscale complex that extended gracefully up the mountainside from the beach itself. Like other enterprising Greeks who wished to avoid pay-offs and a mountain of red tape, he had paid hard cash in German marks to acquire the property. Intended for the Scandinavian, German, and Italian tourists who crowded Corfu's beaches in summer, each landlord painted his apartment bright yellow or creamy white and bedecked it with Mediterranean foliage, which appealled to the tastes of the more affluent northerners.

Of course the tourists came only when the weather was good and the sea was warm enough for swimming, so during late autumn and early spring he and Sophia were free to luxuriate at Glyfada in a style normally beyond their everyday means. Seldom, in fact, did the Greeks who owned these apartments live at anywhere near the standard that such dwellings seemed to suggest. Their lives were consistently more humble, as they depended upon the infusion of stronger currencies to carry them through the entire year.

Sophia wanted the apartment to look inviting for their guests: that was good for business. But she also loved to come here with Modestos and Yanni. Over a simple meal on the apartment's bougainvillea-clad terrace, they laughed and sang along with the songs being played on the radio. They looked down on Glyfada Beach and across the cove as the setting sun spread color over the cliffs below Pelekas Village and Agios Gordis. Sometimes she wished they could move out of their apartment in the city and come to Glyfada to live year round, but of course that was not practical. The Glyfada apartment brought as much rent as all three rooms at the Puthena *dhomatia*, and she knew that even the considerable sum that Modestos collected from renting the Glyfada apartment to summer tourists would not entirely meet upcoming expenses, and that that was a source of great worry for her husband.

When they arrived at Glyfada, Modestos showered and changed into fresh clothes that Sophia had brought for him. He slicked back his hair, shaved and splashed on a bit of *eau de cologne*. Sophia rearranged the ends of her curly hair that the wind from the open car window had left in mild disarray. She pinched her cheeks then put on bright red lipstick to contrast her black eyes and hair. Once attired, they were off to Taverna Loyiza Hara-Theou.

Together they walked casually down the path to the shore. In nearly full darkness they could see pinpricks of light coming from the cliffside villages of Pelekas and Lefkimi. Anchored half a kilometer offshore, the lanterns of fishing boats were barely visible. Both Modestos and Sophia took off their shoes as they went along the deserted beach. The sand on their bare feet was still warm from the day's generous sunshine, and the gentle lapping of the waves on the shoreline eased away the tensions of their weeklong separation.

Loyiza Hara-Theou was a traditional *taverna*, with half a

dozen tables inside and another ten tables under an arbor of mature grape vines. When the weather was fair, the cook grilled meats and fish outdoors, and often roasted whole lambs in an open pit of coals near the masonry grill. At the door the taverna's owner, Diakatos Leonidas, took Modestos's hand and shook it firmly.

"*Yasou, yasou*, my friends! Why have you stayed away so long from Loyiza Hara-Theou?"

"I've been to Athens on business," Modestos told him.

"*Athina*? *Eisai trelos*!" "You must be crazy," said Leonidas. "But perhaps it's better to be crazy than poor."

Modestos only shrugged.

Sophia said, "Modestos has been on board ship all day. I'm sure he has an appetite."

"Of course you are welcome to come to the kitchen, my friends, but allow me to recommend the lamb tonight," suggested Leonidas. "It's just off the spit, and Stephanos says it's a good one. Very juicy!"

Modestos said, "Yes, Leonidas, bring the lamb. Everything. Bring us pita and *tzatziki*. And salad and cheese pies, too!"

Leonidas shouted across the room to a young waitress. "Katerina, bring my friends fresh wine!" He turned again to Modestos and Sophia. "Enjoy, my friends," he said. Then he withdrew.

Looking round the dining room, Modestos observed that only two other tables were occupied. Around one table sat a group of four rural men drinking coffee, clicking worry beads, gossiping, and playing a game of backgammon. Their weathered faces displayed the quintessential features of mariners or shepherds or farmers. Dark, cracked lips held home-rolled cigarettes of strong tobacco. Their clothes were simple. They wore no rings or other jewelry. As they cast the die and moved the pieces over the playing board, Modestos could see that their hands were thick from a lifetime of physical work, and he realized that they were probably the last generation

33

of Greeks to live life guided by such temporal traditions. Such a prognostication was made all the more apparent to him by a young, attractive Scandinavian couple seated across the small room, each one self-assured, resolute and venturous. And though he had never been to northern Europe, he understood that the differences between his country and Belgium, Holland, or Denmark must be appreciable.

When the waitress brought the wine and fried cheese, they began to eat and drink at once. Right now eating was more important than talking. To Modestos, wholesome food and drink meant more than basic nourishment: wine became blood; bread turned into brains; meat built strong muscles. And the marvelous oil from the olives (on Corfu there were no less than ten olive trees for each man, woman, and child) made all the other elements somehow work together in a sublime harmony.

But the food had to be fresh—no chemicals, nothing artificial! At Loyiza Hara-Theou there was never any doubt about the quality of the food. Diakatos Leonidas bought everything locally—chickens, eggs, cheese, vegetables, lambs. The wine served at the taverna was pressed from grapes grown on the hillside behind the restaurant. The lemons on the tables were picked each day from Leonidas's trees. The herbs with which Stephanos seasoned the meat grew in urns outside the front door. And no fish was ever brought to table more than a few hours out of the sea. That was Leonidas's rule. Like Modestos, he understood that good food made for the beginnings of a good man.

Katerina was not long bringing the main course. She also served tomato and cucumber salads with feta and oil, and that rather strange yet delightful combination of yogurt, garlic, and cucumbers know as *tzatziki*. For a time all concentration was on eating, but finally Sophia broke the silence. "I have waited long enough," she said. "Tell me what Stratiotis wanted from you."

"He wants me to go to Cyprus," Modestos said solemnly, not lifting his eyes.

"Cyprus?" was her incredulous reply. "No, Modestos. Not Cyprus. I thought Macedonia."

"With a post at Cyprus they will make me a captain in the army," he said. "And there is plenty of money, too!"

No amount of casual behavior was about to pacify Sophia's doubts and concerns. Not amused by this unexpected revelation, she said, "You're not considering it, are you?"

"I *must* consider it," he said.

"But you would be gone for months at a time. Macedonia is not nearly so far away. But Cyprus! Ah, perhaps you might be able to come home at the Feast of Saint Dimitri, or on the Epiphany. And how am I to handle Yanni? You know he's out of control. If you are far away, no telling what he might do!"

He tried to reason with her. "Let's not forget why I am considering the position." With his eyes he motioned toward the four old men sitting in the corner. So typical of their generation and of countless generations past, they appeared tragically trivial by emerging standards. Then he gestured at the fine, young Danes. Thankfully, they were oblivious to the fact that they were part of his awkward comparison.

"What are you trying to say?" Sophia wanted to know.

"The future is right in front of every Greek, but most are fools," he admonished. "God gave them sight, but they refuse to see. What is it that we want for Yanni's future? Those old goats in the corner are from our past, Sophia. Those young Danes—just look at them!—they are the future."

"Perhaps in Denmark," she dismissed. "But Greece is still full of fishermen and shepherds and half-hectar farmers. The *helpful* European Community says to Greece: Come now! Be part of our great economic alliance. Free trade. More tourism. But I tell you, Modestos, in

Maastricht they know very little about the Greek people. No cooperation, no trust! Twelve Greeks, thirteen opinions! Just how do they propose to turn an ass into a thoroughbred, eh?"

Modestos put down his fork and wiped his mouth with the napkin he'd stuffed inside his collar. He sipped his wine before answering his wife. "Think whatever you want about the European Community, Sophia, but the truth is that money causes changes. Maybe it can even change an ass into a horse. No doubt the Greece of today is not the same Greece we knew as children. There have already been changes—many changes! I believe it is very important for Yanni to attend the university at Bari. And in order for that to happen, I must find a way to pay."

"But Cyprus, Modestos. You'll be lucky not to get your throat cut."

He lowered his voice and leaned his head close to hers. "Stratiotis believes there is a threat of war on more than one front. If such a thing were to happen..."

Sophia glowered at him, as if he were personally responsible for all the non-sequiturs in Balkan politics. "Of course I am upset about the prospect of you leaving. And I am worried for Yanni. It's no secret that there are those who would not hesitate to put a gun in his hand."

Modestos was certainly no man of war. Conversely, he delighted in the processes of life: robust wine shared with a time-honored friend, or a vigorous swim in the chilly waves. This was the man Sophia loved! Not this stranger, so recently emerged, that carried the weight of the world upon his back. Once they had enjoyed life in a place that the ancient poets and the gods themselves had favored and chosen as their home. Somehow purity had been compromised. She knew not when; she knew not how. But Sophia remembered when they were Yanni's age and believed with all their hearts that the world was friendly and just. Then they had been certain that they would live forever.

After dinner they walked along the beach in the moonlight until after one. They sat on the shore where the water met the sand and buried their bare feet in wet mounds, absorbed in the essence of land and sea. It was special to be Greek. And Corfu sustained a mystery older than memory itself. As man and wife they were approaching their silver anniversary. Their son was nearing manhood. His emergence into adulthood would mean big changes—not only in his life, but in theirs as well. But tonight they had the sea and stars and mountains. They had the warm breeze to blow upon their faces, and they had the scent of the precious earth to reassure them. Tonight they had one another. And tonight that was enough.

CHAPTER 4
COMPLIANCE OF SEDUCTION

AT SCHIPHOL AIRPORT IN AMSTERDAM, Doran passed through Passport Control and Customs without pause. In the main terminal he located the exchange kiosk and traded several hundred American dollars for Dutch guilders. He bought a *strippenkaart* from an automated vendor then took the underground train into the city.

Unprepared for the utter mania at *Centraal* Station, he conceded that absolute fatigue probably contributed significantly to his impression of a scene that seemed truly bizarre, if somewhat surreal. Strewn throughout the station were the greasy belongings of transients and impoverished souls—mostly young heroin addicts. Amidst the commotion of everyday pedestrian traffic, Satan's legions lived in their own grime, damned and lagging in lethargy: shocking, repelling, vacant and hungry. Apparently the Dutch police tolerated vagrancy.

Outside the station, the *Damrak* extended before him. The boulevard divided the city into distinct hemispheres. Experiencing the commotion of urban Europe for the first time, he tried desperately to assimilate everything in his midst. Of course that was not possible. Novel sensations pelted him like raindrops from some long-anticipated cloudburst, and he wanted only to quench his thirst in this torrent of fresh impressions.

At *Stationsplein*, yellow trolleys gathered near an archway that led onto the *Damrak*. He watched as traffic hurtled by in a relentless blur. An incomprehensible fantasia bombarded his senses. It was three-thirty on Friday afternoon as he watched Amsterdam's status quo: chaotic pedestrians; black-haired, leather-clad punks; rent boys and alcoholics; a junkie lost in a Procol Harem reverie that nobody else could hear anymore; a clown handing out balloons; businessmen on their way to the Exchange; hearty women riding staunch bicycles; paradigms of fashion; a bevy of young backpackers camped out on the pavement in front of the station, gnawing on *baguettes* and slugging wine and bottled water. Dark skies threatened rain, and the spires and gables and cupolas of the Dutch skyline appeared to be melting like the hot wax of a candle. In such a sleep deprived vision he grasped the pre-psychotic reality of a Van Gogh cityscape. Holding his breath for a moment, he tried to re-establish his equilibrium, but his emotions gave way, and idiotic tears of joy and relief formed in his eyes as he noticed four stone baboons and twenty-two carved owls staring down at him from the facade at number 28 *Damrak*, the welcoming joke of sculptor Mendes da Costa.

Feeling nearly overcome by weariness, he moved through this strangely harmonious symmetry populated by unfamiliar beings. Entering the *Dam*, the crush of traffic fed his reticence, but the bells of the carillon pealed out a vaguely familiar melody that encouraged progress.

Searching in circles was not a wholly unfounded pursuit in his recent experience, and he determined finally that the street for which he was looking, Radhuisstraat, extended directly off the *Dam*, behind the Royal Palace. He continued across a walking bridge toward a bend in the busy boulevard where several small hotels were located.

After walking up twenty-nine narrow stairs to the lobby of Hotel Gallery, he found a heavy-set, swarthy gentleman seated behind a desk that was noticeably too small for him. He was immediately aware that the hotelkeeper was looking him over, silently trying to ascertain something relevant or important. "I am looking for accommodation," he told the man.

"Only you?"

"That's right," he said. "I arrived at Schiphol this morning from the United States, and I'm very tired."

"Are you American?"

"Yes."

"I have one room left," said the hotel manager in an accent that was certainly *not* Dutch. "It's on the top floor. Many stairs to climb, but it's quiet. You will sleep well."

"I'm happy to have it," said Doran. "Everyone else on the street is already full."

"I always keep one room back," said the clerk, implying that he was not inclined to rent it to just anyone who happened to march up the stairs. "May I have your passport, please? It will take only a moment for me to record the number." The man held out his thick, well-scrubbed hand, and Doran noticed that he wore several gold rings on his rather cumbersome fingers. "My name is Dr. Sudarek," he informed. "As you can see, I am not Dutch. I come from Egypt. Presently, I am not allowed to practice medicine in the Netherlands. A matter of license, you understand. So I manage this hotel. Have you come to Amsterdam on business? Or is your visit for pleasure?"

"I am here for the business of pleasure, I suppose," said Doran.

The doctor looked mildly perplexed by his statement. "I suppose that is best," he allowed graciously. "How long will you be staying in the city?"

Doran shrugged. "I'm not certain. First I must rest. Then I'll look around. Coming here from the station,

Amsterdam appears to be a fascinating city."

"Oh, yes!" said the doctor, his eyes wide with the delight of understatement. "There are many sides to Amsterdam. After you rest, come see me. I will point out sights you should not miss. Perhaps I can direct you to some inauspicious corner. Maybe there is a surprise waiting here for you. One can never predict such things, I believe. But come with me now, I will show you the room."

Carrying his leather bag, he followed the Egyptian doctor up sixty-nine more dizzying stairs. The dimly lit passageway was confining and precipitous, and over time the building itself seemed to have reconstructed its architectural lines. One could no longer be certain of either attitude or stability. Walls seemed to lean against their true center of gravity, and corners intruded at unlikely junctures.

With heart pounding from the climb, Doran entered his room. To call it modest would have been a generous assessment. In America, he assessed, this sort of lodging might well have served as a flop. Though in truth it was just old and worn, not dirty. With a single, sagging bed, a small table and a scarred armoire for furnishings, the dreariness of these quarters was disappointing. The colorless carpet was threadbare and pathetic, the paint was peeling in places, and it was obvious that the electrical wiring was an afterthought. The light from the overhead fixture was much too harsh, but both windows looked down on the busy Radhuisstraat, four floors below.

"Okay?" Dr. Sudarek asked.

"Yeah, it's okay," he said, only half believing his willingness to accept such lodgings on his first night in Europe.

"Are you hungry?" asked Dr. Sudarek.

"I don't know," he said. "My internal clock is confused. One simply forgets to eat."

"I understand," said the doctor. "I have a Turkish

41

friend around the corner who makes good kebob. I will have a sandwich sent up for you."

"Thanks," said Doran.

"You want a drink, too? I have gin and Amstel beer downstairs."

"No, thanks. I have a few mini-bottles of Remy-Martin from the plane. The sandwich will be fine. Then ten hours of sleep, and I'll be ready for Amsterdam."

Dr. Sudarek laughed. "I'm not sure anyone is ever ready for Amsterdam, Mr. Seeger. But *bon appetit*, and have a good rest. Talk with me in the morning and I will have a few ideas for you."

Fifteen minutes later a young woman, also Egyptian, brought the promised sandwich. At first bite Doran was acutely aware that the lamb on pita bread was quite unlike the meat to which he was accustomed at home. It was more robust, richer tasting, and the fat was not trimmed away to the point of paranoia. He drank some brandy, wiped his mouth on the sandwich wrapper, and then moved to the window overlooking Radhuisstraat. Sitting on the windowsill, he watched the street scene below. Shops were closing for the evening, and lighted trams glided along tracks carrying commuters and students and shoppers home. Two lovers lingered on the bridge where the street curved toward *Dam* Square, and a sad, old woman in ragged clothes panhandled coins from passers-by.

Darkness fell, and the mysterious-sounding bells of the Westerkerk tinkled a far-away, circular song each quarter hour. Neither moon nor stars were visible tonight. It was too cloudy. Sniffing the air, he silently predicted it would rain all night long.

He was still up and taking a sponge bath in the basin when the bells chimed eleven. Though in a state beyond exhaustion, he was certain he could not yet sleep. This dissociated consciousness was like a waking dream. Myriad images paraded before him with an impact that was certainly unique, and presumably significant. What seemed to congeal was a curious collage of disjointed impressions: an unexpected odor, the timbre of distant bells, a fluid atmosphere. He lay down on this unfamiliar bed in the attic loft of the Hotel Gallery.

Of course, many questions remained unanswered. Was this journey, with all its piquant symbols, merely an experiment arranged by some deeper expression of self? Were these varied images simply projections of his own mind's prism, refracting different aspects of character?

Hours later (or at least he perceived it so), he awoke to the unlikely sound of a small herd of sheep or goats being driven over the cobblestones outside his window. The vinegary presence of the lamb he had eaten lingered on his tongue and lips, and from out of the shadow world pealed the music of Ludwig van Beethoven. He suddenly realized he had been dreaming in a foreign language, though while conscious he spoke only English. He opened the shutters, which he did not remember closing, and leaned out to have a look. It was the twentieth century. Amsterdam was a modern city. In what temporal realm had he awoke?

MEETING HIS SECOND DAY IN EUROPE, Doran thought a night's sleep had remedied his stupor. He was wrong; his sensibilities remained somewhere over the North Atlantic. He looked out the window to the street below. It was Saturday morning, it was spring, and it was raining in Holland.

Above the tops of the leafy trees that lined the Keitzersgracht he could see the bell tower of the Westerkerk with its golden crown and simple cross. Then he remembered the mysterious ghost herd from his dream, only it had not seemed like a dream when he'd sat up in bed, thrown open the shutters, and leaned his head out the fourth story window to determine the true source of the clatter.

The shower room at the end of the hallway was vacant,

so he gathered his toiletries and towel and went to bathe. When finished, he dressed, then walked downstairs to the communal breakfast salon.

"*Daag*, Mr. Seeger," said Dr. Sudarek. "I hope you rested well."

"I feel much better," said Doran.

"Would you prefer coffee, tea, or chocolate this morning?" asked the host.

"Coffee, please."

"There is also bread, cheese, and cold meats, as well as fresh fruit. Please serve yourself," he said with a short bow.

He filled his plate with food and ate a heavier meal than the average European might have eaten at breakfast. Since he'd come downstairs rather late, he was soon the only guest not yet finished with the morning repast.

"Where will you start your exploration this morning?" asked Dr. Sudarek.

"I thought I would begin by following the canals," he said. "It would appear that they define the city in ever widening semi-circles, like the ripples in a pool."

"A fair analysis," said Dr. Sudarek. "Amsterdam is a compact city, and walking is easy and safe."

On the *Dam*, he found the Saturday flower market. The many stalls were filled with glorious tulips and cut lilacs, and from a vendor in front of the *Nieuwe Kerk*, he bought a single carnation. He pinned it to his collar, then found a bench from which to watch the activity. He tried to make sense of the dour expressions on the faces of the many young people sitting on the steps of the Queen's Palace, but he was unable to penetrate their stoicism.

All the while, high above the *Dam*, a collection of water deities in bas-relief was tirelessly worshipping the Maid of Amsterdam. With the full cornucopia of eighteenth century trade overflowing at her feet, the figure of 'Peace' resided endlessly beneath the squat, copper dome, holding an olive branch in one hand and the staff of Mercury in the other. The likeness of Atlas buckled under the weight of the modern world, and the Dutch, in all their ingenuity, had seen fit to furnish him with iron rods to make his special hell a little more bearable.

Doran wanted to see the paintings of the Old Masters: Vermeer's subtle interiors; Jan Steen's depiction of Dutch family life; and the incomparable portraits of Rembrandt. But he had not come to Amsterdam solely to examine and study the collected art and antiquities. His examination centered in the present tense. Once outside the Rijksmuseum, he wandered along the scenic Herengracht, or 'Gentleman's Canal,' with its rows of tall and stately, gabled houses built from wealth acquired during the city's Golden Age.

On his way back to Hotel Gallery, he passed through a neighborhood known as the *Jordaan*. Many of the streets were named after flowers, but the narrow alleyways and old working-class, brown brick houses gave the quarter a dank, enclosed feeling. Here souls brooded; and your neighbor was likely to be your aunt or uncle.

As he navigated through wet streets he could hear a punk band practicing nearby. He stopped to listen, but as the buildings were situated so closely together, it was nearly impossible to trace the sound of the echo. Like a confused rat in a maze, he chased after phantom drumbeats and nebulous bass lines, to no avail. He was about to abandon the search when a pealing guitar solo helped him zero in on the basement where the tumultuous music was boiling over with rage, desperation, dreams and oblivion.

He walked down the cellar stairs to listen outside the door. The words were all in riotous Dutch, so he did not understand their meaning; but the music was tough and hard, the notes and musical phrases condensed and wrapped tight as a bale of wire. These bloody and wounded drum beats were as unnerving as an arrhythmic heartbeat, and a curious ensemble of techno-synthetic instruments seemed to be converging on some point of critical mass, at first catastrophic, then circling round to some implied reassurance.

Trying the door, he found it unlocked and boldly pushed it open. The chamber was mostly dark and smelled of hashish and mildew. He squinted to see in this vat of murky water. Four phosphorescent eels swam in well-measured frequency through waves and particles of tubular light. Like the avant-garde culture in which they lived, these four musicians found themselves suspended in mid-song, like a troupe of trapeze artists caught with insufficient momentum to execute a critical maneuver. For a time no one noticed him standing there, but when the song finally degenerated into chaos, the sallow-faced, leather-clad singer approached. His knees nearly buckled under the weight of his own ruin, his sense of direction battered by some *blitzkreig* of distortion generators, bizarre harmonics, and drugs. Careening and glassy-eyed, he looked sickly in the smoky basement of Calvinism's worst nightmare.

"*Daag*!" he said.

"Do you speak English?" Doran asked.

"*Ja*, I speak a little English," he smirked. "But since I was born here in the *Jordaan*, some Hollanders say I don't even speak very good Dutch."

"I heard your music and came to listen," Doran offered.

"Do you want to come inside?" the singer asked with a playful, gap-toothed smile. Doran followed as he turned and walked into the crypt. "Where do you come from?" he said.

"The States," Doran answered.

"My name is Axel Van Zoet," he said.

"I'm Doran Seeger." He put out his hand. "I don't want to intrude. Are you sure you don't mind?"

Axel shrugged and took a bottle of Teacher's from inside his leather jacket. He offered Doran a drink.

"No thanks," he said.

"You sure? It's okay, I don't care."

"I'm fine," said Doran.

"What brings you to Amsterdam?" the singer asked.

With an inconclusive expression on his face, Doran only shrugged.

"Hashish? Heroin? XTC? Other drugs?" Axel persisted.

"Nothing so easy to find," said Doran. "Perhaps a rare piece of art—or a memorable scene."

"Well," said Axel, "the graffiti is good in Amsterdam. But contemporary art... Too many clichés for true art to survive."

"What are your lyrics about?" Doran asked.

"Stress, tension, loss of control," said Axel.

Before going back to their music, the four band members smoked hashish. Though he'd not done so in years, Doran took a puff or two when they offered him their water pipe. The sweet smoke went into his lungs like a wrecking ball, but after a moment of adjustment he reached a new equilibrium.

Axel offered the whiskey bottle again. "Are you some sort of artist?" he asked Doran.

Again Doran declined the whiskey. "By trade I was an engineer," he explained.

"But not anymore?" Axel prompted.

"Maybe not," said Doran.

"I am trained as an architect," Axel revealed, "but for now I prefer to fuck around with this music." He shrugged. "Fewer constraints, more room for expression."

Doran nodded.

"What kind of art are you searching for?" Axel wanted to know. "Do you mean Vincent Van Gogh? Or Rembrandt? Everybody who comes to the Netherlands wants to see Van Gogh and Rembrandt. But there are many other possibilities."

"Of course I want to see Van Gogh..."

"Look!" declared Axel. "Maybe you would like to see some very unusual art. It has to do with mechanics and theater all at once. This group of artists—or maybe like yourself they are actually engineers—is doing something very different, I believe. There is a performance tomorrow night. I think you might be interested, Doran. What do you say? Do you want to come along?"

"Why not?"

Axel smiled and nodded. "Meet me here tomorrow at seven o'clock. First we'll go to Café Chris for supper, then we'll go to Harveyery Theater. I know you will not be disappointed, Doran."

HAVING RETURNED TO HIS ROOM, Doran opened the window, for he liked hearing the bells of the *Westerkerk* chime each quarter hour. But tonight he did not turn on the light as he undressed and lay on his bed. His thoughts rolled and tumbled out of control, back to his recent past. He saw before him certain *specs* of a motor he had once designed to drive a gimbal, or to move an optical lens—*Element #6* for the Laser Doppler Rangefinder. In the beginning those for whom he worked would not verify the motor's true purpose. They were vague and evasivean insult to his intelligence and creativity. Many times he had asked that they simply tell him the truth.

Then came the so-called threat—inevitable all along: movements, threats and counter-threats, ultimatums, build-ups. The Cruise missiles flew and the smart bombs exploded. In a matter of hours much of Baghdad was in rubble, and a quarter million people lay buried under desert sands, never understanding what had hit them.

All during that first night of televised air raids Doran had puked until his horrified body was limp and dehydrated, and still he could not expurgate the guilt. Nowadays, sometimes sleep did not come so easily.

LIKE IN THE INTERIOR OF VAN GOGH'S

STUDIO, Doran's visceral workplace was filled with empty bird's nests, old mud-stained shoes, broken chairs, fallen limbs, and filthy peasant's caps. Walking from his hotel, with the cold north wind biting at his already crimson earlobes, he slipped inside the gray building on *Paulus Potterstraat* and spent the afternoon with the dead artist. From every picture, letter, receipt and scrap of hand-written paper, Vincent whispered: *"You cannot be at the pole and the equator at the same time. You must choose your own line..."*

To Theo's frustration, Vincent was forever giving away his small stipend to people less fortunate than himself—if indeed such persons were to be found! Left alone and misunderstood in Arles by the artist Paul Gaugin, Vincent preferred oblivion to the constant fear of epilepsy and shot himself point blank in the stomach. Waiting three days to die, he lay back on his bed, bleeding, and smoked his pipe. Fragrant wreaths of tobacco smoke gathered in swirling clouds about his head, and the painter died amidst his own yellow vision.

It was five o'clock when Doran left the museum with flexuous Van Gogh visions freshly imprinted upon his mind: crows and wheat fields; dour and oblique-looking peasants eating potatoes; terrace cafés; Vincent's bedroom; landscapes; skeletons; and the red and green and orange portrait of Vincent himself, his ear bandaged, looking quite mad.

Outside it was raining again, and Doran walked quickly up *Paulus Potterstraat.* Along the *Singelgracht* he finally took refuge from the mist inside a cozy tavern on the *Leidseplein.* He ordered Heineken's and sat at a corner table. The smoke from the cigarettes and pipes of a dozen other drinkers filtered out the clarity he sought to invoke.

And yes, tonight he had an unlikely engagement with the rock singer/architect, Axel Van Zoet. He had no idea what to expect. That was fine. He took a sip of beer. Then another. He looked at his palms to discover oil pigment stains of the primary colors, some reactionary stigmata. He bit his lower lip in reflection and searched for help. No one in the tavern saw the tears falling from his eyes.

CAFÉ CHRIS HAD BEEN IN BUSINESS on *Bloemstraat* as a beer tap since sixteen twenty-four. Axel Van Zoet's studio stood just a few doors away. Outside the café, a spray of purple tulips grew in window boxes and set off the clean lines of the well-maintained building. The interior was finished with dark wood paneling. The lighting was subdued. Doran offered to buy dinner for his host. Axel was a little surprised but did not decline Doran's offer to pay. "Look," he said, "this isn't much of a place. Only simple food and good beer."

"I'm not particular," said Doran. "It seems just the right place tonight."

"*Ja*, just right," he confirmed.

They took seats in the far corner of the *tapperij*. There were no menus on the plain wooden tables, only several pre-determined suppers written in Dutch on a blackboard behind the bar. Axel translated the possibilities for Doran, and the guest settled on a mushroom omelet with grilled onions. Axel ordered a crock of fish stew with brown bread. They each had draught beer.

Axel lit a cigarette, and Doran examined his companion's poignant features. Axel's sallow face, his pointed chin, and his hollow cheeks all suggested simple artistic poverty. His dyed, jet-black hair was long and scruffy at the neck, cut short and uneven at the temples. A defiant cowlick bristled without apology from the crown of his head. Under his black leather jacket he wore a t-shirt with faded lettering that read, "N.L. *Centrum*".

"Actually, Amsterdam is small scale," Axel said without prompting. "Very domestic and very complaisant. Of course all the good little hippies believe it's an open society. It's not that at all. In Amsterdam we live very close together. That is the real reason for social tolerance."

"To an outsider it appears that no one is in control,"

Doran observed.

"Ah! Now you've touched the real issue," said Axel, quite pleased. "Look, there are many forms of control. Just as there are many variations of freedom. Freedom or control by degrees. That's what we're really talking about, don't you agree?"

"I'm not sure I follow."

"No, my friend. Let me explain. Amsterdam is the great experiment in controlling people by giving them everything they want. If you want hashish or pot, they say go ahead, it's okay. If you want heroin or cocaine, they look the other way. Sex? Here it's lost all enchantment. In the end it comes down to economics. Same as in America. A commercial."

"So you're telling me you don't necessarily agree with the Dutch system of permissiveness..."

"Look, eventually the pendulum will swing back the other way. It's predictable. First right; then left. Right. Left. But it's all a great distraction, isn't it? Meanwhile, bigger issues remain. But tension is building. Don't you feel it, Doran?"

"I'm a foreigner here," said Doran.

Axel moved closer, putting his face just inches away from Doran's. "Of course. But if you stay here awhile, if you live the peculiar life that Amsterdam offers, I'm sure you'll begin to understand that it's all a grand seduction. That's it! All the hippies are lapsing into comas, and the Punks are kicking butts and screaming 'Anarchy!' There's no anarchy. It's only made to resemble anarchy. What's really going on is control. It's *compliance by seduction.*"

Doran recognized that he, too, had been seduced by promises of recompense—both direct and subliminal—bribes and rewards that, once attained, never quite satisfied. The pervasive feeling of emptiness that resulted grew slowly but steadily into an accustomed, dull ache, completing a slavish circle. But no longer was he willing to chase after phantom redress, there had to be something that might restore to him a measure of dignity.

The food arrived and they ate quickly. Then it was time to head for Harveyery Theater.

The night was very damp, and the wind blew relentlessly off the waterfront. While Axel wore a knee-length Navy coat against the weather, Doran had only a cable-knit sweater to break the wind. Quite unaccustomed to such raw weather, he drew his arms over his chest and shivered as they scuttled through the mist. Each pedestrian bridge they crossed was outlined with strings of white lights that defined the course of the waterway and led eventually to an undisclosed vanishing point. Such scenes offered Doran an obscure exercise in perspective, but there was little time to linger, scant opportunity for analysis.

"Just what are we about to see?" Doran asked Axel.

"It's a performance by a consortium called Survival Research Laboratories, or SRL for short."

"Sounds serious," said Doran.

"Well, it is and it isn't. It's a metaphor, yes. But it also tries to stand all on its own. You see, the world theater maintains drama and tension through the perpetuation of greed and injustice and so forth. In this allegory, everything comes crashing down. So these performances are about creating more problems than they solve. It is theater with machines as characters, and each time the audience must be sacrificed."

Before fifteen hundred open-mouthed onlookers, Harveyery Theater was transformed by the dozen members of Survival Research Laboratories into something resembling a prehistoric chasm, populated by nightmarish, four-meter-high, mechanical creatures: steel dinosaurs; friction threshers; shock wave cannons; erector set mania. Born of inverse ingenuity and a blow torch mentality, these fortified joints and welded junctures, these dancing skeletons, flame throwers, and catapults were apparently built only to collapse upon themselves. Their mechanical sounds were primordial: shattering glass; fire bombs; cargo exploding; scaffolding crashing; animal outcries.

As a huge boom swung out over the first twenty rows, spreading scraps of fetid refuse, the audience recoiled in one collective movement. Loud speakers barked unintelligible castigation at one hundred fifty decibels. Axel Van Zoet, the die-hard rock musician, covered his ears and grimaced, while the girl standing beside him tugged tensely at her hair. All the while, the Shock Wave Cannon fired wake-up calls at the audience. Rancid debris rained down like nuclear fallout. Doran laughed uneasily, but as the performance continued he came to realize that the creators of this theatrical whatever-it-was were, like himself, engineers, and this was their personal dare with the world!

"We're witnessing the technocratic world at war with itself," Doran yelled in Axel's ear as Armageddon thundered on stage.

"Yes, but it becomes even more! These machines are at ease in the world the artists have created for them. They take on a life all their own. Ultimately, the personality of the machine exceeds that of its operator."

Here no status quo expressions of talent were manifest. Each person who saw the performance was challenged to make up his own story about what was happening right in front of his eyes. A successful performance meant the development of new idioms!

"I can't imagine a production like this taking place in the States," Doran told Axel. "I'm certain the cops would close it down in minutes."

"Perhaps they would not understand it," suggested Axel.

"On the contrary," said Doran. "I'm afraid they would understand it all too well."

"Art like this is very persuasive, no doubt."

"Sometimes you have to bite the hand that feeds you, I suppose," said Doran, "or else you become just another lap dog!"

Once the performance ended, the crowd filed out of Harveyery Theater, but they did not immediately disperse. Instead, they stood outside the auditorium, waiting for the end of the world. And for a new one to begin... Word began circulating that SRL's fire cannon had been stolen. "With their consent, I suspect," Axel said with a self-satisfied look on his face. "Though of course they will never admit it."

Doran stood by his new friend.

Minutes later he heard a low-pitched hum, followed by several muted popping sounds. In time they could see clouds of black smoke billowing into the chilly night air. Scores of police went running in the direction of the commotion.

"I knew *something* was bound to happen," commented Axel.

"I don't understand," said Doran. "What is it?"

"Five minutes walk from here there was a long-time squat. Not anymore."

For they'd burned the entire ghetto to the ground!

CHAPTER 5
L'ASCENSION

THE BUILDING IN WHICH ALARICE VAN ZYL LIVED was one of a Modernist complex resembling six dice in mid-tumble, each tremendous cube balanced precariously on one corner. Gisela Van Zyl knew that apartments in the *cubiswonung* were in high demand, and that her sister was lucky to live there. Gisela, herself, did not appreciate their slick appeal. Though a common base seemed to support the lopsided structures, she was never quite sure of her balance once inside these peculiar buildings. Taking shelter from the rain, she rang her sister's bell.

Alarice answered the door immediately, and without offering any greeting, Gisela ducked inside. The apartment felt warm. Gisela took off her raincoat and hat and hung both on a rack near the door. She wandered into the parlor and flopped down on an easy chair. The sweet smell of a freshly made confection filled the apartment. "What are you baking?" Gisela asked.

"A crumb cake," Alarice answered.

"When will it be out of the oven?"

"It's out already. Would you like a piece?"

"With coffee, please," said Gisela.

In truth, Gisela saw her sister infrequently. They might cross paths at a family gathering, or in passing at their parents' home; but all in all their sisterly kinship was full of unknowns.

Today, at Alarice's invitation, Gisela had walked twenty minutes from her parents' apartment on a rainy Sunday afternoon to visit her sister and discuss the odd possibility that they might travel together. Only two days before, her mother had casually introduced the idea, and the notion had taken Gisela completely by surprise. Their family was unaccustomed to traveling for pleasure, and her sister hardly seemed the adventurous type. What was this about?

Gisela noticed various travel books on Alarice's coffee table. Leaning forward, she began studying a map of Greece. Alarice brought the small repast.

"You really are serious about traveling," Gisela said.

"Of course I'm serious," said Alarice.

"You've never traveled before," the younger sister observed.

"All the more reason to go now." Alarice settled herself on the sofa near Gisela so they might look at the same page of the open book.

"Mama says you want me to come along," Gisela said as she sipped her coffee.

"It would be extravagant for you to have a summer in Greece before starting at the university," said Alarice.

"Papa will never allow it," Gisela said dourly.

"Mama knows how to take care of him," advised Alarice.

"I can't believe she's offering to pay my way!" Gisela declared. "What's the catch? What's going on? Did you and Mama devise this scheme to keep me away from home this summer? For what reason I can't imagine."

"Nothing of the kind," said Alarice as she began paging through the color photos in the travel book. "I told Mama that I'd decided to go to Greece for the entire summer. I was expecting resistance, but she surprised me by suggesting that I take you along. I admit that I was skeptical at first, but the more I thought about it, the more I liked the idea. What do *you* think, Gisela?"

"I don't know what to think," said the younger sister.

Alarice recalled the summer before she had gone away to the University at Leiden. She had spent the entire time cultivating anxiety. "Don't be a dolt, Gisela!" she admonished. "Just look at these pictures! It's the opportunity of a lifetime. I wish I had traveled when I was your age."

"Why?" Gisela asked sincerely.

Alarice explained, "Once you've finished studying and settle into a job—or maybe start a family—you become absorbed, and time hurtles by. One day you look in the mirror and barely recognize the person staring back. Such things are hard to imagine at nineteen, but it's true. Perhaps you say to yourself, 'Okay, not so bad. There is still plenty of time. It's not as if I were old and decrepit. Important things are put off another year. Maybe two, or three, or ten...'"

"You sound a little desperate, Arrisa."

"Desperate? I don't know about that. But I'm glad I've decided to do this. Please come along, Gisela."

Gisela's gaze was distant. Had she already begun this fated holiday in fantasy? Or was it something else altogether? "We're going to Greece; you and me. Imagine that!" she said. She turned to Alarice and smiled. "May I have another piece of cake?" she said.

"Coffee too?" asked Alarice.

"Please," said Gisela.

Together they began reading the travel articles that Alarice had collected.

IN MID-APRIL, the Van Zyl sisters packed their rucksacks and set off by train from Rotterdam to the busy and cosmopolitan Midi Station in Brussels. There they made a connection that took them through Belgium and deep into the heart of Alsace Lorraine in France. Now that they were out of Holland, Alarice was feeling increasingly positive about having her sister along for the summer holiday. She smiled to herself as she acknowledged her mother's keen insight. Truly, she did not know Gisela. No doubt they were as different as they were alike.

Gisela's attention was fixed for the moment on minor personal grooming, so without being too obvious or staring rudely, Alarice took the opportunity to consider her sister's appearance. Whereas her own features were round and pliant, Gisela tended to portray a no nonsense persona. Recently she had dyed her hair jet black and allowed her brows to grow thick. The counterfeit hair color, along with her insolent style of applying eyeliner, mascara, and eye shadow, set off her pale complexion in a way Alarice found unflattering. Gisela usually dressed all in black, striving for an image she perceived as invulnerable. She tended to wear silver jewelry instead of gold, though such adornment was always minimized.

Alarice studied her sister's strong yet nimble hands as Gisela rifled through her small purse looking for her stiff-bristled hairbrush. Her sister's hands were not unlike her own, though the manner in which she moved them—with an unreasonable sense of urgency—seemed to contrast with Alarice's own natural gift of fluidity.

Following the course of the Rhine River, the train made brief stops in Luxembourg, Saarbrucken, Metz, Nancy, and the French university town of Strasbourg. There, the two sisters got off the train and spent their first night on holiday.

From the modern station they walked to the city center. Near the cathedral they found a satisfactory room at the Hotel Michelet. Their quarters were a bit dark and somewhat cramped, but they only meant to stay a couple of nights before continuing their journey south, so the accommodation was accepted without complaint..

At a small bistro called *Le Coq Rouge*, both girls had the

plat du jour, a dish of pasta with poached salmon in rich cream sauce. After eating *mousse au chocolat* for desert, they paid their bill then sauntered together, holding hands, along the scenic promenade next to the River Saar. Many people were out, strolling and socializing on this warm springtime evening, and the tour boats were operating as well. Young, athletic Frenchmen came rowing by in their kayaks, and a troupe of clowns entertained children next to the boat launch. Alarice and Gisela sat on a bench, taking in the lucent glow of the evening.

"You know, it won't be necessary for you to watch over me," Gisela said casually.

"I hadn't intended to," said Alarice.

It was still quite warm at midnight so they went to bed with their window open. A lethargic breeze lilted through their room as they lay on top of their beds. Gisela's nerves were volatile, active, and untamed. Her sister's spirit was porous with the prescience of circumstances she could not yet define. The ringing of the one o'clock church bells soothed away all resistance to sleep. Sensations turned into dreams, and their fates were sealed.

THE NIGHT TRAIN FOR THE COTE D'AZUR was not scheduled to depart until after midnight. After eating a light supper, Alarice and Gisela returned to the station. There they spent the evening reading French and Italian fashion magazines in the *salle d'entente*. There were few travelers in the waiting room, and time passed slowly for the girls. Alarice found that reading in poor light made her eyes burn. Gisela tried drinking coffee to keep herself buoyant, but sometime after eleven she surrendered to fatigue. Slouching in her chair, she let her arms go limp, and cultivated a rather blank expression of boredom.

A few minutes before midnight, the arrival of the train was announced over the loud speaker. They collected their luggage and moved out onto the platform; and as the sisters prepared to step onboard the train, they were nearly run down by a disembarking, blond-haired, bleary-eyed traveler carrying a single over-the-shoulder bag. Standing eye to eye with Alarice, he seemed to be tongue-tied for a moment, then said apologetically, "Pardon me, I'm just trying to make a connection." The sincerity conveyed in his blue-gray eyes gave Alarice a moment of pause, and she was somehow powerless to move aside. "*Geen dank.*" "Don't mention it."

The train conductor helped the two sisters find the sleeping compartment reserved for them, and wasting no time, they crawled beneath the sheets and blankets. As the train pulled out of the station, the rhythmic clattering of the wheels moving over the tracks invited dreams. They lay quietly in the darkness, tired but content.

THE NIGHT TRAIN FROM STRASBOURG TO NICE made its way over the French Alps, then into the Rhone Valley. There it turned south and lumbered through the darkness toward Provençe and the sunny Mediterranean coast of France. Alarice and Gisela slept right through the pre-dawn stops at Avignon and Marseilles.

At morning's first light, Gisela awoke and wriggled from beneath her covers. She rubbed her eyes and brushed away the few stray hairs that tickled her face. Raising the window shade to see how far they'd come, she observed the lush Mediterranean landscape. "Arissa, come look outside!"

At the resort town of Juan les Pins, the dark evergreens and palms and gargantuan aloe plants contrasted against the sun-drenched coast and the cerulean color of the sea. Captivated beyond all expectation, Gisela suddenly realized just what she had missed not having traveled. She resolved immediately that this summer-long excursion would be only the first of many more to come.

"Arissa, wake up and come see. It's fantastic!"

Alarice took a moment to gather her wits then climbed down the *couchette* ladder to see what so enchanted her sister. Looking out the window at the characteristic seaside town, she too might have been caught up in its ambiance had she not felt curiously unsteady on her feet, and overcome with a sour stomach and an incessant ringing in her ears.

Gisela took one look at her sister and became alarmed by her pale complexion. "Arissa, you look awful. What's wrong?"

"I *do* feel terrible," Alarice confided.

"Are you sick?"

"I think it's from sleeping on the train—all the rocking and swaying as we crossed the mountains. I'm sure I'll feel better once we're out in the fresh air. How much longer till we reach Nice?"

"Not far," consoled Gisela as she consulted the SNCF timetable. "Antibes is next, then *Gare Nice Ville.*"

Though they arrived in early morning the station at Nice was already bustling, and Alarice and Gisela lingered only long enough to procure a map of the city. As they made their way up Avenue Thiers, Gisela was feeling strong and confident, while Alarice was simply happy to be off the train and out in the sunshine.

A short distance from the station they rented a charming *cuisinette* at the Hôtel des Medicis on a back street called Rue Herold. As the maids had not yet finished cleaning the vacated rooms, it was not possible for the girls to occupy their *chambre* for yet another hour, but the perky, red-haired woman at the reception desk invited them to leave their luggage in her care while they went to a café for *petite déjeuner.*

"My sister is ill with motion sickness," Gisela told the *hôteliere.*

"Perhaps a walk by the sea, along the Promenade des Anglais, will help you feel better," offered *Madame* Medici. "It is not far. Only ten minutes, *et voila!*"

"*Merci beaucoup, Madame,*" said Alarice. "I'm certain we will find it with ease."

The girls walked up Rue Herold to the tree-lined Boulevard Victor Hugo. With its stately hotels and elegant apartment houses, the avenue called up a bygone era of sophistication and affluence. They proceeded up Avenue Jean Médecin, finally reaching the Promenade des Anglais by the sea. They found a bistro and had *café au lait* and croissants for breakfast.

"This is so unexpected," Gisela said to her sister.

"What surprises you?"

"Travel! I'm feeling infected by the novelty, and I'm afraid there is no cure."

"I wish that were my only ailment," said Alarice.

After breakfast they walked back to the hotel. Alarice continued to feel dizzy and needed to rest. Fortunately, their room was ready when they returned, and *Madame* Medici personally escorted them upstairs and got them settled. Once they were alone Alarice undressed and went straight to bed. Within minutes she fell into a heavy sleep. Gisela took a shower and unpacked her belongings. She watched over her sister without panic, and they remained inside their room until Alarice woke up around two o'clock.

Venturing out to a corner market, they bought groceries to prepare meals in their tiny kitchen. They bought meat and cheese, salad, and ice cream. A freshly baked *baguette* stuck out of their sack like a flagpole with its French colors retired at evening. A bottle of *Bordeaux Superieur* had cost only fourteen francs. Ah, to be living a Frenchman's life!

On their second day at the Cote d'azur they awakened to bright sunshine and a mild temperature. And even if it was still too cool for lazy afternoons in bikinis at the seashore, Alarice and Gisela resolved to stay in Nice for several days. Touring every little corner of the old city, they stopped in front of the magnificent Triton Fountain in the *Jardin Albert* 1*er*. Standing under a trellis of yellow roses, they watched *savant* Frenchmen, and were fascinated by the *petite* coquettes with ingénue looks and 'C'est moi' attitudes. Later they shopped at one of the many expensive boutiques to try on a *chic* outfit that their Calvinist upbringing and practical Dutch perspective would never allow them to buy at such a price.

Alarice and Gisela were truly enjoying the *vie Francais*. They visited the Matisse Museum and climbed the hill where the ruins of an old Roman fortress were preserved in a park-like setting. There they could look out at the Riviera, or north into the hills above the city. In evening they went out to Scarlet O'Hara's on Rue Adroit, after ten, to drink and dance with the suave, unattached Frenchmen. Or, if they were feeling particularly exhausted from touring, they lay about in their room watching French television until they fell asleep in their clothes.

Sunday was a holiday throughout France—*L'ascencion*! Around noon they headed for the square in front of the cathedral off Rue Rosetti, near the three-block-long flower *marche*. The old city was alive with a traditional celebration. As worshippers filed out of the cathedral after mass, a comical brass band played on the square in front of the church. A beggar danced happily with a little girl as a woman passed a hat among hundreds of onlookers. Everyone, it seemed, had a bouquet of flowers. The smell of roasting fowl, as well as other delicacies, filled the air.

Alarice and Gisela gadded about back streets, too narrow even for a Reneault. Shamelessly, they peered up staircases and into open windows, eavesdropping on family life dramas as they unfolded with bravado or tenderness or humor. An elderly couple, with shopping bags in hand, came unsuspectingly out of a doorway just ahead of them—he with a baret and worn leather sandals and a mustache like a push broom, and she with a flower print dress and head scarf to match. A chilly, startling wind from the sea came whipping up the enclosed corridor, and without warning lifted Gisela's skirt above her thighs. "*Mon Dieu*! *Mon Dieu*!" she exclaimed as she replaced the material around her legs. *"On m'a certainment consigne a l'enfer pour l'eternite!"*

The old couple looked up in alarm. The woman drew a cross over her breast as the couple hurried by with eyes lowered, and the sisters laughed until their sides ached.

Throughout the city bells rang, music played, and families gathered for food and conversation. In France, it was a day for small gifts and for *socca* and Beaujolais at an outdoor cafe. Alarice and Gisela sampled Niçois pancakes made from couscous and drank fruity wine at a small wine bar in *Vieux Nice*.

"Everyone is so happy today," Gisela bubbled.

"So it's only right that we celebrate, too," said Alarice.

"Mais oui!" squealed Gisela.

"Where do you want to go next?" asked the older sister.

Gisela responded with an unfledged look. "I haven't even begun to consider it," she said.

"For once in our lives we are totally without chains," said Alarice. "We can go anywhere, do anything. We have the entire summer. Plenty of money."

"Oh, I know," Gisela swooned. "But here on the Cote d'azur I wake up each morning and the sun is shining. Not like home. No dark clouds, no rain or north wind. Just the sea and this happy lifestyle!"

"Of course there's no hurry to get to Greece. First we must pass through Italy, and just imagine what lies around the bay, Gisela. The Cinque Terre and Florence and Tuscany!"

"Tous les jours, je t'aime France!"

"You can be incredibly silly," Alarice laughed.

"Oui, oui, ma seour. Mais quelquefois tu es alors serieux! The men of Italy await our arrival with a sense of anticipation that makes them ache. Believe it!" she blushed. "It's true! However... Firenze must be beautiful indeed. And we deserve a room with a view, don't you agree?"

"Mais certainment!"

"And I may find myself lost in the charm of Tuscany, drunk past all remorse on Chianti Classico. *Si, bello*! *Domani, domani, domani...*"

"I think you are drunk on *this* wine, Gisela."

"On the wine and on *L'ascencion*, too!"

CHAPTER 6
THE FAMILY THROMOS

HAVING STOPPED AT A LEGENDARY WELL IN LEFKIMI to fill two containers with the best water on Corfu, Modestos arrived at his mother's apartment in Puthena Village just before noon. He hauled the heavy containers up the stone steps at the *dhomatia* and set them inside Aphrodite's doorway. A returning prodigal, he hugged and kissed his mother and asked if she had everything she needed.

"Why haven't you come to visit me?" she asked sorrowfully.

"I told you, Mama, I had to go to Athens on business."

"I do not always remember things," she lamented. "What kind of business do you have in *Athina*?" she wanted to know.

"Communications work, Mama," he said.

"At least you came home," she said.

"Why wouldn't I come home?" Modestos bantered, knowing well that his mother's reference was to her husband and his father.

"Do you want to eat, Takis?" she said, moving to her

66

cooking. "Of course you want to eat."

It had always appeared to Aphrodite that her younger son, unlike his siblings, had never been able to get enough to eat. No matter how much she fed him, his stomach would not grow large. Nevertheless, after fifty years she had not abandoned her cause. Her pots had been simmering since before dawn.

A week in Athens had robbed Modestos of vitality, and even the meal last night at Taverna Loyiza Hara-Theou had not completely replenished him. Aphrodite fed him his favorite grapes dipped in honey, and Modestos poured himself cupful after cupful of the pure Lefkimi water. Later, Aphrodite served him a huge plateful of *stifada*, for she alone understood the portions he needed to consume.

"How is Sophia?" Aphrodite asked. The old woman truly liked her daughter-in-law.

"Wonderful," he said rather absently as he continued eating.

"And what about Yanni?" the grandmother wanted to know. "When is Yanni coming to visit me?"

"He will come this afternoon," Modestos promised her. Aphrodite's mood brightened at the prospect of her grandson's visit. In truth, Modestos had no idea when Yanni might visit, but with Aphrodite's memory being what it was—or was *not*—perhaps it really did not matter whether the boy actually showed up or not.

"A demon woke me out of my dreams early this morning," Aphrodite proclaimed out of nowhere.

Modestos looked curiously at her. He would rather have ignored such manifestations of superstition from his mother, but he felt helplessly obliged to ask the anticipated question: "What demon, Mama? What are you talking about?"

"He was trying to break down the door and drag me away. But my candle never went out. I hissed and spat and threw down a curse, God forgive me."

"Who would want to bother you so early in the

67

morning?" Modestos pressed, trying to ascertain what might actually have happened.

Aphrodite's expression turned contrary and she shook her head skeptically. "This was no ordinary man, I'm certain. A demon! I'm sure of it. Yes! He came right into my dreams. He woke me from a sound sleep with a voice like a cold wind." She shivered at the remembrance.

"Maybe you felt a draft," Modestos proposed.

Aphrodite's look was scornful. "You are full of mockery, aren't you, Takis? But someday you too will be old."

Modestos tried to conceal his resignation. "All right. All right," he said. "Tell me what happened."

"Tell you what? There's nothing more. He ran away," said Aphrodite matter-of-factly.

Modestos chuckled and said, "Maybe you are not so vulnerable after all, eh?"

Aphrodite grunted and turned away for the moment as her son returned to his plate. His voracity still amazed her. She cut him more bread and refilled his glass. She sighed as she lowered herself onto a chair opposite her son. "Takis, I never sleep well anymore," she complained.

"Why not?" he asked brightly, through the eyes of his own relative youth. "You have no worries."

"No worries… But with age come memories. And memories are not always kind, Takis."

"Has your life not been a full and blessed one?" he asked. "I do not understand, Mama. What are these memories?"

The old woman's eyes went moist. Transported back to a time more dependent on her own energies, her gaze was the result of an inverted viewpoint. "I often recall the holidays," she told him. "Especially Easter—it was always my favorite one. Each Good Friday, Constantine butchered our best milk-fed lamb for roasting, and on Easter Eve, before midnight mass, we ate the *magaritsa*, the Easter soup. For Greeks the eggs have been a symbol of rebirth ever since Adonis, but out of respect to God we color them red to represent Christ's blood. Inside the church, the priests gave each person a lighted candle, and we walked in a procession through the village, then around the church three times, holding our candles, careful not to let the flame go out all night long. Oh, it was a beautiful sight! Do you remember how it was, Takis? But you were so young..."

"I was young, Mama. But I remember."

"Nowadays, I think God is ignored by young people," she observed, full of lament. "Where is the respect now? I see young women from all over Europe coming to Hellas—more every year, I believe. Where is their modesty? They walk through the streets naked with no shame at all. I hear them curse the Lord as if He were a pig. I don't understand this disrespect, Takis. Such immodesty makes me tremble. Oh, it is not the Greek boys and girls; it's the other ones!" she accused as she symbolically washed her hands clean of the intruders.

Whether or not Aphrodite realized it, her grandson was one of this new breed that frightened and repelled her. Yanni was throwing off tradition at a rate that even Modestos found staggering, and the father had begun to think his son was becoming over-burdened with fashionable European and American clichés, almost to the point of farce. He wore these new tastes and habits like a suit of clothes several sizes too large, though of course he had no mirror to see how ridiculous he really looked.

"Times have changed, Mama," Modestos observed.

"Yes... You have many important things to do, don't you? And soon the tourists will come again, and you must fill your rooms. You must make money for Sophia and for Yanni. This modern world! Now my son goes to *Athina* for business. What business? Not the business of his old and feeble mother, eh?"

Modestos wiped his mouth with his napkin and rose from the table. He kissed Aphrodite on her forehead and thanked her for lunch. He wanted to tell her that her life was not over, that her existence still had meaning. But just how was one to sell such an observation? Instinctively, he had the sense not to attempt consolation. Promising to visit her again tomorrow, he went out the door and walked down the stairs leading to the garden.

The bougainvillea vine that crept up the stucco wall that guarded the steps was beginning to flower. Soon the glorious red blossoms would cover the whitewashed walls of the *dhomatia*. Modestos strolled to the end of the walkway and looked up and down Christopher Street, Puthena's high road. The sun was warm this morning, and a gentle breeze was coming off the sea.

Ah, the air smelled so fresh in springtime! The rainy skies had cleared, and the village women were hanging bedding and rugs over balconies and beating out the winter's accumulated dust. Nearly everyone grew geraniums in pots or used olive oil tins.

The restaurant owners, too, were whitewashing buildings in anticipation of the coming tourist season, and a group of laborers was giving the dome of the church a fresh coat of blue paint. Modestos observed a sinewy farmer bringing his winter harvest of roots on the back of his donkey to the outdoor market, and a gang of boys was playing with a soccer ball in front of the Bank of Greece.

He walked up the street, past the *Poste* and the currency exchange, to Taverna Rankios. There his friend since boyhood, Giorgos Zervas, was busy cleaning the umbrellas used to shade the tables in the garden of his restaurant. Modestos stood unnoticed underneath the pergola at the garden's entrance.

"*Yasou*, Zervas!" he greeted. "Stop working for a little while and have coffee with a friend."

Giorgos looked up from his labor and saw Modestos standing at the threshold. "*Yasou*, my friend. What brings you here on such a morning?"

"A good son must visit his mother, eh?"

Zervas put down his sponge and approached his friend. Smiling broadly, he acknowledged, "Aphrodite is truly amazing."

"She may outlive her namesake," joked Modestos.

"It is good, though," said Zervas. "We should all have such a long life, don't you agree?"

"God willing," Modestos allowed.

"Tell me," said Giorgos, patting Modestos on the shoulder, "how is Sophia? And how is your boy, Yanni?" Giorgos put two cups on a table and motioned for Modestos to take a seat.

Settling back Modestos declared, "On the surface everything is fine, I suppose."

Giorgos looked at him somewhat indulgently. "What do you mean, on the surface?"

"Yanni is running wild," lamented Modestos. "He refuses to be serious about his studies. He only wants to drink and ride his scooter and have parties with foreign girls. I never know what to expect from him anymore. Things are different from when we were his age, eh?"

"Some ways yes, some ways no," conceded Giorgos. "The devil was in me when I was Yanni's age. But yes, Thromos, some things *are* different. Just open your eyes in the morning and you wonder where it is you have woken up. But listen! What are you complaining about? Life is better for us than it was for our fathers."

"Do you believe that, Giorgos?"

"Of course I believe it. And you believe it, too!"

"Aphrodite is becoming disoriented," related Modestos as he sipped coffee from a demitasse. "I hear it in the way her voice quivers."

Zervas sighed philosophically. "Look," he said, "it is always that way for old people. Their time has passed. It's a different world now, Takis. Like it or not, you can't deny it. Now stop worrying. You'll put a hole in your stomach. Soon we'll both be up to our ass in rich tourists, then you won't have a spare minute to yourself."

71

They passed an hour talking and relaxing in the warm sunshine. After saying good-bye to Zervas, Modestos strolled casually through the village. There he encountered Father Dimitri, the village priest. He greeted the cleric and walked onward.

Arriving at the crude fishing harbor, he sat upon the pier. There was hardly anyone about due to the season. Absently he cast a few stones into the water and watched the ripples expand. The concentric circles grew larger and larger, until finally they disappeared altogether. Surely, he thought to himself, a specific event had its greatest impact at its onset; and like the ever-diminishing frequency of these man-made ripples, eventually the energy of any cataclysm was absorbed into the pool. Once the process was complete, the original condition was lost forever. Or in the case of a changing culture, at least consigned to memory and legends.

Acknowledging the active roll he was playing in this so-called cultural transformation, Modestos felt a certain sense of shame. But he was also a pragmatist. Giorgos was right. Like it or not, the intense competition had begun. Of course Aphrodite was confused and frightened. And Sophia persisted in wishing it was not so. But the young people embraced this revolution with a such a zeal that metamorphosis had already become a virtual certainty.

He walked back to the village where he'd left his car. Sophia had remained at Glyfada to go for an afternoon swim, but by now she was probably back at the city apartment cooking supper. Modestos was eager to see Yanni, so he started for Corfu Town.

LOCATED ON MUSTOXIOLOU STREET, between the commercial center and the harbor, the third floor, two-bedroom, walk-up apartment occupied by the Thromos family was built in Corfu Town's Venetian Quarter before the turn of the century. It included a gracious parlor with twelve-foot ceilings, a formal dining room with a crystal chandelier, a kitchen with space for a small washing machine, and a single, pie-shaped bathroom. In this densely populated neighborhood of government offices and foreign embassies and consulates, Modestos, Sophia, and Yanni had lived for the past eight years.

Entering the apartment, Modestos immediately noticed that the window shades were drawn. Sophia was fanatical about fresh air, so Modestos found it odd that the apartment was dark. Gatos, their small black cat, greeted him near the doorway, and meowing softly, rubbed its body against Modestos' pant leg. Modestos lifted the feline to his chest and spoke tenderly to it. "You pretend to miss me, don't you? But it is my dinner cooking on the stove that you really want!" He set the cat down gently and went to the kitchen. Lifting the lid of a simmering pot, a sumptuous aroma rose to his nostrils. Sophia was cooking *briami*, a vegetable dish consisting of eggplant, peppers, tomatoes, squash, and potatoes.

Walking through the parlor, he entered his bedroom. There he found his wife lying on the bed, not quite asleep. Immediately she was aware of his presence. "I didn't hear you come in," she said. "How is Aphrodite?"

"She will live to be one hundred," said Modestos as he unbuttoned his shirt to change. "Are you all right?"

"*Kalá*," she said. Just a little tired."

"Did you swim this morning?" he asked as he slipped out of his slacks.

"I tried," said Sophia, "but the water is still too cold. Two more weeks until it's warm enough."

"Just as well," said Modestos. "I have painting to do at the *dhomatia* before the season begins. Where is Yanni?"

"He's in his bedroom. He's not feeling well."

Modestos raised one eyebrow.

"When I arrived home at eleven-thirty," Sophia explained, "the apartment was dark and Yanni was still in his bed. I asked him what was wrong, but he was evasive. He looked dehydrated, so I made him drink some water.

That was a couple of hours ago."

Modestos bent his right arm at a perpendicular angle and pantomimed a man drinking from a wineskin. Sophia nodded in frustration. It was not her aim to conceal the truth; she was just as determined as Modestos to see the boy right his ways.

"I could smell liquor on him," she revealed. "Takis, what are we going to do?"

Modestos Thromos had no trouble expressing his good moods; but conversely, and unlike many other Greeks, he had never been one to fly into rages when he was angry or frustrated. He sighed as he sat on the bed.

"This is becoming a contest of wills," he said to Sophia. "He desperately wants his independence, even if having it ruins him. But that is an old story, eh?"

"He is nineteen years old; we cannot follow him everywhere he goes!" she said. "If he means to make trouble..." Sophia turned up her palms and shrugged in resignation.

"We must hold onto him a little longer," said Modestos. "If we give up now, everything could be lost: his chance for an education; his religion; his opportunity to make a family of his own. Maybe even his health if he continues to drink!"

Modestos took down fresh slacks and a clean shirt from his wardrobe. He dressed quickly. "I will have another talk with him," he said.

The father knocked once, softly, at his son's closed door. He received no reply. For a moment he considered leaving the boy alone with his misery, but decided instead to push open the door.

Yanni lay on the bed looking pale. His voice emerged from a protracted yawn. "Welcome home, Papa," he said.

Looking at his only son, Modestos felt a rush of paternal pride, and took a moment to unravel Creation. Yanni's face was lean and brown, his expression sultry. His thick, dark eyebrows and plaintive features enhanced his quixotic eyes. His smile came fast and easy, if a little sad.

"I'm happy to be home," Modestos admitted, "but I'm sorry to hear you are not well."

Not inclined to comment on his self-induced malady, Yanni waited for whatever was to come next. He was well aware that his father's thoughts were often collected during extended periods of silence.

"In Athens I met with a very important general," Modestos began.

Yanni looked puzzled. "Trouble?" he asked.

"Trouble has many disguises, eh?" observed Modestos thoughtfully.

"Do you think there might be a war?" Yanni asked.

"Who can predict the future?" said Modestos. "Let's hope it's not your concern. You will be at school in Italy."

"I know you wish I would be more serious about my studies," said Yanni earnestly.

Of course it was true, but Modestos was not in the mood to underscore weaknesses. "You will have a fine future, Yanni. I have confidence in you."

Yanni had not performed badly at the *gymnasium*, but he was tired of going to school. Now the entrance exam for the Italian university lay before him. Certainly it was his obligation to perform well to please his parents, though it had become obvious that Yanni was *not* inclined to scholasticism. The summer-long issue of exam preparation was one he avoided whenever possible.

"Sophia is cooking *briami*," said Modestos. "Are you up to it?"

Yanni nodded. "I am feeling much better now," he related.

Modestos smiled knowingly at his son. "First the party, then the payment," he said. "Ah, there is always payment, eh Yanni?"

Modestos stood up to leave the room, then turned back to the boy. "Would you mind helping me tomorrow with some painting at the *dhomatia*?" he asked.

"Tomorrow? No problem!"

"And Aphrodite was asking for you this morning. You are her brightest star, you know. So let her give you lunch. It will probably add another year to her life."

"*Nai, nai*," said Yanni. "No problem!"

AH! Surely this was a spring morning to rival any spring morning since the gods had taken corporeal bodies and walked on earth. The sun already shone brightly overhead as father and son drove out of Corfu Town, past the Neapolitan houses, the French style colonnades, and the British cricket field at the esplanade. With paint cans, brushes, and rollers stowed in the trunk of Modestos' car, they were ready for a day of labor.

Modestos sounded the horn as he sped round a tight curve; and an old man bringing flowers and fresh vegetables to market on the back of his donkey put his hand over his heart and called out a greeting as they passed him. "*Yasou! Yasou!*"

Entering Puthena Village, Modestos did not try to repress or discount his feelings. Though he now lived a more cosmopolitan life in Corfu Town, Puthena Village would always evoke memories of his boyhood.

In his mind's eye he could see the barber shop where his mother had taken him and his older brother three times each year, paying precious cash for professional haircuts— once before Easter Sunday, once before Epiphany, and again on the occasion of each child's Name Day. Many of the old places were gone now, replaced by souvlaki stands, motorbike rental shops, *Bureaus de Change*, and other conveniences that existed solely for the tourists who came by the thousands each summer.

But the church and the outdoor market, the dock house where the fishermen cleaned and repaired their nets, and the *ouzeria* where the sluggards gathered to boast and tell lies: these places remained. These were the scenes that defined his boyhood village.

This morning he enjoyed the smell of freshly-baked bread and confections coming from the ovens where Panos, the village baker, stood outside the door of his shop with a broad smile on his lips and flour spilled over the front of his apron. Modestos also detected the aroma of roasting meats coming from the open windows and doorways of the handsome homes. A pack of five scrawny dogs gathered in front of the only butcher shop, sniffing in restless anticipation.

And many of the *nikokyra*, the housewives, were about on this glowing morning, happily doing their shopping, or simply gossiping with neighbors and friends. The more industrious women scrubbed down steps and walkways. With pales at their sides and brushes in hand, they were dedicated to the task of restoring order from the seasonal chaos of dust and grime, and intent on putting the mark of redemption squarely upon a fallen world.

Widows and old women were dressed all in black, each having lost somebody she loved—be it husband, brother, or son. They sat out on balconies and doorsteps, sunning their faces after having remained inside throughout the rainy season.

Aphrodite had not always lived in the apartment above the *dhomatia*. In fact, Modestos had bought the building with his savings and moved his mother there when the family's home was given to his sister Tassoula at the time of her marriage. It was understood to be the oldest son's responsibility to care for elderly parents, and since Modestos' older brother had died tragically at a young age, the duty had fallen upon him. It was one he bore with a sense of irony, but surely no resentment.

When father and son arrived at the *dhomatia* the first thing they did was visit Aphrodite, who was busy watching over her simmering pots and crocheting some innumerable piece of handiwork. With thick, slightly arthritic fingers, she worked her needles in and out, producing a bit of lace for an unknown beneficiary. With the passing hours she meditated upon the repetitive stitches as if they represented the accumulated circumstances of her life. Her apartment was filled with such creations, tugged loops and painstaking tassels, stitches, beads, and knots. Many of these patterns were handed down from her mother; others were manifestations of her solitude or grief. The few handcrafted items she had not given away lay stored in her chest, protected in leaves of camphor.

"You tell me lies!" she croaked at her son.

"What lies, Mama?"

"You said Yanni would come yesterday. So I waited and waited. No Yanni!"

"I was ill, *Mamou*," Yanni explained as he went to her and kissed her on each cheek.

"But now you are well?"

"*Oráia!*" he assured her.

Soon they were ready to begin their work. Modestos prepared the paint while Yanni unrolled the drop cloths. With brush in hand, Yanni white-washed the outside of the *dhomatia*; Modestos painted the shutters and doors and handrails blue as he sang along with the folk songs being played on the Government-sponsored radio station.

"Papa," said Yanni with exasperation in his voice, "your singing is idiotic! Like Yannis, the *vlakos*."

"Your fascination with all things foreign keeps you from appreciating the traditional ballads," said Modestos.

"So much tradition is nothing but an embarrassment," Yanni answered cynically. "It belongs inside museums."

"*Oxi*, Yanni, you are wrong."

"The twenty-first century demands that we change or be left in poverty and squalor," said Yanni definitively.

Though he would have preferred it was not so, Modestos knew his son's assessment was basically correct. He worked in an office as a technician; his father's father had been a shepherd. "So much serious debate is bound to give a person a headache," said Modestos trying to lighten the moment.

After a morning's work they changed into casual clothes and sat down to lunch. Aphrodite had cooked *pastitsio*, and the aroma of the baked macaroni, tomatoes, and bechamel sauce made their mouths water. Modestos stuffed his napkin into his shirt collar and took his knife and fork in hand. He covered his *pastitsio* with ground cinnamon and spread sheep's cheese and oil over his coarse bread. He drank several glasses of spring water without pause, then several more of red wine with his meal. Yanni, on the other hand, ate more delicately than his father. He placed his napkin on his lap, not over his chest. And with slender, long fingers he maneuvered his utensils with grace. Rather than devour his food ravenously, he tended more toward his mother's manners. Both men ate generously, while Aphrodite herself would not touch a bite.

"Very soon," Modestos said to his mother, "the tourists will be arriving."

Aphrodite summoned up her phlegm, as if to spit on these intruders. "I have never liked it! I never wished for it," she said. "Takis, you come and go at all hours of the night. You bring strangers to stay in my house. Why?"

"I do it for money, Mama. So Yanni can attend the university in Italy."

"Italy!" she said with contempt. Again she gathered the essence of her disdain inside her mouth. "And Germans... Of all people! I'll never understand. But I am too old to influence you now, Takis. Soon I'll be dead."

Modestos did not try to disagree with the obvious.

After lunch Modestos and Yanni walked round the bay to the resort town of Gouvia. It was not a long walk, and the tendency to meander was rewarded by feelings of well-being. They passed a boy selling dried apricots, and Modestos bought a small basketful for them to eat as they went.

All during the morning Modestos' mind had been on Sophia. To say the least, she was skeptical about him leaving Corfu for a stint in the army; nevertheless, she was being very brave regarding the possibility. Caught up in the dilemma himself, he had not remembered to bring her a present from Athens. He thought he had detected disappointment on Sophia's face the other night when he'd not produced some small token of his love and appreciation. He knew she would never hold such an omission against him, though he wanted to make amends quickly. So he went inside a small shop selling imported toiletries to have a look around.

Inside the shop he considered several items, but the longer he looked, the more indecisive he became. He tested perfumes from France and Italy, sniffed at lotions from Germany and Denmark, read as best he could about the extraordinary results one might expect from the mudpacks and facial scrubs from Sweden. The shopkeeper tried to be helpful, but it was Yanni who seemed to know his mother's personal tastes best and suggested an ornamental box containing three different French *savons du toilette*. Modestos made the purchase before walking with Yanni back to Puthena village to finish the painting.

CHAPTER 7
AN AFFAIR IN VALAIS

IT WAS AFTER SEVEN when Doran emerged from the station at Brig in Switzerland. Towering over the river valley, the peaks of Belalp and the Glishorn still wore snowy caps in mid-April, though at lower elevations alpine blossoms were already prolific. Verdant forests encompassed the ancient settlement and provided sanctuary for owls and cuckoo birds, while on the valley floor the Rhone River made its way toward France. To Doran, this modern yet quaint, German-speaking village seemed at first glance agreeable to accommodating another curious traveler, so he ventured into town.

Along Victoriastrasse, three and four-story stone buildings with elegant facades curved graciously with the bend in the busy boulevard. Steeples with weather vanes and golden crests topped half-timbered towers, and onion-top domes were covered with slate tiles. Colorful awnings shaded each shop display, while old-style street lamps hung from ornate, wrought iron supports. Forming a queue in front of the station, taxicabs and yellow postal buses with destination plaques such as 'Rosswald' and 'Naters' took on passengers, and then departed with a tooting of their horns.

Up the tree-lined Bahnhofstrasse he went, a bounce in his step that seemed oddly unlike his own familiar, loping gate. This evening he could not stop smiling as he glimpsed his reflection in the glass of a shop window. How happily out of character he felt, playing the unlikely role of a transient with two pairs of jeans and a pocketful of traveler's checks!

Now two weeks into his trip, Doran had gained a measure of confidence in his natural abilities at navigation and integration. Fearlessly climbing a winding set of stone steps and entering a vast foyer, he came to the door of *Frau* Lydia Nanzer, where he inquired about a room. Wiping her hands on her flower-print apron, the grandmotherly woman took up her set of keys and led him to the second floor. There she offered him her best room.

Throwing open a set of French doors, *Frau* Nanzer invited him onto a balcony that overlooked the village church and its garden and cemetery. Doran complimented her on her home, and though she did not speak English, she seemed to understand. Taking a final look around the room to make certain he had everything he needed, she seemed satisfied. Graciously, she took her leave, closing the door behind her.

Tossing his bag on a chair and flopping down upon the bed, Doran suddenly realized he felt quite hungry. At the front of the *pension*, a modern *gasthof* was serving German-style food, so he washed up, changed his clothes, and walked round to the front of the building. He seated himself at a table on the terrace, for the evening was a splendid one.

Doran's German was pathetic, so with a rather comical approach to sign language and no small commitment to pointing, he tried to make himself understood to the attractive waitress. At the pinnacle of his idiocy, she began laughing good-naturedly. "Sorry to make you struggle," she said in English. "Do you understand the menu at all?"

"Hardly," Doran confessed.

"Do you have a big appetite tonight?" she asked, smiling.

"I haven't eaten since breakfast," Doran told her.

"Allow me to bring you the *Bauernschmausteller*," she suggested. "I know it will be just right."

"I'm in your hands," said Doran, smiling through his embarrassment.

Watching her turn and walk away, he admired her long legs and shapely figure. She moved without resistance, and Doran guessed that she knew he was watching her. Over the rim of her stylish glasses she peeked at him and impishly raised an eyebrow.

A few minutes later she brought him a stein of beer, and Doran asked her name.

"Trudi Heberling," she told him. "What's yours?"

"Doran Seeger."

Trudi seemed savvy and sophisticated, though thoroughly approachable. "Enjoy the beer," she said. "I will bring the food shortly." She was off again to serve the other tables.

Unlike the Netherlands, no unseemly element was visible here in *Valais*: no sense of desperation; no insatiable taste for the avante-garde. On first impression, Swiss society seemed to operate with foresight and efficiency. There were no drunks in the parks; there was no trash lying around. In fact, Doran had seen a power plant near Montreaux that made the boast, '*Energei vom Abfalle*!' Energy from garbage!

Trudi brought the *Bauernschmausteller*, a sampling of sausages, a portion of baked ham still on the bone, a pork cutlet, and sauerkraut. "*Guten appetit!*" she said.

Doran ate purposefully then lingered over his drink. Not once did the waitress try to hurry him. Though she did glance his way each time she crossed the terrace. Her look was very friendly, and Doran thoroughly enjoyed the flirtation.

"*Gut geschmeckt?*" she later asked as she cleared his plate.

"I beg your pardon."

"How was the food?"

"*Wundebar,*" he said. Though slightly hesitant, he ventured, "How late do you work?"

"Why do you want to know?" she teased.

"I was hoping we might go somewhere for coffee or schnapps."

"You want to have coffee with me?" she said, surprised.

"Unless you're married, or not available," he stumbled.

"I am not married," she said, now playing the coquette.

They smiled as they surveyed one another. Trudi broke the silence. "I will be free at half past the hour. I'll bring you another glass of beer if you want to wait."

"Wonderful," said Doran.

FRUSTUCK, HERR SEEGER!" "Breakfast is served!"

Doran opened his eyes sluggishly to the morning light that came gently through colorful curtains. Trudi Heberling lay in bed beside him. She'd made love to him most of the night, and then recited aloud the poems of Rilke in her sleep.

"*Kein Frustuck heute, Frau* Nanzer!" he called.

Doran heard the old lady chuckle as she descended the stairs, then the bells from the church chimed nine o'clock. Trudi purred as she rolled over and barely opened her big, black eyes. "Ah, *Guten Morgen, Liebchien,*" she said in her dusky voice. She snuggled closer to him and kissed his neck.

Wrapped in down and gathered by the arms of affection, Doran reconstructed the events that had led to this encounter. It was his experience that dependencies often developed far too quickly for his liking, and this particular situation already had obvious limitations.

"Why have you come to Switzerland?" Trudi asked

him.

"What makes you ask?"

"Perhaps you are running from the police," she lured. "I might imagine something sinister or intriguing. I understand crime is rampant in America."

Sorry to dismiss your fantasy, but my only crime is that of complacency," he said. "I'm in the process of reconstructing my foundation."

Trudi's singular expression offset intimacy for the moment. "A curious task for a person your age," she observed.

"I think so, too."

"A strong foundation is essential, I believe, but nobody who is inherently weak makes such passionate love, *Mein Herr*."

Doran cleared his throat in embarrassment. "I'm sure you must know a place where we can have a leisurely breakfast," he said in diversion.

"Of course. But first I must shower."

"I'm customarily slow to wake up," Doran told her.

"I'm not fussy. I will be only ten minutes."

Underneath blue umbrellas in front of *Hôtel du Commerce*, Doran and Trudi lingered over a continental breakfast. Rather than talk about himself, Doran commented redundantly about the beauty of the Alps.

"Perhaps we can go for a hike in the mountains today," Trudi suggested as she finished her Nescafe. "I can show you the old timbered village where I live. The footpaths go everywhere. If you like, we can take some fruit and cheese and wine and hike all the way to the *Rosswald*."

"Splendid!" said Doran.

Beginning at the cemetery, which surrounded the little church at the foot of the massive alp called Glishorn, they started up the footpath that led through the old timbered village, then into the lush forest, and finally over the Simplon Pass. Even in Switzerland this village was an anachronism, yet the scene was vividly alive with animals

85

grazing in their backyard pastures, wild flowers growing untrimmed near a fence post or a wooden gate, and doors adorned with antlers or tin-sculpted *objets d'art.*

Doran became absorbed in taking high-detail photos, so Trudi walked ahead. Once Doran shot the final exposure on his roll of film, he slung his camera over his shoulder and wandered along the twisting lanes. Around an inclining curve he discovered Trudi chatting with a robust, elderly gentleman dressed in a plaid shirt and baggy trousers held up by red suspenders. The cuffs of his pants were tucked into calf-high rubber boots, and he wore a conical cap with a long black feather sticking out of its band. Doran approached with deference. The old man's greeting was punctuated by the fairytale twinkle in his eye.

"This is my grandfather, *Herr* Joseph," Trudi introduced.

"*Guten Tag, Mein Herr,*" said Doran. "My name is Doran Seeger." They shook hands.

"Joseph has lived his entire life in this village," Trudi explained.

"*Dieser Dorf ist sehr schon,*" Doran complimented. "*Sehr interresant!*" "Your village is very beautiful and quite interesting."

"*Ja! Dieses Bauen sint zeitgemass. Die Heiden lebt hier seit das Mittelalter. Das ist wahr!*"

Doran looked to Trudi for a translation. "My grandfather is not impressed by all the *new* buildings in the town of Brig," she told him. "Joseph says the buildings in the old village are not up to date, but there is a reason they endure. You see the Pagans have lived here since the Middle Ages. Long ago the Rhone River was much more powerful, and every spring the run-off from the melting snow would flood the valley. That is why the shepherds built their homes on the ledges of the Alps. But the valley has not flooded for many years. Now the train runs beside the water."

The old man's perception was keen and he had no

trouble determining precisely what Trudi was telling her new friend. *Herr* Joseph seemed to show resignation to some ill-conceived approach that he had long ago determined he was powerless to change. *"Diese Christliche Leute leben mit einer falsch Sicherheit!"* he told them.

"The Christians live with a false sense of security," Trudi faithfully interpreted.

"So your grandfather is not Catholic?"

"Sometimes old and new can co-exist," she said.

Herr Heberling conducted them on a short tour of the village, showing Doran the house where his grandfather was born. Not a hundred meters from the house of Jopseph's grandfather stood the house where his father had lived, and where he, himself, was born. And just across a green pasture, where half a dozen goats grazed the long grass, stood *Herr* Heberling's house. There he had lived with his wife Hilde until she died seven years ago. Now she rested in the cemetery at the church. But Joseph rarely visited her grave. He left the weeding and candle lighting and flower placing to Trudi, since his own daughter, Ilse, was also dead.

Behind his chalet-type house, *Herr* Joseph grew a garden of onions, chard, spinach, and tomatoes, as well as many, many flowers. With a wave of his thick hand, *Herr* Heberling invited his granddaughter and her friend to step into his root cellar. From a dusty shelf he took down a one-foot-square black box shaped like a suitcase. *"Zauber,"* he told them, the German word for magic.

Doran and Trudi followed the old man as he walked back into the garden. He moved to the low wall that separated his garden from the kindergarten next door. Half a dozen children were playing in the adjacent yard, and *Herr* Joseph tenderly implored them, *"Tanzen sie jetzt zu meinem Musik, schones Kinder!"* "Dance to the music, my pretty children." And he opened his magic box to reveal an old gramophone and two well-worn records. *Herr* Joseph cranked the machine well, and the scratchy music delighted the children and sent them whirling. Innocent and unselfconscious, they danced round and round, their hands together, forming a dizzy, Picasso-like circle. Their laughter spirited the birds in the trees that surrounded the garden. Grandfather Joseph's gramophone had performed its magic again, linking past, present, and future.

A few minutes later the gramophone was back in its black case, and the children had returned to their original game. *Herr* Joseph led the way back to the root cellar, where he proudly showed Doran his cache of bottles. "*Trinken?*" he offered.

He took down a bottle filled with clear liquid. "*Wasser*," he explained as he handed the open bottle to Doran. Somehow, Doran knew this libation would not prove so benign, but he would not dream of refusing the old man's gesture of friendship. He took a deep drink and hoped such indiscretion would not result in blindness. "Schnapps!" he croaked as he passed the liquor back to its maker.

"*Apfel gemacht*," *Herr* Heberling told him. They each had several more swallows, and over these drinks a bond of friendship was sealed.

After bidding *Herr* Heberling '*auf wiedersehen*,' Doran and Trudi slung their rucksacks over their shoulders and continued their hike. Light green meadows offset the darker color of the sweeping stands of fragrant larch trees; and the the remaining snow fields in the higher mountains was contrasted by the verdant springtime hue.

Reaching the *Rosswald*, they spread a blanket in a grassy pasture well off the road. In the distance they could hear the sound of a waterfall, and a breeze blew through the tops of the tall pines. They lay together on the blanket, and Trudi nonchalantly stroked Doran's hair.

"Your grandfather's affection for you is obvious," Doran said.

"*Ja, das wahr...*" Trudi unlaced her hiking shoes and removed her socks. She put her bare feet over the edge of the blanket and allowed her toes to explore the long blades of grass. Her round face was full of healthy color from their three-hour walk in the sunshine. "I was only thirteen when my parents died in an avalanche," Trudi revealed. "I was devastated, but I never had a moment of doubt that Joseph and Grandmother Hilde would take care of me. After I lost Grandmother Hilde, it strengthened the bond between *Herr* Joseph and me. Now I suspect he needs me more than I need him. Of course I will not fail him. He is so dear to me." Trudi sighed deeply. She brushed her eye to clear a teardrop shed long ago. "Forgive me, Doran," she implored needlessly. "Perhaps we should lighten the atmosphere, or a dark cloud might come, and there is no place here to take shelter." She reached inside her pack and began assembling their lunch.

Arriving back at Brig, they walked through town to Garni Glishorn, for it was nearly time for Trudi to go to work at the *gasthof*. Ever since landing in Brig, Doran's attention had been focused solely on his newfound friend. "Will I see you later?" he asked Trudi.

"Ah, this has been a full day—a wonderful day!" she said. "*Mein Arbeit lauft bis elf Uhr*, so perhaps it is best that I go home tonight. *Zu schlaffen!*" She kissed him sweetly on each cheek. "I will call on you in the morning," she said.

"You mean I must stay alone tonight?"

"Perhaps *Frau* Nanzer would be willing to give you some comfort," she chuckled.

"What a thought that is," Doran said.

On the balcony at Garni Glishorn, Doran held a sketch pad on his lap. His gaze was drawn to the massive hillsides dotted with chalets. Beyond the homes lay the huge snow fields. The handsome church dominated the foreground, and all around the old neighborhood tulips and lilacs and cherry trees were in bloom. Doran watched a woman hoe her garden behind an ancient stone wall. A young collie tied to an iron railing near the churchyard stairs watched some workmen in polite excitement. With a variety of colored pencils he absorbed himself in the quasi-artistic task of documenting such common scenes of Swiss village life. Though less than accomplished as an artist, Doran gained a wide perspective from this balcony. It offered a unique vision of the culture in microcosm. As he sketched, the church bells began to ring, and two dozen women filed out of the chapel after evening mass. Among them was seventy-five-year-old *Frau* Nanzer. Many of the pious women paused at the gravesites of departed relatives. Some placed flowers by the headstones or cleared away weeds and debris. This was their daily ritual of remembrance. In Valais the dead were not forgotten.

Doran fell asleep in his chair as the moon rose over the mountains. When he awoke, the yellow globes of the streetlights revealed images in chiaroscuro of the ancient buildings across the street. He heard a voice softly calling him. Trudi stood on the walkway below the balcony.

"I saw you sitting there," she said. "I thought I would say good-night."

"I was asleep in my chair," Doran explained. "Do you want to come up?"

"It's late. I should go home," she said with the light of the moon reflected in her black eyes. Then she turned and headed up the *wanderweg*.

NEXT EVENING OVER DINNER, they noticed a crew of workers assembling a stage in front of the Hotel Victoria, and they asked the waiter what festivities were planned. He told them there was to be a performance of *Rigoletto* that night by the renowned *Salzberger Marionetten Theater*. "We must stay for the opera," Trudi determined.

The musicians arrived as the bells chimed eight o'clock. The players tuned their instruments and the conductor took the podium. Introductions were made, and the orchestra began the overture as fading rays of sunlight shone through irriguous clouds and bathed the mountains in a wash of misty color. To the delight of the audience, the splendidly costumed, two-foot-high, wooden characters made their appearance on the stage, each in strong voice. The children danced with glee as the spirited music began, and the middle-aged *Hausfraue* tapped their puffy feet to the rhythm of the music and held hands with their husbands. Doran stood behind Trudi with his arms wrapped round her small waist, his cheek pressed close to hers. "Everyone comes out," he said. "They come to be together and talk to one another. They laugh together. They share their happiness and their troubles."

Two hours later, as the charming production concluded, storm clouds gathered over the Rhone Valley. Thunder echoed off the mountainsides, and the rain came down in sheets just as the final chord sounded. The downpour sent everyone scurrying for cover. Up darkened cobblestone streets Doran and Trudi ran with no hope of staying dry. Trudi shrieked, and Doran was surprised to hear the sound of his own laughter as huge drops drenched him. The wet stones glistened in the yellow light of the street lamps, and the forest loomed above on the terraced hillsides. Their shoes became soaked, and their pant legs were wet up to the knees. When they reached Garni Glishorn, *Frau* Nanzer was waiting with the key to Doran's room. "Such a shame the rain came so early," she commiserated. "There was to be a fireworks display after the opera. Now the children will have to miss it."

"Too bad," said Trudi. "I think it will probably storm all night long."

Frau Nanzer nodded. "*Guten Abend, Lieben!*"

"*Guten Abend,*" said Doran.

MONDAY MORNING DORAN AND TRUDI walked together through town to the station in Brig. After standing in line to buy Doran's ticket, they sat quietly and waited on the platform for the train to take him to Italy. Even though they had known one another only a short time, each realized that parting would not be easy. They

91

could promise to write, or visit one another in the future, though in all likelihood such promises were good only for consolation. It would simply have to be enough for each to remember fondly this time they had shared.

When the train arrived, Doran brushed Trudi's cheek with a kiss before hugging her deeply.

"Let's not make this difficult," she said. Sentimental tears welled in her eyes.

"I don't know what to say," Doran choked.

They kissed once, and then Doran picked up his bag and got onboard the train.

CHAPTER 8
SACRIFICE AND THE SWEET LIFE

NO DOUBT THE ITALIAN CULTURE was accomplished on many levels at elaborate facades, and that fact became immediately evident to the Van Zyl sisters at Menton on the French/Italian frontier. On the French side of the border the buildings were freshly painted, the windows washed, trash swept. But like a day-old rose, faded beauty was apparently no less beautiful to the Italian eye, and a cracking wall, or a piece of ruined tile, or a bit of peeling paint only fanned the fires of romance.

Wearing starched blue uniforms and proposing some pseudo-authoritarian pride with their impeccable posture, the Italian *Carabinieri* came aboard the train and delayed its progress an entire hour while conducting a perfunctory passport check. Neither Alarice nor Gisela was impressed by their over-groomed braggadocio.

Once away from Menton, the train lumbered past beach-side resorts and sun-drenched villas. Built into the hillsides and surrounded by stands of cypress trees and palms swaying in the Mediterranean breeze, these nineteenth century estates were painted the color of fresh cream and topped by terra cotta roofs, like cinnamon sprinkles over cappuccino.

At Genoa, the police were waiting on the platform with bomb-sniffing German Shepherds. The dogs sniffed at skirts and pant legs without apology, while their keepers' expressions remained stony and unsympathetic.

"I need to stretch my legs," said Alarice.

"I'll go with you," Gisela offered.

Stepping into the corridor, Alarice leaned out the window and breathed in the heavy seaside air. Traveling only a few hours, the climate was noticeably different from Nice. This air was like Vin Santo, a thick, amber wine made from grapes dried on straw in the hot sun, then aged well past maturity. Here the air was saturated with sea lore and superstition and religion. "What do you think?" Alarice asked her sister.

"Sort of run down, but maybe it's too soon to judge," said Gisela.

Intensely curious toward cultural differences, they watched the younger Italian women as they moved across the platform. In Italy the unmarried girls were all lines and angles. Poignant yet peripheral, they were at once falsely seductive with their sultry expressions and painted red lips. With black eyeliner, plunging necklines, and skin-tight, hip-hugger jeans, they appeared dangerously impassioned, yet frightened.

At Pisa, a springtime shower had just ended and the air was laden with moisture. Skies were big in Tuscany, and by early afternoon the gathering clouds often rendered the sweet rains that brought bounty in Titian colors.

Riding through the marvelous Valley of the Arno, past ancient villages built similarly into the terraced hillsides, with churches and bell towers at their meridians, and fallow vineyards cascading over the undulating landscape, Alarice and Gisela observed the rural stone houses with their red slate rooftops and small gardens. Their peculiar walled-in geometry spoke in curious riddles to countless ancient land disputes. Nothing here was equilateral, all dimensions coming up odd when considered through the sextant.

"I can't help wondering what it might have been like growing up in the shadow of the Madonna," Gisela remarked.

Alarice was feeling almost intoxicated by the perfect balance of land and sky, hill and valley, forest, farm, and vineyard. Drinking in the utter sensuality of lineament, she was contrasting gradient values of a single color. "Our Dutch sensibilities demand more reason," she told her sister. "We are grounded in the physical world, after all. Without the dikes we would be swept under by the sea."

They arrived tired but still in high spirits at the Stazione Santa Maria Novella in Florence. From the piazza in front of the busy terminal they walked up the Via Nazionale as clouds gathered for yet another downpour. With a single crack of thunder the heavens opened. Up came the umbrellas of those on the sidewalk—red, white, and green—the colors of Italy's national emblem.

Wet to the skin in a matter of minutes, the sisters walked over rain-slick cobblestones and through murky puddles up the Via Faenza, often pressing themselves against the buildings to avoid oncoming autos. The facades of these three and four-story structures looked graceful but timeworn, with iron oxidation bleeding through the exhaust-stained stucco. Heavy doorways led into dark and mysterious foyers, where teenage lovers were making out, and sculpted gargoyles breathed malevolence from their places above ornate thresholds.

The entryway at number seventy-seven was somewhat lurid and gloomy, but Alarice and Gisela were forewarned about Italian exteriors. Besides, Pensione Lelli had come highly recommended by friends in Rotterdam. So they crowded themselves and their luggage inside the tiny elevator and rode to the second floor. There they found a handsome young man at work behind the reception desk.

Amidst a flurry of activity he was calling out instructions to a bevy of young women dressed in work smocks. Seeking clarification of their specific duties, they approached their supervisor, ranting in breathless Italian and waving their hands and arms madly. Like a cop at a busy intersection, the young man sent the housekeepers in various directions, each with new instructions.

Then he turned to Alarice and Gisela. "*Buon giorno, Signorini,*" he said with an almost imperceptible bow. His clothes were stylish and his grooming impeccable. Gisela nudged Alarice with her hip. The gesture was in place of a more direct comment regarding the host's obvious sexuality.

"Hello," Alarice said in English while ignoring her sister's gesture. "We understand you might have a clean room for us."

With feigned embarrassment the reception clerk related, "My English is not good. I am very sorry."

At that moment, yet another employee interrupted with a problem needing immediate attention. Language flew about like debris in a windstorm, climaxing finally in a clap of thunderous innuendo. Off she went with glaring eyes, and the young man's practiced composure returned as if the interlude had never occurred.

"Excuse my rudeness, please," he apologized to Alarice and Gisela. "We are very busy today. Now, how can I help you?"

"Do you have a clean room?" Alarice repeated.

"Clean room..." He rolled the words around on his tongue as if tasting new wine. "Ah! *Si, si, si. Uno momento, per favore.*"

Leaving Alarice and Gisela standing in the red glow of the reception area, the clerk exited with all the grace of a dancer moving off-stage. Evidently he meant to attend to some task necessary for their accommodation. They passed the time by examining the many artistic posters that decorated every wall in the room: a masked figure reveling through the fog-draped streets of Venice during Carnival; a young girl bathing her feet in the waters of the Trevi Fountain in Rome; horsemen carrying colorful banners at the Palio procession in Siena.

A short time later one of the housekeepers approached. Speaking Italian (which neither sister understood well), she directed them to leave their luggage and come with her. The sisters looked curiously at one another but shrugged off their doubts. They followed the maid down a dimly lit hallway, into a closet-sized room obviously used for storing linens. The girl handed each of them a smock and began issuing what they perceived to be instructions for work.

"What's this? What's this?" Alarice asked her sister.

Gisela began laughing. "For some reason they think we have come to work as housekeepers."

"But this is ridiculous!" Alarice said as she tried to hand back the apron. The Italian girl would not accept it. "Come on," Alarice said, "let's get out of here!"

The maid in charge of outfitting the newcomers threw the smocks onto the floor, shook her head in exasperation, and cursed in Italian. "Giuvanni!" she called.

Alarice and Gisela walked back up the hallway, determined only to collect their luggage and be on their way. The housekeeper came along behind calling for Giuvanni. When they reached the reception area they encountered the clerk. Confused, he looked on as they gathered their bags to leave. The maid tried to explain what had happened when she had tried to show the new employees their tasks.

"Please wait," Giuvanni beseeched. Approaching the girls, he plaintively asked, "What is the problem?" He put his hand upon Gisela's shoulder. "I thought you said you were here to clean rooms. Have I misunderstood?"

Gisela looked at Alarice and broke out laughing. Then Alarice began laughing, too. "We asked you for a *clean room*," Gisela explained. "We are not here to work as maids. We are tourists!"

"*Dio mio*!" said the clerk, rolling his eyes. Then he explained the twisted meaning to the housekeeper, who was, by this time, quite beside herself. She, too, began laughing.

"I am so humiliated," said Giuvanni. "I hope you can forgive me. You must accept my finest room. Let me escort you," he said. He gathered their luggage in his arms. "There is a marvelous view of the *Duomo*," he went on. "And the light comes gently in the morning. You will see!"

Indeed, the room was exactly what they might have hoped for—simple yet elegant, with a marble floor and a fourteen-foot-high ceiling. Happy wallpaper displaying cherubs and satyrs led to a border of gilded molding. A superb collection of tastefully modern Italian furniture brought the room into the present tense. "I hope the room is to your liking," said Giuvanni. "And again, please accept my sincere apology."

"No need to humble yourself any further," said Gisela.

"You are very gracious, *Signorina*. But let me explain. You see, many art students come to study in Firenze, and Signor Lelli, the owner of this *pensione*, feels an intense desire—No! Call it an obligation!—to help aspiring artists. For years he has employed students here at his *pensione* as housekeepers and clerks. To help them make ends meet. So, you see, even as my mistake was one of ignorance for language, still it was a natural one."

"Are you also an artist?" asked Gisela.

Giuvanni lowered his eyes to look at his hands. Folded at his waist, Gisela could see that the skin on his fingertips was dry and cracked. "I make an effort at sculpture," he said.

"Thank you for renting us this beautiful room," Alarice offered. "It's right out of Forster's novel."

"Say no more, please. It is the least I can do."

Though she was not altogether certain of Giuvanni's sincerity, Alarice was unwilling, for the moment, to allow such doubts to ruin the spontaneity of the encounter. Besides, she could see that Gisela liked him.

"Is this your first time in Italia?" he asked them.

"Yes, it is," said Gisela. She was beginning to flirt with her eyes. "And it feels wonderful!"

"Of course I could never be impartial. Italy is my country." Giuvanni's Etruscan eyes flashed with pride as he spoke of his heritage. "Where is your home?" he asked.

"Rotterdam," said Alarice.

"I have not visited there myself, but I am sure it is very beautiful, too," he said. Though Giuvanni's features took the light in the room benevolently, the source of this light was not obvious. If blessings could be luminary in nature, perhaps certain human beings were natural repositories.

"Very different from Italy," Alarice observed through her preoccupation.

"Perhaps you will allow me to be your guide during your stay in Firenze. So I might make amends for my foolish mistake."

"That is very kind of you," said Gisela.

"Please, the pleasure will be mine," said Giuvanni, first unabashedly assessing Gisela, and then turning his eye to Alarice. "Are you close friends or are you sisters?" he asked.

"Sisters. Though we are ten years apart in age," explained Gisela. "But how did you know?"

"If it is not obvious by your appearance, your mannerisms reveal the relationship," he confirmed.

"It seems," said Gisela, "that you have seen in ten minutes what we have missed our entire lives."

IN GISELA VAN ZYL'S OPINION, the young art student, Giuvanni Capello, was handsome, gallant, and very sexy, a fact she belabored to her sister all during their first afternoon and evening at Pensione Lelli. The elder sister's admiration for their newfound friend and guide was somewhat less exuberant. Still she could not help agreeing with Gisela. "He is charming and suave," she said, "but I think you should be cautious of him."

Next morning, Giuvanni Capello awakened the vacationing Dutch sisters with a polite knock on their door. He announced that breakfast would be brought to their room in thirty minutes, and then withdrew. The sisters rose, showered, and dressed before Giuvanni returned, and when the promised repast arrived, they lingered with their host on the terrace over coffee and pastries.

After breakfast, they set out on a tour of Firenze with Giuvanni as guide. A short walk led them to Brunelleschi's Duomo of Santa Maria del Fiore Cathedral, still resplendent in tinctures of pastel green and pink cast against a glossy backdrop of Carrara stone. With its arched circles, its cupola, and its ingenious double-shell supports, the cathedral was dedicated to the glory of God, though it said more about human accomplishment.

Along with Giotto's two hundred seventy-four-foot Bell Tower, the octagonal Baptistery finished the Holy Trinity. The Baptistery's cavernous interior seemed cold and empty to Alarice.

"It is four hundred seventeen steps to the top of the Lilly Tower," Giuvanni told them. "Not quite as high as the *Duomo*, but I like the view of the city much better. You *must* climb to the top."

Though the girls were accustomed to walking, the climb to the top of the Bell Tower was so physically strenuous that they had to pause often to catch their breath. This was no less true for Giuvanni. Having lived in Florence his entire life, he was not inclined to make such an ascent without ample provocation. And while he had not exaggerated the view from the pinnacle, still the two Dutch sisters were his primary motivation for making such an exhausting climb.

From the top of the tower they could see all of Florence, as well as the Tuscan hills to the west of the city.

The red tile roof of the Duomo seemed almost at arm's length, while pedestrians and traffic moved along on the street below. The ultimate lowlanders, Alarice and Gisela were left breathless and dizzy by the vista.

"Each time I make this climb I am more amazed," said Giuvanni, lighting a cigarette and profiling himself against the hazy landscape.

"The cathedral, the Baptistery, the Tuscan hills—it's all so beautiful!" said Alarice.

"It's as if we've been transported back in time and we are standing in the midst of the Renaissance," said Gisela.

"In the year Fourteen hundred," Giuvanni explained, "Firenze was quite different than the other city-states throughout Italy. The city was a republic of merchants and bankers. Such gentlemen aspired to fine living, and began to cultivate a liking for secular books, which were, until this time, hidden away throughout Europe."

"Where were these books concealed?" Gisela asked.

"Anywhere and everywhere," said Giuvanni, extending his arm across the breadth of the continent. "Perhaps Lucretius might turn up beside a cookbook inside a Swiss monastery; or maybe Cicero's letters to Atticus were discovered in some burial vault."

They walked to the north side of the tower to take in the view from yet another perspective.

Giuvanni continued: "Florentines of the early Renaissance had the impassioned desire to surpass their own efforts, no matter how lofty their accomplishments became. They favored versatility over specialization. Consider Leonardo da Vinci! He was certainly a master painter, architect, and inventor—*pazzo-matto!*"

For a time Giuvanni gazed over the edge. Eternity was imminent, but the present promised rewards as well. "What do you think, Signorini? Shall we walk onward to the Palazzo Medici or the Uffizi Gallery?" he asked.

"The Uffizi," said Gisela.

Through labyrinthine streets in austere light they went,

to the Loggia della Signoria. There the cobbled courtyard of the Palazzo Vecchio was encircled by clay pots filled with profusely blooming wisteria and tuberose. Blissful Madonnas with their innocent *bambini* looked down through the ages from the heights of marble cornices, and the venerable 'Fountain of Neptune,' with its base of bronze and its water nymphs, satyrs, and horses' heads, inspired an unanticipated spiritual fever in Alarice. Just off the piazza were the wings of the Uffizi.

Inside the museum the zenith of the Italian Renaissance was revealed. Alarice paused ten full minutes before Botticelli's 'Birth of Venus.' Her emotions overwhelmed her. In her heart it was the first day of spring as Zephyrs bore the goddess to shore upon the shell of a clam.

Nearby hung 'Mars and Venus,' the artist's mythical conception of god and goddess. Full-bodied in their Heavenly garden, they were attended by characters with pointed ears, horns, and animal haunches. Such archetypal images posed questions that Alarice was *not* presently prepared to contemplate. Her sense of future remained as cloudy as the leaden skies over Holland, but the thunder of the Renaissance now echoed in her consciousness. *Mi pare rinascere*, she thought to herself. I have been reborn.

In her state of reverie she lost track of time. Where were Gisela and Giuvanni? After a short search she located them in the main hall, talking quietly on a bench in front of a window that looked down upon the Ponte Vecch*io*. Incorporating the image of her sister and the young Italian sitting close together, Alarice found herself surprised by their intimacy. She approached slowly, careful not to invade some private moment. "It's getting late and the museum is about to close," she told them. "Take us someplace for dinner, Giuvanni."

IT WAS THE SOCIAL HOUR BEFORE THE EVENING MEAL, and the Piazza della Signoria was mobbed with people of every age and description. Standing face to face and waving their hands, they discussed politics, or business, or domestic issues. A dozen kids played with a ball near the fountain, and lovers pressed themselves together, trying to find anonymity in plain view of hundreds.

Over the Ponte Vecchio they walked—once the butcher's bridge, now taken over by gold merchants. This bridge—most famous in all of Florence—was the only bridge over the Arno spared by Hitler. "It is said that once the Arno flowed red with the blood of slaughtered animals," Giuvanni told them. "Now it is hopelessly polluted. In *our* world, sacrifice is unavoidable."

In weak shafts of watery light, Fellini's clowns gathered once more to pass the early evening by acting out a well-rehearsed farce of sin and repentance. Oscar Wilde had written that Italy was a country full of actors, the least of which were on the stage. Was the Piazza Santo Spirito the real theater for Italian melodrama? Dealers were selling heroin and syringes on the steps of Brunelleschi's graceful chapel, while the *Carabinieri* looked on with aplomb.

In the piazza, the girls, along with their indigenous escort, were merely waiting for Ristorante Natale to open for dinner. It had been a day for encountered wonders, albeit an exhausting one, but the ever-engaging Giuvanni Capello was showing no telltale signs of fatigue. He seemed intent on detailing the original *Bonfire of the Vanities*.

In Natale's dining room, conversations were vivacious. Glasses were raised in salutation, drained and refilled. The older men were dressed in brown suits and heavy shoes, while their wives wore flower print dresses, which tended to over-emphasize plump thighs and buttocks. The young people, however, were dressed in attractively cut linen clothes—expensive fashions designed in Milan.

Alarice and Gisela allowed Giuvanni to order dinner. They began with a sienna-colored soup of peppers, green olives, and herb-seasoned croutons, followed by a spinach salad covered in olive oil. Next came ravioli served in cream-and-tomato sauce. Their main course was grilled trout cooked in oil and lemon, and two bottles of Suave wine made them feel mellow after an exciting day.

After dinner they lounged over cappuccino and biscotti. Many of the diners had finished eating, paid their bills, and left the restaurant, but Giuvanni was in no hurry to go. He talked on and on about Federico Fellini's cinematic accomplishments, explaining in detail the conflicts that led Steiner to take his own life in *La Dolce Vita*. Looking directly into Alarice's eyes, he quoted: "Sometimes at night the darkness and silence weighs on me. Peace frightens me—perhaps I fear it most of all. I feel it is only a facade, hiding the face of Hell... We need to live in a state of suspended animation. Like a work of art. In a state of enchantment. We have to succeed in loving so greatly that we live outside time. Detached. Detached!"

Gisela yawned and said, "I'm afraid *I'm* feeling outside time. It's been a long day and I'm about to collapse. I must excuse myself."

"But the evening is young, Gisela," Giuvanni protested.

"You and Alarice stay out, I don't mind. But I'm going to have a short walk then go to bed."

"I won't be long," Alarice told her sister.

On her way back to Pensione Lelli, Gisela stopped briefly in the Piazza del Duomo to marvel again at the magnificent cathedral, this time under spotlights. She was standing in front of the *Duomo* only a moment or two when three young boys approached her. They were excited and hopping about. "You are beautiful," said one brashly. "Where are you from?" asked another. "Marry me!" implored the third.

Gisela smiled indulgently. The boys were harmless—perhaps fourteen or fifteen years old. But in a matter of seconds two friends joined them. Suddenly, three more lighted like pigeons come to roost. "Go away," she told them gently. "*Basta, basta!*"

With egos firmly intact, they danced round and round her, leaving Gisela no route of escape. "Come dancing with us, pretty signorina!"

"I'm too old for you. Shoo, shoo, shoo!" she told them with a smile on her lips. And they went away laughing as Gisela walked back to the pensione.

At Ristorante Natale, Alarice and Giuvanni had finished their second after-dinner drink. The light of the candle at table center cast a glow over Giuvanni's face, and the reflection of the flame flickered in his black eyes. Alarice found herself drawn to the fire.

"Tonight we are Paolo and Francesca," he told her.

"Ah, but Francesca hungered to know the Divine, and through her singular love for Paolo, she condemned herself to Hell."

"Perhaps one can never know the Divine," Giuvanni speculated. "Only the 'Holy and glorious flesh.'" He drank the last of his brandy as Alarice called for the check. All things had their price.

"You see the flesh as consecrated," she observed.

"Sometimes." His approach was not a weak one. "Would you come to my studio tonight?" he asked.

"Yes. I will come," Alarice said as she settled the bill.

They undressed in near darkness, amidst marble busts and torsos, half-sculpted. An amber light from the street shone through the tall windows, and Alarice could see her lover's tensile body. He was self-possessed, like 'David' in the Academia. Perhaps he was a chameleon. To Alarice, it had become obvious that Giuvanni had many secrets, upon most of which she had no desire to intrude. She felt consumed by some anguish of body and spirit, and her long, dreary loneliness, cultivated by degrees at home in the Netherlands, begged for respite. Two spiders, they spun a web of hesitation. Finally, Giuvanni moved to kiss her. They were completely alone in blackness.

A single tear in the corner of Alarice's eye magnified the encounter's detachment, but Giuvanni was so blind in his hollow passion that he did not notice her insularity. Their fingers touched, then their torsos. She felt his breath upon her neck. The room was spinning, and Alarice could not stop it. She did not want to stop herself. This was Brunelleschi's vanishing point.

How little we own our bodies, she thought as Giuvanni took her to his small bed. The linens were cool but not fresh; they held the smell of many nights spent alone. The springs groaned, and the echo in the cavernous room reinforced the superficiality of the act. His self-love and his bitterness covered her like a wet blanket, and in the end his lassitude shone through the facade of grand machismo. It was a fight to the end. And she tried to lie with feigned sweetness when he looked to her for approval.

Afterward, Giuvanni dared to smoke, but neither would breech the dense silence that gathered round them. Alarice thought of neon Madonnas as she felt his hand upon her breast. She closed her eyes and waited for Extreme Unction. There was no chagrin, nor talk of justification.

"I believe someday I will commit suicide in order to avoid a living Hell," Giuvanni said.

"But you are Catholic," Alarice reminded him. "And suicide is a mortal sin."

"I am only Catholic in this world," he said.

Perhaps Giuvanni's statement was some sort of purge. This boy longed for the confessional with his guilt and his morbid fantasies. Alarice recalled what he had said earlier this evening as they had crossed the Ponte Vecchio: sacrifice was unavoidable. She was only glad that Gisela had not wound up where she lay.

CHAPTER 9
THROMOS WOMEN

SOMETIMES MODESTOS arrived at his mother's apartment early enough to take her to the cemetery, but other times he was late and Aphrodite had to walk to the edge of Puthena Village where her firstborn son was at rest. Even though the morning light was perfect and the day was warm, Aphrodite wore her black scarf over her head. Her shawl covered her shoulders as she walked, step by careful step, all the way to the graveyard.

By the time she reached the cemetery, Aphrodite wanted to curse her swollen ankles, but not in the presence of spirits. Somehow she knew she would always be able to find Kostas' marker—even if she went totally blind! How many mornings had she come here to light a candle, say a prayer, and talk to her dead son?

"A stranger came to my door right out of my dreams, Kostas. At first I thought he was just a drunk or a troublemaker. Now I know it was a spirit. Too bad I never saw his face, eh?"

She opened the glass case on top of her son's headstone and, striking a wooden match, re-lighted his eternal candle.

"Too many mysteries confound me in old age," she complained. "I will never know what happened to your father, Constantine Thromos." For the moment it seemed as though the influence derived from Aphrodite's desire and frustration enveloped the small cemetery.

"Lifetimes are filled with comings and goings," the revenant commented. "Kostas, is that you?" the old woman called.

"Don't you recognize me?" he asked.

"Your picture is faded now, and my eyes fail me. Oh, I am ashamed to say it, but sometimes I don't remember your face."

"Constantine died in Italy," he told her. "You have known it for decades."

"I never knew for certain because they did not send his body. Instead, I was told lies. They expected me to believe their stories. Of course, I never believed them. But I made no trouble. I suffered in silence. Tassoula barely speaks to me now. Modestos wishes I would die so he can use my apartment for his *dhomatia*."

"Modestos is the son that every mother would wish for," appraised the long-dead brother.

Aphrodite spat on the ground—not directly over the grave, but off to one side. "How can you presume to know these things, Kostas? You've been forty years in the ground!"

"Yet you continue to come here day after day, year after year. You speak to me as if I were alive. I know I have not been quick to answer you."

"You have always been here, Kostas."

"With the faith of a saint, you keep my candle burning."

"This is the duty of a mother. Tell me, who else would do it?"

"Perhaps it is not important," he dismissed.

"Of course it is important, Kostas. But now I must go

to the butcher. Modestos is coming to visit later, and you know your brother's appetite. Now that you have made yourself obvious, walk along with me."

"*Oxi, materamou*, you walk ahead," said the spirit. "Don't worry, I'll catch up with you…"

IT WAS NOT ALWAYS EASY to understand or embrace the myriad changes taking place in Greece. But what choice did a smart woman like Sophia Thromos really have? Selective posturing was all but impossible; one either lived in the old world or the new one. Perhaps some women her age would choose not to believe that the new ways were inevitable, but Sophia was certain that, in the end, they would prove to be the foolish ones.

"Money! It is always money nowadays!" Modestos would complain when he felt tired, overworked, or frustrated. Sophia recalled that, when they were children, their parents had needed almost none. Now the persistent need for money encroached upon every aspect of their lives. Sophia knew that Modestos would all but kill himself trying to earn the money for Yanni's education, though she suspected her husband's stomach would never stand the strain. He always tried to minimize his discomfort, but lately the progression of his ulcer was all too obvious. This new life—and all that it entailed—was eating away at him from the inside.

Sophia was not altogether certain she wanted Yanni to attend school in Italy. From her point of view, his maturity was in serious question. Parties and foreign girls and drinking: those were Yanni's chief interests. Yet Modestos remained firm in his intention to send the boy away to school. Sophia dutifully acceded to her husband's intense commitment. She became determined to find a way to help him pay the cost.

"Will you be going out tonight?" she asked him.

"There is a ship due at the port later," he told her. "It is probably still too early for tourists, but I thought I would meet the boat anyway. You never know."

"True," she said passively. "I thought I might go walking along the Esplanade with a few friends. For fitness... Thalia Booras invited me. They go every Wednesday night. You don't object, do you?"

"Why would I?" said Modestos.

Now Sophia had only to deal with her lie.

ACROSS THE STREET FROM THE HOTEL ATLANTIC, in front of the high wrought iron gate where all newcomers emerged from Customs, Modestos waited at the port, anticipating the arrival of the Espresso Venicia. Many nights over the years he had met ships from Italy, and each season he enjoyed welcoming these eager-faced strangers, these *xenos*, to his homeland. Through fresh impressions reflected in their eyes, he saw Kerkyra anew, again and again. It was Modestos' aim to provide more than simple lodgings at his *dhomatia*. Equally important was the sharing with his guests of his partisan understanding about Corfu's unique personality.

Tonight the air was still and humid, and the lights from two docked military ships reflected upon the black water in the harbor. The presence of the two vessels—one Greek and one American—called to mind Modestos' meeting six weeks prior with General Stratiotis. Indeed, if he went away to Cyprus, he would miss hosting these summertime travelers, and Sophia would have to take charge of the *dhomatia*.

"Our life here is an honest one," he murmured to himself. "What is to become of these simple pleasures?"

On the horizon he could see the lights of the foreign ship approaching. For Modestos, the echo of the Italian ferry's horn was the harbinger of yet another season.

CHAPTER 10
A SERENDIPITOUS CHOICE

AT THE TOWN OF DOMODOSSOLA on the Italian-Swiss frontier, Doran boarded the Milano Express. He stared out the window as the train began its long, slow climb up the mountainside. From pristine fields of eternal snow, clear streams thundered down the mountain slopes. Twisting and turning trough narrow valleys, they sought out the lakes of Ticino.

As the long train ranged south from Como toward the hazy farmlands of Lombardy, Doran took only a passing interest in the changing scenery. Sentimental memories of the past few days pre-occupied him. One-night stands were not his style anyway, but Trudi Heberling's touching sincerity had made it especially difficult for him to climb on board the train and simply continue on his journey. Perhaps he would see her again, perhaps not. That was for the future to decide. Yet even now he understood that she would always occupy a special place in his memory.

At eleven forty-five, the train reached the outskirts of Milan. Block after block of post-war apartment buildings defined urban sprawl at its worst. Doran was happy he had not chosen this city as his first Italian destination.

The train remained in the station well beyond its scheduled departure time, but Doran had no reason to question Italian punctuality—at least not until all the lights inside his car were abruptly turned off. The conductor offered no explanation. Nor did anyone else. Looking out the window, he observed that activity on the platform had diminished noticeably. What was going on?

The remaining passengers in the car began to grow restless, and Doran suddenly realized that not a single train had departed since his arrival. One by one, passengers got off the train and started walking up the platform.

Doran waited fifteen more minutes in ignorance before he felt compelled to get off the train and investigate the reason for the delay. Just as he had suspected, not one train was running. Engines had shut down, and car after car was dark. Perhaps there had been a massive power failure, he speculated. That might explain it. He marched up the long platform into a huge common hall. The station was full of travelers. Of course Doran could not yet fully interpret displays of intense cultural emotion, but there was certainly no mistaking the presence of trouble. He found a row of ticket windows and took his place at the end of a long line. It was thirty minutes before he stepped up to the window for service. "Do you speak English?" he asked the clerk.

"Leetle beet," said the clerk..

"Why have all the trains stopped?"

"Train strike" was all the agent said.

"I have a ticket all the way to Rome," Doran explained.

The agent only shrugged.

"When will the trains resume?" Doran asked as he leaned closer to the two-centimeter-thick piece of glass that separated him from the ticket clerk.

"Maybe one hour, maybe two days..."

"Where can I find out more?"

"Maybe God knows," the agent said sarcastically. "He is behind window number eight. Try there."

That was obviously the end of the conversation. And the beginning of another long wait at the rear of a very deep line. It was now quarter after two. No sooner had the line begun to inch forward, than the agent closed his window without warning. Nevertheless, the line remained intact. Each traveler was determined to endure the delay in hopes of obtaining information. Fifteen minutes later the agent returned. Progress was painstakingly slow, but Doran too was determined to survive the misery. Finally at the front of the line, he was again politely re-directed, this time back to the window where he had questioned the first ticket clerk. The idiotic circle was now complete.

Gaining no satisfaction, he turned to leave. He was nearly out of the terminal building when a stranger approached him and boldly asked, "*Signor*, do you need a place to spend the night?"

"I am hoping to reach Rome by tonight," Doran told him.

The man shook his head doubtfully. "Tonight, *Roma* is not possible."

"Just the same, I think I'd rather not stay here," Doran informed the Good Samaritan.

"I believe there is one train leaving *Milano* tonight—not for *Roma*, but Verona," the stranger said. "If you want to take it, then you must wait on the first platform."

"Are you certain?" Doran asked.

"*Si, Signor*. But you must hurry. If you miss the train, you will be in Milano overnight."

"*Mille gracie*," said Doran.

"*Prego, Signor*."

AT VERONA the usual commotion of a European train station was absent, for only one train had arrived all evening. Apparently the strike was nationwide. No information window was open. Alone outside the station, Doran must have appeared bewildered, as a woman standing no higher than his chest approached him, asking,

"*Centro? Centro?*"

"*Sì*, hotel." he answered.

She waved for him to follow her.

Walking beside this kindhearted stranger, progress was slow, but eventually she guided him to the Corso Porta Nuova, a wide and busy thoroughfare that led through the medieval archway of the Complesso Monumentale di Piazza Bra.

"*Gracie, Signora*," he said. She lowered her eyes and acknowledged him with a weak smile before moving off.

Even at this hour there was plenty of activity on the piazza. The numerous outdoor cafés along the Liston were busy serving food and drinks, while boys played a spirited game of football near the central fountain in front of a pillared municipal building. Lovers strolled and talked intimately near the old city ramparts, and groups of men congregated to argue and smoke.

Doran located Albergo Bra and rang the bell. A voice answered in Italian over the intercom. How could he make himself understood?

"Do you speak English?" he implored.

"Leetle beet" came the response.

"Do you have a room free?"

"Nothing in life is free. How many nights?" The voice sounded almost accusatory, not at all friendly.

"Considering the train strike, probably several nights," Doran said.

Apparently he had given the proper reply. He heard the electric latch unbolt, granting him entrance into the building. "Take the lift. *Piano secondo, prego!*" said the voice on the intercom.

The foyer was dark and unattractive, and the elevator was something he might have expected to find in a warehouse. He had to manually operate the steel lattice doors, and when he pushed the button, the car lurched into motion with an alarming jolt. As if the machine carried some time-honored grudge, the pulleys and cables creaked and groaned in protest all the way up to the second floor.

The elevator doors opened onto a small but surprisingly attractive lobby. Polished marble floors gleamed, while ornate mahogany furniture warmed the overall effect. A rotund man with a shaved head and eyes that seemed to bulge behind thick glasses greeted Doran vociferously as he stepped off the elevator.

"Ah, you are American!" he exclaimed. "Welcome! Albergo Bra is the home of many Americans while they visit Verona."

"Thank you," said Doran. "I realize I'm arriving late. I hope it's not a problem."

"No problem at all," the man shrugged. His garrulous attitude seemed to have softened markedly with the determination of Doran's nationality. "Due to the train strike we have a rare vacancy," he informed.

"Yes, the strike," said Doran. "I was on my way to Rome. That proved to be impossible. I took the only train leaving Milan, and here I am."

"Life is full of detours," the host offered.

"I suppose," Doran said half-heartedly.

"I am the night clerk at this hotel—a respectable position, no doubt," the host rambled as he showed Doran to his room. "But I was not always a night clerk. Once I was a painter!"

Arriving in front of a closed door, he stopped. Due to his weak eyesight, he had trouble inserting the key into the lock. Doran waited patiently behind the night clerk.

"Yes, I was a painter! But I had no model. So I became a masseur. I have fine strong hands, don't you agree?" He turned and held them out for a cursory examination. "But, alas!" he confessed. "I had no clients." He turned up his palms and cocked his head. "Life tempts a person with promises," he concluded.

Finally he unlocked the door and showed Doran inside the room. "I hope you are pleased, *Signor*," he said.

AFTER A NIGHT'S SLEEP, Doran was hungry for breakfast. The hallway leading from his room to the breakfast salon was dark and his steps echoed on the marble floor. Coming into the reception area, he was hardly prepared for the vision before him. In a land accustomed to the presence of angels, there, behind the reception desk, sat the most stunning fourteen-year-old he had ever seen.

The night clerk came abruptly around the corner looking haggard from his night watch. "Eh, Franco," said the girl in a voice too low for her years. Barely acknowledging her at first, Franco reprimanded her for flirting with the American.

In the breakfast parlor, Franco served the repast dressed in his sleeveless t-shirt and rumpled, brown slacks. "You will pardon me if I work in nude chest," he said to Doran as he brought a basketful of bread and a plate of soft butter. A moment later he returned to fill the bowl-sized coffee cup. "*Caffe latte*," he narrated as he poured. The brew was incredibly potent. It probably had enough caffeine to generate the energy needed for a medium-sized city. By the time he had finished his breakfast, Doran's heart was palpitating like a werewolf and his legs felt as if they had springs.

Out in the morning sunshine, Doran buzzed and howled through the Complesso Monumentale, the medieval portal that led into the Piazza Bra and the old city. He began his tour in the stately courtyard of the Castle of San Martino, which led directly to the Ponte Scaligero, a turreted bridge that spanned the River Adige. Along the Corso Cavour he visited the Church of San Lorenzo and the Church of the Apostles. Through the Porto Romana he walked, turning right to the Coliseum. The day was hot, and by the time Doran limped through the Piazza di' Signori he was dizzy with the sight of ornamentation. Feeling hungry and thirsty, he lighted at a small outdoor café. There he watched children playing in front of the Fountain of the Madonna of Verona.

He ate cold meats, bread, and salad with vinegar and oil as he quietly contemplated the glorious results of past inspiration: divine columns and heavenly frescoes; a Venetian winged lion; the Campanile. "*Signor!*" he called to the vain and ingenuous-looking waiter who stood most visibly to one side of the café.

A slender man with beautiful skin and slicked-back hair approached with movements so fluid that Doran could not help pining momentarily for his own younger body. "*Si, Signor...*"

"*Per favore, mi porti una caraffa Valpolicella.*" Doran handed the waiter one thousand lire as a tip before the fact. "Bring the good wine," he said in a non-accusatory, matter-of-fact voice.

"*Si, Signor,*" said the waiter as he took the bill. "*Gracie!*"

Laying his daypack upon the table and discovering that one of the table legs was uneven, Doran wondered: Why do so many tables at outdoor cafés possess this ingratiating defect? These tables always seemed to shift at just the wrong moment, combining sauces never meant to commingle, spilling water or wine. Somebody had tried to stabilize this particular table by stuffing a pink, folded-up piece of paper underneath the offending leg, with little result. He reached down and dislodged the paper. Unfolding it carefully, Doran determined that it was some sort of handbill—an advertisement for a vacation residence on the Greek island of Corfu. It read:

PENSION APHRODITE THROMOS
Welcome to our beautiful island.
If you would like a clean, comfortable room, studio, or apartment,
come to visit Pension Aphrodite.
It is located at the seaside village of Puthena,
only five kilometers away from Corfu Town.
Two or three bedded rooms, private bathroom, hot water,

KITCHEN FACILITIES
(TO ECONOMIZE ON YOUR HOLIDAY)
Here you will find all you need: Beach, pools, bars,
Disco, restaurants, super markets, bike rentals, etc.
And of course many new friends.
Come and have a happy time.
(Bus No, 7, San Rocco Square.) TEL. 341539.

Doran put the flier in his pocket and decided to go with serendipity. After finishing his meal and half a liter of wine, he walked to the train station to better determine the status of the strike. He felt light headed in the afternoon heat and humidity, and his face became flushed as he emerged from beneath the chestnut trees on the Corso into the bright afternoon sunshine.

When he reached the station it became obvious that all difficulties were now in the past. Encouraged by his own sense of anticipation and fortified with a new sense of resolve, he approached an agent at the information window. The agent explained that such sabbaticals were but one more embarrassment concerning Italian efficiency; indeed, an oxymoron, like the ingenious but comical insignia placed on the engines of all *FS* trains—a *speeding turtle in a puff of smoke*!

"From which port do ferryboats sail to Greece?" he asked the clerk.

She told him: "Boats leave from the port of Bari or from Brindisi, but this early in the season the service from Brindisi is more frequent."

That settled it. How simply things resolved! He was going to Greece. Without hesitation he reserved a couchette on the overnight train.

SUNNY, SEASIDE, BRINDISI felt altogether different from Northern Italy. The air was dry and palm trees swayed in the pleasant breeze. Each day, beginning with the arrival of the first night train at nine-thirty in the morning, Brindisi began swelling by degrees with one-day visitors about to embark for Greece. The town had one main street, the Corso Giribaldi, which stretched one kilometer from the station to the pier. The local people on the street, as well as those standing outside their shops trying to hawk itinerants, greeted passers-by with a smile and a sincere *"Buon giorno!"*

Halfway up the boulevard, at a bar already filled with sailors and dockworkers drinking shots of Sambuca, Doran found himself a breakfast of eggs and flaky croissants with hot, black coffee. The repast was welcome even if the company was a little suspect.

After he finished eating, he went straight to a ticket office for his fare to Corfu. There the agent booked him on the two o'clock sailing of the catamaran, Dolfino. She guaranteed Doran that the Adriatic crossing would take no more than three hours.

From the ticket office he made his way up the Corso Giribaldi to the Embarkation Office. From there he paid a visit to the Port Police for a passport check. Once he had finished all his official business, he located a comfortable bench on the wharf. He sat in the sunshine to sketch and await the crossing.

CHAPTER 11
A GOOD MAN

AT TEN-THIRTY IN THE EVENING, Alarice and Gisela stood with two hundred other people in the sweltering hold of the ferryboat Espresso Venicia. The boat's air-conditioned upper deck had been closed off, and the Greek Immigration Officer had sent them into this iron Purgatory. As they waited for the ship to dock, sweat covered their faces and stray hairs hung limply round their foreheads. Because the porters had already started the engines of the cars in the hold, the noxious auto exhaust commingled with the all-too-pungent aroma of two thousand live chickens in wooden crates. The smell was awful, the air stifling. The ship was two hours late.

Having weathered rough seas, passengers could now hear the ship's horn repeatedly announcing their arrival. To Alarice, it sounded ancient and rheumatic. Still they were forced to wait. And wait. Group impatience, Alarice decided, had a sour smell.

When the boat finally docked at the pier, it sounded as if it had run aground. The mega-ton ramp lowered, and unable to resist the human momentum, the two sisters tumbled off the ship and onto the wharf. They gulped thesweet air in relief. This was Corfu, Greece.

Here few political formalities existed, yet to Alarice and Gisela nothing seemed obvious. Their fellow travelers quickly dispersed, and the two sisters remained nearly alone on the dock. Alarice's eyes searched the lighted signs across the street, but she saw nothing immediately useful. In such unfamiliar surroundings she was thankful to have the companionship of her sister.

Then they heard a voice. Both girls tried to search out the source of the message, but they could see only a gray silhouette behind an iron bar fence. What was he saying?

"Come to my village. I am a good man."

Curiosity was their mission here, but caution was their cultural bias. Nevertheless, they approached the stranger to learn more.

"I live in Puthena Village—only seven kilometers up the coast!" he explained. The girls could see the stranger's face in the incandescent glow of the street lamp. He was well groomed and neatly dressed. "Everything you need is there," he went on. "A beautiful beach. A market. I can offer you a private apartment. Very nice, you will see."

"The ship arrived late," Alarice told him. "We have no Greek money."

"No problem! No problem!" He now spoke repetitively, with urgency and emphasis. "You need money, I give you money. No problem. Tonight you stay at my apartment; tomorrow you exchange money in Puthena. I will show you everything."

So here, in one split second, they were obliged to somehow determine if this was indeed a gratis opportunity or some sort of trap. Maude had always told them not to go with strangers. But Maude had never come to Greece. Perhaps the point was moot from the beginning: it was late and they had no other offers. The momentum of travel compelled them to trust the moment.

Minutes later, after clearing Customs, they found

themselves crammed into a beat-up Suzuki compact with their benefactor at the wheel. To Gisela, the Greek seemed to be talking non-stop as he dodged pedestrians and steered around a couple of scrawny dogs. From the back seat of the car she tried to make eye contact with Alarice. Dismayed at their daring, she silently solicited her sister's reassurance that they had not managed to maneuver themselves into a very tight corner. Alarice could say nothing under the circumstances, so Gisela looked out the window, wide-eyed.

The night air was balmy and sentient. Motorbikes were thick as locusts in August. Their eager host was a flurry of imperatives. And even though everything in her midst seemed remarkably strange, Alarice knew that her instinct to come to Greece had not been wrong. She could not predict what might happen but she acknowledged the unshakable sensation that she was in precisely the right place at the right time.

"My name is Modestos Thromos," said the Greek.

"I am Alarice Van Zyl. This is my sister, Gisela."

"Where do you come from?" he asked in English.

"We come from the Netherlands," said Alarice.

"Ah!" said the host.

On their way to Puthena Village they passed several country tavernas. With music playing and the catch of the day cooking over coals, it appeared to Alarice at first glimpse that the Greeks were inexorably motivated after dark into social interaction. Nobody, it seemed, stayed locked up behind closed doors.

"You come from Italy today?" Modestos questioned them.

"Yes, Brindisi." Alarice was doing the talking.

"Ah, Brindisi! And the sea was not so good, eh?"

"Rather rough, actually."

"Too bad. Maybe you are hungry, yes?"

"In fact, we are very hungry."

"Okay!" he said. "A little farther along this road there is

a market. I doubt they are still open, but never mind. I know these people. No problem! You understand? We stop there and I buy bread for you. And cheese and wine too! You like bread, eh?"

"Of course. But you don't have to —"

"Okay," he dismissed.

A moment later he veered off the road onto a dusty driveway in front of a ramshackle building. Instructing the girls to wait for him in the car, the Greek jumped out and ran inside. Amazed by the stranger's energy and by his benevolence, there seemed little else for the girls to do but surrender themselves to his good will. Still, doubt remained in Gisela's mind.

"Arissa, this guy might be a little crazy. Are you sure this is all right?"

"I don't think he's crazy. Just high strung. Besides, it's eleven o'clock. We're not familiar with Corfu, and he's offering lodging."

"We could have gone to a hotel," Gisela said.

"You surprise me," Alarice told her sister. "Why not find a little adventure?"

Gisela shrugged, too reticent to press her point.

Modestos poked his head out of the shop's doorway and waved a thick loaf of bread in the air. "Okay?" he inquired. Alarice nodded acceptance. The Greek went inside again, only to emerge carrying not one, but two loaves, a one-and-a-half liter plastic water bottle filled with wine drawn right from the cask, a block of feta cheese, a bottle of olive oil, fresh garlic and basil, and a bag filled with fourteen eggs laid that morning. "Enough for tonight, I think," he said. The girls were astonished into silence.

After a short ride up the island's eastern coastline, they arrived at Puthena Village. Modestos's simple apartment proved a welcome reward for their trust. "On the roof is a solar collector," their host proudly informed them. "For hot water at any hour of the day or night!"

As Alarice and Gisela waited on the patio, Modestos

darted about like a nervous mouse, making certain their quarters were spotlessly clean. By the time he had finished sweeping entryways and fluffing pillows the hour was approaching midnight, but the host's supply of energy seemed boundless. It seemed to be his practice to smooth over rough spots that did not yet exist.

And it seemed also as though he were treating them more like long-lost relatives than new tenants. With one arm he lifted both rucksacks as he led the girls to their apartment. All the while he carried on a running narration.

Sparing every luxury, their humble flat consisted of a bedroom, a rudimentary kitchen, and a bathroom with a hand-held shower. The whitewashed bedroom was furnished with twin beds, a wardrobe, and a small desk. In the kitchen a portable, two-burner propane stove was installed upon a countertop. There was an ancient refrigerator, a table and chairs, and a fold-out bed that could, in times of overcrowding, be used as sleeping space for a third person.

Modestos asked, "Is the apartment okay?"

"It's fine," said Alarice.

"Very nice," Gisela complimented politely.

"You are my guests," said Modestos. "Anything you need, just tell me. You can stay here one night, or you can stay all summer. It's up to you."

"We don't even know how much the room costs," said Alarice a little nervously.

Shaking his head and smiling broadly, Modestos proposed, "Tonight, you make the price. If you want to stay longer, the apartment costs five thousand *drachmae* each night. Not so much to pay, eh?"

Gisela made the mathematical conversion with due amazement, while Alarice thanked Modestos for his timely hospitality.

"I will check on you tomorrow," he told them as he headed for the door. "When I come back I will bring spring water from the mountains. For now, I hope you have a pleasant holiday here at Corfu. *Kali nichta*, my friends!"

It was well past midnight, but after dining on half a loaf of coarse bread with feta bathed in olive oil, and consuming a significant portion of the dark red wine, the girls felt tipsy and restless and decided to put off sleep. Walking through the village they observed that the tavernas were still lively, but they found themselves quite alone on the nearby beach. They lay out on the fine sand calculating the astronomical paths of less than familiar stars. The sea had grown calm, and the sound of gentle waves washing ashore soothed travel-weary nerves. It was Alarice's mission here in Greece to forget. And to remember...

They were out early next morning, changing guilders for drachmae, shopping for groceries, exploring the village and the pier. By noon Modestos had not returned to collect the rent, nor deliver the promised spring water. The sisters passed the afternoon relaxing at Puthena Beach.

Late in the afternoon Gisela was awakened from a nap by a knock on the door. She was alone in the apartment; apparently Alarice had gone out. Expecting to see Modestos when she opened the door, Gisela was surprised to encounter a very handsome young man instead—a Greek boy who seemed as thrown off guard by her presence as she was by his. He stared at her with an intensity that matched the force behind her reconnaissance. For a moment neither said a word. There was only silent assessment and blind recognition. Gisela held her breath and waited.

"My name is Yanni Thromos," he said, not too shyly. "Excuse me, but my father asked me to bring you this container of spring water. He gets it from the well at Lefkimi. Personally, I don't know why he does it. I can't taste the difference between this water and the water that comes from the village well in Puthena. But he says it's better." Yanni shifted his weight onto his right hip and lifted his chin. "What is your name and where do you come from?" he asked.

"My name is Gisela Van Zyl. I'm from the Netherlands. I'm here with my sister, Alarice."

"When did you arrive?"

"Late last night," she told him. "Your father was very kind to us."

Yanni nodded. With obvious innuendo he asked, "Where do you want me to put it?"

Gisela rolled her eyes. She did not mean to encourage his audacity. Or did she? With soft, brown hair and warm, tawny skin, she could not deny that she found him terribly handsome. His eyes seemed to convey some forbidden invitation. Yet she could tell instantly that Yanni was good-natured and gentle—a bit like his father perhaps. Gisela had heard stories about the Greek *kamaki*—young fellows who combed the beaches during summer and preyed upon foreign girls for sex and money. Surely she was much too savvy for such a tactic.

"You can put the *water* in the kitchen," she told him a bit sardonically.

"If there is anything else you want—anything at all—I am personally at your service," Yanni said with feigned gallantry. Gisela stepped onto the patio with him. The sun was not so intense now, but the evening sky was full of light.

"Thank you. And be sure to thank your father for the *special* water."

"Good holiday to you," said Yanni. "Maybe I will see you at the beach tomorrow."

"Perhaps," said Gisela coyly.

Yanni shrugged as Aphrodite eyed them both with suspicion from her second floor balcony.

Next morning, Gisela and Alarice walked lazily in their Espardrilles along the main road through Puthena Village, all the way to the small beach at the far end of town. Shallow and clear, the water in the sandy cove was quite still today, a sure sign that summer was not long in coming. Alarice had brought along a rather thick novel to read; whereas Gisela had become absorbed in the creation of her travel journal. This morning she wrote:

'Perhaps someday I will be reading these words back in cold, gray Rotterdam, but I doubt it. I love traveling—it's so much fun! Greece is very special. It is only our second full day at Puthena Village, but already we have established the facile routine of going to a small cafeteria in town to have our breakfast of Nescafe, bakery items, and Greek-style yogurt.

I have learned a few Greek words:
Kalimera - Good morning
Kalinichta - Good evening
Ena - one
Mono - only
Exo - out
Endoxi - okay

Also:
Effharisto - thank you
Parakalo - please, you're welcome, excuse me.
Effharisto, Hellas!
Alarice and I have rented snorkel masks and fins—what fun it is swimming in the shallow waters of the inlet! We can sunbathe bare-breasted here—everybody does it. I'm not at all embarrassed. And we can see much of the coastline of Albania from the beach at Puthena.

I've met a Greek boy named Yanni Thromos. He is the son of the man who owns the apartment we have rented. He is handsome and clever, though not particularly serious—a perfect summer romance, I think. Ha! He should be so lucky. But I'm hoping to see him again.'

By three-thirty the sun was very intense, and Alarice decided to go back to the apartment for a shower and a rest before dinner. "Are you coming with me?" she asked Gisela.

"I don't think so," the younger sister answered. "I can't seem to get enough of the sun and surf. I think I'll stay out a while longer. Don't go to dinner without me though."

Alarice gathered her belongings and walked slowly back to Puthena Village. Gisela put on her snorkel mask and fins and went for a swim in the still chilly water. Looking back at the shore from fifty meters out, she could see that the beach was only sparsely populated. Soon many students would finish their university terms and begin migrating south for their holiday. She was anxious for the excitement to begin.

After a thirty-minute swim, she pulled off her fins and walked across the beach. There she lay down on her grass mat to dry herself in the warm sunshine. Gisela closed her eyes and drifted between consciousness and whimsy. She went on dreaming until a shadow dimmed her vision. Opening her eyes, she was startled to see Yanni Thromos standing over her, looking down.

"I didn't expect to see you," she said as she sat up and covered her top.

"Why not? I told you I would come," said Yanni.

He was wearing tight-fitting Levis and a tapered white shirt that set off his olive skin. To Gisela, the taught lines of his figure were quite sexy, and she was embarrassed that she might seem too obvious in her admiration. "I thought you were only flirting with me," she told him.

"I'm not like that. I'm a serious guy."

"Seriously on the make," she scoffed.

"Do you like this beach?" he asked her.

"It's beautiful," she said, sifting sand through her fingers. "At home we don't have sunshine like this."

"I know a better beach," Yanni told her. "It is called Glyfada. It's on the west side of the island. Would you like to go there tomorrow?"

"Just you and me?" Gisela asked.

"I will take you on my scooter."

"Why not?" said Gisela.

Yanni put up his thumb. "I will come for you around eleven o'clock tomorrow morning," he said.

GISELA AND YANNI spent the entire next day at Glyfada Beach, body surfing over the rolling swells, snorkeling at a quiet inlet, and tanning themselves on the fine warm sand. Around one o'clock they ate pizza and drank Coca-Cola under the awning of a snack bar, then headed back into the surf. When the sun slipped behind the mountains around seven o'clock, they dressed, climbed onto Yanni's scooter, and roared thirty kilometers over narrow roads to the community of Ypsos. There they danced and danced at the *J'ai Moi* Disco with a couple of hundred high-spirited French kids. After midnight they moved on to a more sophisticated jazz club.

Gisela thought Yanni was fun but too intense. Their first kiss was full of melodrama, and Gisela started laughing before it ended. Even with his ego quite bruised, Yanni was hardly one to withdraw in defeat. He kissed her again—immediately. This time there was nothing inept about his advance.

Before dawn they lay out on some flat rocks on a promontory above the sea just north of Ypsos Town. Through the morning haze Gisela saw the lights of Corfu Harbor seventeen kilometers up the shore, as well as the twin fortresses around the curve of the bay. She heard the crowing of triumphant cocks and the mournful braying of a forlorn donkey. Owls called from deep within the olive groves, and gulls fished near the rocky shoreline below.

Gisela took a brave swallow from the bottle of ouzo they had been drinking ever since leaving the nightclub. Without meeting his eye, she passed the bottle to Yanni, and he swallowed the liquor without a thought for tomorrow. Maybe she would decide to never go home to the Netherlands. Perhaps she would become a professional itinerant. If she were lucky, she might meet a wealthy Frenchman with a yacht, and they could sail about the

Mediterranean, from Crete, to Stromboli, to Tangier. Nevermore would she endure the cold damp winters in Rotterdam. She might even escape a life of drudgery working in her father's export business. Gisela could see that such a life had not proved especially inspiring for her sister. Sadness had crept over Alarice like a storm from the cold North Sea. She was happy that such problems were sufficiently distant, and Gisela turned to Yanni and asked, "Don't you ever sleep?"

"Why? Do you want to go back to Puthena?"

"I'm exhausted," said Gisela.

Yanni shrugged his shoulders. "No problem," he said.

"No reason to feel rejected," Gisela told him. "I had a fantastic day. We have plenty of time. I'm not leaving tomorrow, you know."

"You want to see me again?"

Gisela smiled at his puppy-dog insecurity. She leaned over and kissed him on the cheek. "What do *you* think?"

Yanni Thromos smiled warmly before sliding down the loose rocks. Once he had both feet on the ground he held out his arms, and Gisela slipped willingly into his grasp. She was swept along with the wind in her hair and her heart still pounding, through Ypsos Town, down the twisting road by the side of the sea.

CHAPTER 12
A GODDESS IN DISGUISE

ON A GOLDEN EVENING IN MAY, Doran stepped off the bobbing catamaran at Corfu Harbor. The water shimmered in Ionian light, as ancient twin fortresses kept a vigil from individual jetties that defined the harbor itself. Walking toward the building that housed the Immigration Office, Doran could see the Hotel Atlantic across the street, as well as the Esplanade, which arced around the pier.

Clearing Customs was a matter of a stamp upon his passport, and exiting the Point of Entry building, he was surprised by a woman who approached without caution and offered to rent him a room in her home.

"I have already arranged accommodations at Puthena Village," he speculated. "I need only to make a phone call," he told her.

"Okay," she said. "You can use my phone. Follow me."

She led him to a news kiosk just beyond the iron bar fence. Inside, her husband sipped black coffee from a demitasse. She uttered a few commanding words in Greek, and without concern he offered a telephone with no dial or push buttons. Acknowledging the language dilemma, Doran showed the woman the pink handbill and asked, "Would you mind helping me with the connection?" She took the receiver from him and rattled off the number to the operator. A moment later Doran was speaking with Yanni Thromos.

"I have a handbill advertising rooms in Puthena Village," he said.

"You need a room?" Yanni asked. He was having a little trouble with the speed of Doran's English.

"Yes. Do you rent rooms near the beach?"

"Good beach at Puthena," Yanni said. "Where are you now?"

"I've just arrived on the catamaran," Doran told him.

"My father will meet you in front of the Hotel Atlantic," Yanni promised.

"How long?" Doran asked.

"Twenty minutes. I go to find him now."

Doran was not at all certain his point had been made; nevertheless, he thanked the couple who operated the kiosk, then walked across the street to await kismet.

Thirty minutes later a car pulled up alongside the curb and stopped. A middle-aged man with olive skin and slicked-back hair jumped out of the driver's seat and asked in Greek-style English, "You are the one who called for a room in Puthena Village?"

"That's right," said Doran as he picked up his bag.

The Greek immediately put out his hand and introduced himself. "My name is Modestos," he said.

Doran shook his hand. "I am Doran Seeger," he said.

"You come from America?" Modestos inquired.

"Yes," said Doran.

"Which state?" Modestos wanted to know.

"Texas," said Doran for the sake of simplicity.

Modestos nodded in quasi-recognition. "Ah, Texas!"

"Have you been there?" Doran asked as Modestos took his bag from him and stored it in the trunk.

Modestos shook his head. "I've lived my entire life on Corfu. Is this your first time visiting Greece?"

"Yes," said Doran.

"Then welcome to my country. Corfu is a beautiful island. But you will see for yourself. How long do you plan to stay? A few days? A week? Maybe all summer if you like it."

Doran shrugged as Modestos sped away from the pier.

"Puthena Village is only seven kilometers up the coast," Modestos oriented. "What kind of accommodation do you need? An apartment? A studio? Maybe just a sleeping room?"

"A room will be fine," said Doran.

"I have a nice room," he said with a satisfied look on his face. "You will see."

In minutes they were out of the city, and Doran was relieved that the air was cooler in the countryside. Dark silhouettes of tall cypress trees defined the narrow roadway, and the outline of distant mountains rose out of the haze. The moon was visible in the pale blue sky. As Modestos turned off one highway onto another, the sea came into view. Such images seemed to emerge from deep within Doran's personal sense of longing and were recognized as they went rushing past some subliminal reference point. He breathed deeply, trying to absorb something significant and palpable.

"Since I arrived on Corfu," Doran told Modestos, "everyone I've met has been kind and helpful."

"We have a tradition in Greece. It is called *philoxenia*. It encourages Greeks to treat visitors with perfect hospitality," Modestos explained, "because any guest might be a god in disguise. For Greek people, being together is the object of everything!"

"I'm a bit overwhelmed," Doran admitted.

Modestos spoke to Doran almost as if he were speaking to a brother returning after a long absence. "Some Greek islands are barren places and invite their sons to set off in search of more fruitful shores. But Kerkyra receives wayward sons and prodigals gladly and consoles and heals them. When one returns to Kerkyra, his aching heart is soothed. This I know from experience."

"I've come to Europe as a pilgrim," said Doran. The readiness of his admission surprised him, but apparently Modestos was able to unveil aspects of his purpose that were decidedly subterranean. With his highly personal approach, the Greek inspired catharsis, and Doran felt a little foolish for having been drawn into such a revealing discussion with someone he barely knew.

Once they arrived in Puthena Village, Modestos settled him in an upstairs room at the *dhomatia*. Apologizing profusely for his haste, the Greek explained that he was having some trouble at home with his son and needed to return at once to Corfu Town.

"You can exchange money tomorrow morning at the bank," Modestos advised. "If you need *drachmae* now, I can lend you a few thousand."

"Thanks for the offer," said Doran, "but it's not necessary. I exchanged money in Brindisi."

"If you are hungry, Taverna Rankios is just up the street. Tell Giorgos that you are Modestos's friend. I am sorry that I cannot join you now for a meal or a drink."

"Maybe another time," Doran said as he put his bag down near the unvarnished dresser.

"How long you stay on Corfu?" Modestos asked again.

"I've traveled several weeks throughout Europe," Doran explained. "I need some time to relax before resuming," he said.

"Then maybe we will have time to become better acquainted," Modestos said. "Perhaps you would like to come with me to the mountains on Saturday? he proposed. "To see a different Corfu than most tourists see!"

Doran nodded his acceptance. "Thanks for the invitation," he said.

"I must tell you about my mother," Modestos

continued. "She lives in the apartment next to this one. She is eighty-seven. She lives in the old way and does not comprehend how things have changed in Greece. She often becomes confused, as you might expect. You may hear her talking to herself. Or she may come out onto her balcony and scold you or swear at you. She is harmless. Pay her no attention."

Doran acknowledged the host's instructions.

"Now I will say good-evening. Anything you need, call Modestos. You have my telephone number. And welcome to Kerkyra!"

BEFORE DAWN Doran awoke to the muffled cries of a woman in distress. The woman's message was beseeching in its tragedy as she begged and pleaded with some long-absent source for resolution.

"Constantine, my husband," she wailed. "You lay buried by Catholics in Italy. Having never come home to Hellas, how do you rest? I have seen Kostas in a vision, but you, my husband, have never had the courage to face me. You are cold in your grave, Constantine, and still I have not surrendered dignity. My end may be near, but I have memories—ones you never knew because you were away. You stopped sending us money, and your children grew up poor! After rainstorms, Modestos and Tassoula gathered snails in their little baskets. What a delight—to eat the little escargot! But you never knew. You brought me shame, and now I am glad I shall not lie beside you when my time comes!"

Through walls as thin as the veil that separated Aphrodite from a world that promised comfort and salvation, Doran could hear the sounds of her movements as she rose from her bed and dressed herself.

"Kostas, my son, face your mother! Face me and hear my thoughts. It is true that the Nazis were bastards. They surely meant to starve the Greeks. You were no older than Yanni is now, yet you joined the Resistance. There were

135

others who were willing to serve. Could it be that you loved Hellas more than you loved your mother? If so, I suppose I cannot fault you. But now! I penetrate the *portiere* between us and call out to you. I beg you to show me the way to God. Take your poor mother's arm, Kostas. I am frail, so frail. And, as your brother suggests, I am often confused.

"I tell you this, Kostas: If it were not for Yanni in all his sweetness, I might put a curse upon the modern world. For our people are slowly but certainly losing heart."

SITTING ON PUTHENA BEACH, Doran now understood why the Mediterranean appeared to so many as an ultramarine jewel. This tranquil sea ebbed and flowed between its blue-green and violet moods. Mythological superstars had once populated these isles, self-absorbed in the hemisphere of Creation. Born of sea foam, the daughter of Zeus and Dione today immersed herself in prospect. With hair tucked neatly beneath her floppy straw hat, the woman's bare shoulders were full and round. Her muscular back turned toward Doran, she looked out to sea. What horizon did she search?

Later that afternoon Doran was on the patio at the *dhomatia* helping Modestos pour olive oil from one large container into several smaller ones. Just as they finished the simple task, the girl with the floppy straw hat sauntered up the stone walkway and offered a reserved greeting before going inside her room.

"A handsome girl, eh?" said Modestos as he capped the tins of oil.

"I saw her sitting alone at the beach earlier today," Doran said. "At the time, I thought I recognized her from somewhere else, but I suppose that's not possible."

"Her name is Alarice," Modestos informed him. "She is here with her sister. They were my first guests of the season. They come from the Netherlands."

After the sun went down, and the air turned cooler,

Doran showered, shaved, and put on clean clothes before leaving the *dhomatia*. He walked up the street to Taverna Rankios. There he seated himself at a table that overlooked the rest of the patio. Giorgos Zervas came to his table to personally greet him. "You are Doran Seeger. You stay with Modestos, right?"

"Yes, that's right," said Doran.

"Takis is a good man. I have known him since we were boys at school."

"He's been very kind to me," said Doran.

Giorgos nodded. "Since you stay with my friend," he said, "I bring you a bottle of wine. With my compliments, Doran Seeger!" He patted the newcomer on the back..

At his table Doran sipped the wine and listened to scratchy records playing over ruined loudspeakers. The whirling melodies played on bouzouki progressed in unexpected increments. The notes of the accompaniment exploded like popcorn, as nasal voices sang of legends, allegory, and love.

Earlier that afternoon, on Puthena Beach, the image of a Greek goddess had appeared to him. Only later had he learned that she was actually Dutch. Her name was Alarice Van Zyl, and like him, she was here on holiday. At a table across the patio, under an arbor of leafy boughs, she stared vacantly as she sipped from a bottle of Amstel beer. Two scrawny cats waited near her table, and she broke off a bit of pita bread and tossed it onto the ground for them. The sister of whom Modestos had spoken was nowhere in sight, and Doran found himself in sympathy with her solitary plight. What might he say to a foreign girl in a land strange to them both?

He took his glass and his bottle of wine and approached her table. He knew she spoke at least some English, for that afternoon she had greeted them in that tongue. He said, "I saw you earlier at the *dhomatia*."

She was not challenged by his approach. "Yes, this afternoon. You were helping Modestos with some chores,

I believe. Are you staying at the *dhomatia*, too?"

"I arrived yesterday. My name is Doran Seeger."

"Alarice Van Zyl. I've been here five days," she said. "Would you like to sit down?"

"I don't want to intrude, if you would rather be by yourself," he told her.

"Not at all. Please sit down," she said.

As she watched him in profile, Alarice was struck with the idiosyncratic feeling that this was *not* her first face-to-face meeting with this stranger. Trying to index her most recent encounters, she was at a loss to place him. Still, there was something familiar about his eyes. Was it their color? Or perhaps the way his glance met hers?

Doran saw her smile for the first time. Even consumed by this unexpected enigma, her graceful features seemed to exude comfort and confidence.

"Modestos told me that you are here with your sister," Doran said.

"Her name is Gisela. She is ten years younger than me. My mother persuaded me to take her on holiday. But ever since she met Modestos's son, I've barely seen her."

"Yes, I've spoken with Yanni."

"Actually, I don't blame Gisela at all. He's her age. And he's incredibly handsome!"

"Modestos told me he was having problems with his son. You don't suppose he was referring to your little sister, do you?"

"If my sister is Yanni's only problem, I would be amazed," said Alarice. "Gisela may be high-spirited, but it appears to me that Yanni Thromos is altogether wild!"

"Aren't you worried about her?"

Alarice laughed. "Gisela is old enough to make her own mistakes. Besides, I promised my mother that I would not be her keeper." Alarice took a sip of beer as she regarded him. "You are American, aren't you?"

Doran nodded. "Yes."

"You're not what I've come to expect from

Americans," she said decidedly.

"How so?" Doran asked.

Alarice felt slightly awkward. "How can I say this tactfully?" she postured. "It's your manners. You are more subtle..."

"Is it your experience that Americans have poor manners?" Doran probed.

Alarice paused, took a deep breath, and then began again. "Now I've put myself in a corner. I could blame my blunder on ignorance of English, but that would be a lie. How can I explain what I meant?"

"I'm not offended," Doran reassured.

Unwittingly, Alarice dug a deeper hole. "I suppose most Europeans experience Americans as being quite aggressive..." Then, realizing further ineptitude, she put her hand to her lips. Rolling her eyes in utter frustration, she now sought to untie the tangled knot she had inadvertently created. "This is getting worse by the minute," she lamented. "I know I sound like a boring elitist."

"Maybe you are more a victim of stereotype than you imagine," Doran suggested. "Not every American is like the imbeciles you see in Hollywood action films."

"I feel foolish," Alarice said.

"No need to," Doran dismissed. Then he asked, "Have you ordered yet? The food looks wonderful," he related.

"No, I haven't. Are you inviting me to join you for dinner?"

"Who likes to eat alone?" said Doran.

"Then I'm happy for the company," she said.

Together, they read the menu.

CHAPTER 13
LIVING THE OLD WAY

AS DORAN LOUNGED on the *dhomatia's* patio, Alarice Van Zyl came out of her room wearing her big straw hat—an accouterment that, at least for Doran, identified her even at a distance. She carried a thick, hardcover book. The title was in German.

"Taking a day off from the beach?" he asked.

"I slept late today. My sister did not return home until dawn. We talked for a while."

"And how is her summer romance progressing?" Doran inquired.

Alarice raised her eyebrows. "Rather well, it seems." An awkward interval followed. Then she asked, "What is your plan today?"

"I'm waiting for Modestos," Doran told her. "He invited me to go with him to the mountains on some sort of food finding mission. Apparently, he likes to buy fresh vegetables from the farmers. Perhaps you might like to come along? I'm sure Modestos won't mind."

"I doubt I would be good company," said Alarice.

"This could be a rare opportunity," Doran cajoled.

"Something out of the ordinary. You never know."

"When is he due to arrive?" she asked.

"Shortly, I believe."

"Okay. Why not? I won't be a minute," she said. "I only want to comb my hair and get my daypack. If he arrives before I return, don't leave without me."

"Splendid," said Doran.

Modestos arrived around one-thirty, and they left without delay. Once away from Puthena Village, tourist Corfu changed its face immediately, becoming an island of timeless character. The roadway twisted wildly and without warning, and olive oil coated the blackened pavement, as fruit from the untended trees had given up its essence to the tires of passing cars and scooters. "One must be careful driving around curves," Modestos explained. "Kerkyra's roads are very dangerous. The oil makes it slippery. Every summer many tourists die. Drive too fast. Careless."

Their first stop was at the home of an elderly couple. With bright smiles, they greeted their visitors. "*Yasou, yasou!*"

Modestos spoke to them in the Greek language. Of course neither Doran nor Alarice understood a single word. They moved closer together in the face of the unfamiliar. Each smiled politely, almost apologetically, as if their presence was an accident beyond their control.

Upon a table in front of the simple house were displayed bottles of homemade wine. Glasses were filled for sampling, raised first for a toast to America, then one to Holland.

"There is no better wine than this wine," Modestos told his guests. "The grapes grow on this hillside. They are pressed the old way. The same hand tends the vine and turns the cork. I have known these people since I was a boy."

Then the old woman took Doran firmly by the arm and escorted him inside the rough structure that doubled as her home and weaving studio. She was rightfully proud of her rugs and *flokotas* and scarves, and entreated Doran to buy something with the phrase, "Very nice, very nice... *Nai, nai,* very nice!" He bought a turquoise-colored scarf with interwoven silver threads, which he intended as a gift for Alarice.

Outside, Alarice continued to pace the men glass for glass in wine consumption. When Doran and the old woman returned, the glasses were filled once more. "*Yamas*!" went the toast.

Alarice began to feel slightly dizzy as Modestos suggested, "We buy two big bottles, eh? I pay one hundred *drachmae*, and you pay one hundred *drachmae*."

After making the purchase they said farewell to the vintners. As they drove away, the old man and the old woman each smiled and waved until they were well out of sight.

Their next stop was at the home of a woman whom Modestos had known for many years. Dressed in black from head to toe, the widow looked older than she probably was. Perhaps she wore her tragedy reluctantly, for she greeted her visitors in happy superlatives before escorting them to a row of chicken coops behind her stone house. All the while she clucked and cooed in Greek. The birds inside the wire enclosure—perhaps the widow's only connection with economic solvency—clawed and pecked at the coarse ground, and the widow came out of the coop carrying a sack filled with three dozen eggs. She handed the sack to Modestos, and he paid her for the eggs. Then, with a soft expression on his face and a barely perceptible wink, he handed her another bill—one thousand *drachmae*. Turning to Doran and Alarice, he explained, "I always try to buy the freshest eggs to give to my mother and my sister, and to everyone staying at Pension Aphrodite. It is one small thing I can do."

Further West, Modestos showed them Monasteraki Panayia Theoto*kos*, situated above the famous Corfu resort at Paliokastritsa. The setting was extremely peaceful, and the view from this elevated position was at once meditative, as well as expansive. The drama imposed by patterns of light cast upon the tranquil waters of the swimming cove challenged Doran's vision to see beyond the rocky outcroppings that defined natural limits. Fishing boats and yachts and liners all faded into the illusive colors of the sky, and prismatic shades of pink and gold seemed to blend anew each moment, defying even the artist's definition. The horizon itself was a game of limits that his collection of prejudices insisted he play. All the events of his life thus far, he realized, were like a regiment of exercises designed to stretch the muscles of his insight.

"Take your time. Walk the gardens and grounds of the monastery," Modestos encouraged them. "I am going to have a short nap in my car, if you don't mind. In one hour I will be refreshed and ready to continue."

The monastery gardens were resplendent with all manner of blossoms and foliage, and Doran and Alarice soon became immersed in the beauty and serenity of a holy place. The bearded priests and robed monks were not in seclusion today; rather they were particularly obvious as they greeted visitors, or prayed silently in the shade of an especially lovely plane tree, or recited devotions as they stepped off contemplative circles.

Refreshed from his short nap, Modestos was ready to resume the quest for fresh food. A mere five kilometers up the road they stopped at a third dwelling, this time for cheese. Modestos explained to the wife of the goatherd why they had come. As she led them inside her house to make the purchase, Modestos proposed to Doran, "We buy two kilos. I pay fifteen hundred *drachmae*, and you pay fifteen hundred *drachmae*."

The austerity of the home's interior left Alarice quite speechless. A single room furnished with a bed, a wooden table and a few wooden chairs, a trunk, and a shelf for the wife's candles and saints reflected a bias toward traditional simplicity. Only a blanket covered the doorway.

The goatherd offered Modestos a home-rolled cigarette. Modestos politely declined the courtesy. Doran noticed that the man's skin was tough and brown from years spent working in the intense sun. As the farmer weighed the goat cheese on a scale that hung from the ceiling, he began to haggle with Modestos over price. This was more out of ritual, Doran surmised, than out of any real discrepancy. They came to an agreement; the exchange was made. The woman seemed glad to be rid of them.

On the way back to Puthena Village Modestos was spelling out every English word that struck him as novel: Invite - I-N-V-I-T-E; Material - M-A-T-E-R-I-A-L. He steered the car around curves at breakneck speed, honking his horn in a warning that was perfunctory at best. All at once there was a truck directly in front of them, bearing down. Horns wailed, lifetimes flashed by in a blur, and tires skidded on the oil-slick pavement. After a near head-on collision, they found themselves still alive but perched precariously on the very narrow road shoulder, looking over a steep cliffside. Oblivion avoided this time, Modestos proclaimed, "The first one hundred years of life is the hard part, eh? After that, the rest is easy!" Modestos maneuvered the car back onto the roadway. "Maybe we will meet again in the afterlife," he speculated. "Good food. No need for money. Beautiful beach. No need for clothes. What do you think?"

Before returning Doran and Alarice to the *dhomatia* in Puthena Village, Modestos decided to take a small detour to show his guests the apartment at Glyfada Beach. "I bring my family here for short holidays," he told them. "When we are not staying here, I rent the apartment to *special* guests. You understand? It is expensive, though," he related cautiously. He threw open the patio doors and waited for their reaction.

The view of the sea from this hillside perch was magnificent indeed, and Alarice complimented him on the superb location. "What a dream!" she gasped. "On this balcony, one might forget to go home."

Modestos was quick with a suggestion. "Perhaps you and your sister—and maybe Doran, too—would like to stay here at Glyfada instead of Puthena?" Then he retreated slightly. "Of course if it is too expensive, no problem. You stay at Puthena."

Alarice looked at Doran to determine what he might be thinking. True, they had not known one another long, but she was not averse to sharing such splendid accommodations with him. There were twin beds in the only bedroom, but there was also a trundle that doubled as a sofa in the sitting area. Gisela had been raving about Glyfada Beach ever since she had come here with Yanni; it was not likely she would lodge any protest to this new arrangement.

"What is the charge?" Doran inquired.

Modestos turned up his palms. "For three people," he said, "fifteen thousand per day. A little more expensive than Pension Aphrodite, but much nicer, eh?"

"What do you think?" Doran said to Alarice.

"Of course I have to ask Gisela, but I'm sure she will agree. How about you, Doran? Do you mind moving in with two Dutch women?"

"I'm sure I can endure it," he scoffed. "If it becomes more than I can stand, I can always move out."

"Maybe you would like to stay here all summer," Modestos conjectured happily. "After one week, I make you a better price. I bring you everything you need. No worries. Here you can really relax. There is a good taverna at the end of this beach—Taverna Loyiza Hara-Theou. My good friend Leonidas has the freshest fish on Corfu. You like swordfish, eh? And around the rocks at the far end of the beach is another cove—a nudist beach. Probably where my son spends most of his time," Modestos laughed. "*Nai, nai*, very nice here at Glyfada. Don't you agree? Good holiday, *nai, nai!*"

CHAPTER 14
MOVING TO GLYFADA

LET'S SWIM NAKED," Yanni coaxed.

"Why not?" said Gisela, and to the Greek boy's amazement, she stripped off her tight shorts and tank top.

On a fine beach just north of Paliokastrisa, the moonlight shone on her black hair and silhouetted her figure against the white sand. Yanni shed his clothes as if they were on fire. Clasping hands they ran into the shallow surf until they both fell forward from the resistance of the tide. The chilly water was shocking at first, but each warmed to the other's slippery embrace. They kissed over and over again as they bobbed up and down with the waves in the glimmering luminescence.

They swam in the private cove as the night grew full. Feeling astonished by the depths of their peculiar closeness, they teased, then touched. Wriggling free from Yanni's embrace, Gisela dove beneath the surface. Yanni followed. Once they surfaced, their game began again. Finally fatigued, they came ashore and lay on the beach where the shallow spurge of the surf could wash away the sand from underneath their wet bodies.

Yanni lay on his back with his eyes closed. Gisela propped herself up on one elbow. For her the moment was unstable. As she placed several soft and tremendous kisses on Yanni's chilled lips, the architecture of caution began to collapse. The night air seemed to palpitate uncontrollably. Gisela realized that she was compelled to search out that which she least needed to find. Only a month ago she was numb from comfort in her cold and watery world of dikes and dams. Now some dreamy improbability had swept her into this warmth. She thought of her mother for just a moment before she pressed herself like a blow upon the boy.

The night was warm and they fell asleep in each other's arms. At sunrise they awoke to the sound of a simple Greek song being sung by a passing fisherman.

"Yanni! Wake up and put on your clothes. It's morning!"

The Greek boy scrambled into his pants and sweatshirt. He brushed sand out of his hair and rubbed the sleep from his eyes. He checked to make certain that his scooter was where he had left it. Satisfied it had not been stolen during the night, he turned to Gisela and said, "I can't believe we slept here all night long."

"Take me back to Puthena," she said. "I want to have breakfast with my sister."

IT WAS STILL QUITE EARLY when they arrived back at Pension Aphrodite. Once inside the apartment Gisela was surprised to find Doran Seeger asleep on the daybed in the kitchen. Alarice was fast asleep in her bed, but the American's unexpected presence evoked a series of questions in Gisela's mind. She lay on her single bed but did not sleep. No doubt her sister was proving to be more unpredictable than Gisela might have imagined.

It was late morning when Gisela heard Doran quietly leave the apartment. "Arissa, are you awake?" she whispered. Alarice groaned and turned over. "I think so," she muttered.

Bleary-eyed from the activities of the previous night, each sister respected the other's need for reconstruction. They showered, groomed, and dressed in tolerant silence.

Their favorite seaside café at Puthena Beach was now crowded with those in search of a Dionysian summer, but Alarice and Gisela found an outdoor table and sat down to have Nescafe and yogurt. The sun-kissed water in the cove gleamed like mica, while the Albanian coast remained cloaked in haze. Alarice shaded her eyes as she looked out to sea.

"Why was the American sleeping in our apartment?" Gisela asked her sister without looking her squarely in the eye.

"We were having a party with the Swedish couple who are staying upstairs. We were all drinking a lot of wine and it got late. I suppose Doran just fell asleep on that terrible bed."

Gisela looked less than satisfied with her sister's explanation. "It nearly froze me when I came in and saw him sleeping there."

"Why?" Alarice asked. "He's harmless."

"It's an issue of privacy," Gisela told her. "Besides, he looks like Huckleberry Finn," she observed drolly.

Alarice laughed. "Then it's my taste in men that you're questioning..."

"Are you involved with him?" the younger sister wanted to know.

"You mean romantically? Not really. So far we're only friends. We've had a few meals together, and yesterday we went with Modestos on an outing."

"What kind of outing?" Of course her curiosity was motivated in part by her relationship with Yanni Thromos.

Alarice recapped for her sister the highlights of her day in the mountains with Doran Seeger and their host, Modestos. "Quite a wonderful afternoon, really," she said.

"And after we had finished buying wine and cheese and eggs, Modestos took us to a beautiful monastery above the village of Paliokastritsa."

"I've been to Palio," said Gisela. She did not find it important to divulge that she had slept naked on the beach there with Yanni just the night before.

"With Yanni, of course," said Alarice.

Gisela nodded.

"Did he show you his father's apartment at Glyfada Beach?" Alarice asked.

"No." But the mention of Glyfada Beach piqued Gisela's interest.

"It's fantastic!" Alarice exclaimed. "Much nicer than our place in Puthena. Modestos told us that he only rents it to special guests. He proposed to Doran and me that the three of us stay there. Doran favored moving, but I said I had to discuss it with you first."

"What are the sleeping arrangements?" Gisela asked.

"We will have a private room with twin beds. Doran will sleep on a trundle bed in the sitting room."

"Glyfada is wonderful," Gisela allowed.

"We each pay one third. And Modestos offered a discount after one week. Accounting for that, it ends up being cheaper than the two apartments at Puthena. And much better!"

"Right," said Gisela as she finished her Nescafe. "I'll give it a try. Why not?"

CHAPTER 15
ON THE PRECIPICE
OF A PIVOTAL MOMENT

AFTER TALKING WITH ALARICE, Doran phoned Modestos on behalf of himself and the Van Zyl sisters to accept the host's offer of the beachfront apartment at Glyfada. To Doran, Modestos seemed truly happy they had decided to stay the remainder of their holiday at his special retreat, and he invited Doran and the two Dutch sisters to accompany him and Sophia to one of his favorite restaurants. After the dinner, he promised to drive them to their new lodging. Doran accepted the invitation even before consulting Alarice and Gisela. For he found he enjoyed the Greek's company. The man made sincerity seem easy, and generosity so natural.

Modestos had told Doran he would call for them around six o'clock, but he was already forty-five minutes late. Alarice and Gisela remained inside their apartment, making preparations for the move to Glyfada. Already packed, Doran walked across the street to a small bar and ordered espresso. He sipped his coffee and surveyed the street scene, mentally re-inventing Kerkyra's past. After finishing his coffee, he left three hundred *drachmae* on the table and walked back across the street to wait.

Arriving at the *dhomatia*, Modestos shook Doran's hand and patted him on the back. "Sorry we are late," he apologized. Then he introduced Doran to Sophia.

As Alarice and Gisela came out onto the patio, Modestos commented on the happy transformation of their skin tone. He remarked brightly to Gisela, "Change color, eh?"

Sophia made a cursory inspection of the Van Zyl sisters' apartment, and of Doran's room too, so she might determine what supplies were needed for the next occupants.

Gisela watched Yanni's mother with vested curiosity. She was forceful and free and full of fire—qualities Gisela recognized also in the woman's son. With ruby lips, she smiled at her son's newest girlfriend, conveying friendship while giving away nothing.

Together Modestos and Sophia were like wheel and flint; they made sparks and light. Their flame was undeniably bright, and neither Gisela and Alarice, nor Doran, could help being drawn to their particular warmth.

Driving fast through Pelekas Village, then around the arc of the bay, the breeze from the car's open windows acted as a cooling antidote for the day's intense heat. Bouzouki music played loudly on the radio, and Modestos turned down the volume as a courtesy to his foreign guests. But Sophia's festive mood was not to be denied. She lovingly scolded her husband then adjusted the volume higher again. Modestos gave himself over to his wife's jovial mood, and a moment later he was singing along with the happy music and snapping his fingers in time with the contagious rhythm.

Turning down a one-lane road, they descended along a border of cypress trees. At the end of the road was Etiopia Tryfon. A brick patio covered by a pergola of vines served

151

as the dining area. At the far end of the patio was an outdoor grill; at the near side stood an enclosed kitchen. It occurred to Doran that he had never seen a Greek dining alone; apparently the ritual of food was just as important as the actual taking of nourishment. Perhaps the Greeks found them to be one and the same.

The taverna was crowded, and conversations among the patrons were demonstrative. Music played loudly as the clock struck ten, and there was gala dancing by some of the men and older boys. Photo flashbulbs breeched the yellow light on the patio to commemorate the occasion of a recent christening.

Dinnertime seemed to be the only time Modestos's running commentary on life was calmed. He told them, "Just before dinner talking is no good. I am not so happy then. After dinner my stomach is full and I am happy again. Then talking is good."

Alarice offered an observation: "Greek people—just like Dutch people—have good longevity. It must be the food."

Modestos smiled warmly. "I will tell you a story about that," he said.

"Once there was a man from France who came to Puthena Village, and he observed that many people there live to be very old.

"But I don't have to tell you this. Just look at my mother! At eighty-seven, she is a fine example.

"Nevertheless, the Frenchman went down to the wharf, where the fishing boats dock, and found a very old fisherman there. He asked the man, 'How old are you?' The fisherman replied that he was one hundred twenty years old. '*Sacre blue!*' said the Frenchman. 'Tell me your secret!' The fisherman answered: 'Each morning I eat fish. At midday, I eat fish. Again, for my dinner, every night I eat fish. Only fish—that is my secret!'

"Much impressed, the Frenchman was still not certain he knew the answer to the riddle of long life in Puthena

Village. So he traveled into the mountains, where he located an old goatherd. He asked the smelly old fellow, '*Monsieur*, how old are you?' The goatherd tried to smile even though he no longer had any teeth, and he answered very proudly, 'I am one hundred twenty years old.' Once more, the Frenchman wanted to know the man's secret for long life. The goatherd told him: 'Each morning I eat feta. At midday, I eat only feta. For my supper, I have feta again. That is my secret for a long life!'

"Well, to a Frenchman with a palate so rare and dignified, a diet of fish and feta seemed utterly intolerable, and he determined there must be another way. So he decided to consult yet one more elderly person in Puthena Village. After conducting a survey, he sought out the village priest, whom everyone agreed must be one of the oldest individuals in the village, for his beard was long and gray and he walked slowly with a pronounced stoop in his shoulders. The Frenchman asked the priest, '*Mon pere*, what is your secret for a long life?' Of course the Frenchman was expecting the priest to tell him that prayer was the only road to longevity, but instead the priest took him aside and told him, 'If you want to know the truth, *Monsieur*, first thing every morning I have sex. At midday, I have sex again. And at night, more sex!' 'How old *are* you, Father?' the Frenchman asked, somewhat astonished, but truly convinced that indeed the priest had the real answer for which he was searching. The priest shrugged and said, 'I am thirty-five, my son!'

"Perhaps some mysteries were never meant for understanding, eh?"

Everyone laughed at Modestos' joke, and then the Greek began to elaborate. "It is true that Greek people live a long life. But for many years we ate only fresh food. Wholesome! Pure!" He wiped his lips with his napkin. With his belly full, he was ready to talk.

"When I was young—only twelve years old—I left Puthena Village to attend school in Corfu Town. This is hard for you to imagine, eh? But we had no high school in Puthena Village, and my mother was determined to send me to the city because she valued education. I lived in one room. My sister Tassoula would come by bus to bring me food. We were very poor—only noodles, bread, a little cheese. Once the bus broke down and she did not come for three days. I was so proud that I starved myself waiting, even though there was a bakery around the corner. When the baker learned about my hunger he scolded me for not asking him for food." Modestos slapped himself on the forehead, still dismayed by his boyhood stupidity. "I could have had anything in that shop, but no! Like a fool I preferred my pride. Still, the food was pure then. Now vegetables and fruits are grown with chemicals and hormones. The meat is not always fresh and clean. That is why I go to the mountains for cheese and eggs and tomatoes. Like this wine: fresh - not old!" He took a long swallow from his half-full glass.

"As a child, life was sometimes difficult. But it was simple. Not like now. You understand? If I can only get through the next few years," he said, "I believe I will live forever. *Yamas*!" He lifted his wine glass again, and everyone toasted to a long life.

Sophia chattered in Greek to Alarice about the difficulties she and Modestos were having with Yanni. She waved her arms, rolled her eyes, and blessed herself and her son, while Alarice rather awkwardly tried to reassure her in some weird syntax that their troubles would soon be in the past.

Of course Gisela could not follow Sophia's lament word for word, though she felt mortified by the meaning she was able to extract. Her red cheeks contrasted against the Italian-made green silk scarf she wore round her neck. Making eye contact with her sister, Alarice rebuked Gisela good-naturedly for contributing to Yanni's supposed ruin.

Looking his guest squarely in the eye, Modestos made Doran a proposition: "You are a serious person," he said.

"Most tourists come to Corfu looking only for a good time. Maybe they want to swim in the sea, or drink a little ouzo. Perhaps they are looking for romance. But you are different. You seem to be looking for something else. I don't know what exactly. But I see you trying to strike some sort of a bargain. And I say to myself, 'This is a serious person!' I like you. And I like these Dutch girls, too."

Modestos leaned closer to Doran and lowered his voice to signify a more intimate camaraderie. "American people help Greek people," he said. "You know, the war. The Nazis. Old news maybe, but Greek people never forget. So maybe you like to stay here all summer long, eh? Really relax. I make for you a better price, my friend. What do you think?"

Touched by the Greek's generosity, Doran did not know what to say.

Modestos continued: "I know we drink too much wine tonight. But I am sincere. I think you know this. So if you want to extend your stay on Corfu, you make the price, my friend. You understand?"

Oh, Modestos, thought Doran. You may be a little tipsy and, as you say, 'happy from so much good food in your belly,' but tonight you are responsibility's chief tempter. Some deeper, more imperative longing argues poignantly for me to anchor my ship here at Corfu. Am I ready for such a twist of fate? Modestos, my friend, why do I feel as though we have known one another forever? Honestly, I do not know how to answer you. Not yet.

Doran Seeger studied each face around the table. His newfound companion, Alarice Van Zyl, suddenly and miraculously understood Greek. Her sister Gisela was relying on him, he sensed, for something yet unstated. Their Greek benefactor and friend, Modestos Thromos, yawned prodigiously, as he'd been at the dock late last night trolling for tourists. And Sophia, Modestos' discerning wife, looked anxious as she imagined the latest exploits of her debonair son. For Doran, these once unfamiliar images had become so compelling that he could only surmise: If I do not tear myself away from this place immediately, I shall remain here forever, forget my concerns and responsibilities, and renounce my personal history once and for all. It was quite late now...

Driving down darkened roads, the car radio played the familiar melodies Modestos had sung since boyhood. Almost unconsciously, he hummed along with the music, while three now-familiar strangers became entranced by the passing shadows of indistinguishable forms. Such scenes rushed past them like the myriad events of someone else's life, black and white snapshots documenting centuries of simple but dignified existence, cradle to grave, cradle to grave. It all felt somehow very personal. How might their place in this parade of stones and souls be ensured, Doran wondered?

The beauty of the lunar light reflected off the waters of the Ionian Sea, and all were spellbound by the power of the moment. Shapes and manifestations were but projections of something much more significant: indeed, something at least temporal if not truly cosmic.

Doran concluded: Sometimes one becomes acutely aware that he is teetering on the precipice of a pivotal moment in his life. If one is vigilant, Greece is full of such moments—moments when the night sky is clear and the stars are dropping into the sea, moments when one unexpectedly meets a stranger and his donkey at midnight on a dark road in the midst of an undulating grove. This ephemeral man walks slowly and a little stooped over, as he carries on his shoulder a faggot of freshly clipped, wild herbs gathered tenderly this night in the selene shadows. He might yell out a heartfelt greeting whose emotional meaning surpasses language itself. Ah! The longing induced by such experiences is bittersweet, but I remind myself with a smart slap and scolding admonitions: Wake up! Pay attention! This is the very moment your entire life has been leading up to. Don't miss it!

Time hung upon eternity's horizon as Artemis waited just beyond the midnight mountain silhouette. Cast abruptly back inside his corporeal body, Doran's first inclination was to panic. But everything was all right. Somebody was telling a joke. And happy music was playing on the radio.

Suddenly, Modestos was braking for an animal in the road, a small furry creature not moving particularly fast. He swerved the car purposefully off the highway then parked on a level ledge. "Fresh food—good eating!" he proclaimed.

He leaped out of the car to give chase to what Doran perceived to be a muskrat, while Sophia enthusiastically yelled words of encouragement to her hunter husband, as if this were some rare opportunity for a delicacy too seldom sampled. Alarice and Gisela sat wide-eyed and incredulous in the rear seat as Modestos ran into the brush, stalking the awkward creature.

A moment later he returned to the car, no kill yet made. He opened the hatchback and took out a large stick. He handed Doran the intended weapon and said, "Okay, Doran: I stop, you hit. Tomorrow we no pay for food!"

Doran clutched the baton tightly and waited. In the front seat of the car Sophia began snickering. The butt of their elaborate joke, Doran held tightly to his gullibility.

"Good eating, eh?" teased Modestos as he started the car.

And once the prank was evident, they laughed and laughed the remainder of the way to Glyfada.

CHAPTER 16
A DISTANT SHORE

AS THE SEASON PROGRESSED THE WATER WARMED, and more and more tourists moved into the beachfront apartments. Gisela and Yanni disappeared for days at a time, while Doran and Alarice spent their days at Glyfada in near idleness on the sandy shore. Their lethargic routine was nearly ensconced when, for the first day in three weeks, the sun did not shine. From the balcony of their beehive condo, Doran made carefree drawings of the scenic coastline. Alarice remained inside the apartment, dedicated to her summer reading.

It was evening when the sky cleared above the mountains, though it remained hazy over the water. Doran's ear was drawn to the sound of distant music, and he looked up the shoreline and saw the glowing lights of Taverna Loyiza Hara-Theou.

"Perhaps we should walk to the restaurant at the end of the beach for dinner," he called to Alarice.

She came out of her room with her hair pinned back. "Good idea. But give me a few minutes."

At Taverna Loyiza Hara-Theou, they sat at a table with a view of the coastline. Over a bottle of white wine they watched the light fade. Dinner was sumptuous and unhurried. For one semester in their lives they had no place to go, nor anyone to see. They watched two Australian fellows playing cards and drinking shots of ouzo. The stars appeared, and couples walking along the beach were discernible only in silhouette. Diakatos Leonidas came to their table and offered a personal observation: "Look through the mist gathered over the sea. There, halfway to the horizon, a fishing boat! The light from the lantern is barely visible. All the tiny specks of light that dot the hillsides around the bay—those are the lights from homes where the women of these mountain villages stand watch for their husbands and sons, sailors and nighttime fishermen."

They lingered at the taverna well past midnight.

NEXT MORNING, they were back at Loyiza Hara-Theou before nine for breakfast. The sun was already intense and the scent of ripe lemons was carried on the sea breeze. Katerina, the waitress, looked groggy. She muddled through the morning chores practicing her ill temper. Leonidas came to their table. "Hello, my friends," he said. "I am happy to see you again so soon."

"We had a wonderful evening last night," Alarice related.

"In the waters off Corfu there is a small fish called Gopa," Leonidas related. This morning I was at the dock and I was able to buy today's catch. Tonight, I will cook them especially for you. Come around nine-thirty."

"Thank you," said Doran, again delighted by Greek hospitality.

After a swim in the three-foot swells and an hour of sunbathing, Doran and Alarice set off to make the five-kilometer hike to the village of Pelekas. Up the switchbacks above Glyfada Beach they went, and at each

159

turn a longer, more stunning vista was revealed. Once the road leveled, they found themselves in a dense grove of olive trees. There, simple stone houses provided basic shelter for those whose needs were elementary. Just as the nets of the fishermen were cast to harvest the bounty of the sea, the nets of these mountain dwellers were spread beneath the olive trees to catch each fallen fruit.

Doran tried to place himself within the accumulated identity of the Greek people. But how could he know what this soil, these mountains, these groves, these stones, or this water might mean to their collective experience? Happy was the old man they saw walking along the road—his cane at his side—who placed his hand upon his heart, a gesture of invitation for the living spirit of Hellas to fall upon these *xenos*. The old man smiled as he turned onto a path that led through the trees. The enigma conveyed in his bright blue eyes sent Doran off on a tangent he would never resolve.

"Greeks walk like no other people," he declared to Alarice. "In each stride is the purpose of five thousand years. Their heritage is of heroic proportions, so no matter what the present circumstance, courage and dignity come naturally to them."

Farther up the road they came to the village of Pelekas, and to their chagrin, the old man who had greeted them earlier sat resting comfortably on a bench in front of a kiosk, sipping a cool drink. He had reached the village by way of a shortcut ten minutes ahead of them. With a jagged-toothed grin, his joke was complete.

Lost within the countless years of its own history, Pelekas was a collage of images: crumbling walls; an ancient rusted lock whose key had been thrown into the sea years ago; a staircase that now led nowhere. Doran and Alarice wound their way through the stone and mortar streets, worn smooth by the feet of pirates and priests, by schoolboys and carts of commerce. Beyond the exposed brick of an old bell tower they came upon a startling view of the sea.

On the edge of the village they found a curious little shop dealing in herbal medicines and occult concoctions. A red-haired Scottish woman, who looked as out of place as a Turk, operated the shop. "Greece cast its spell on me as the Highlands never could," she told them. "Fourteen years ago I left the chill of the North, never to return."

"I love it here," Alarice said, "but I'm not sure I could give up my life in Rotterdam."

"Such decisions are very individual," the shopkeeper conceded.

"I admire your courage," Alarice told her.

The herbalist shrugged off the compliment. "Today I have a small gift for you," she told Alarice. She handed her a cloth bag filled with lemon grass.

JUST BEFORE NINE O'CLOCK, Doran and Alarice arrived at Taverna Loyiza Hara-Theou. Katerina hurried to greet them. "I save this table for you," she said. "You like?"

"Yes, thank you," said Alarice.

They ordered a bottle of Retsina to drink before dinner, and moments later Katerina brought a plateful of flaming cheese called saganaki. "This food is from me," she told them. "You try."

Enjoying the wine, Doran was reminded of Kazantzakis's ephemeral character, Zorba the Greek. 'Now whatever is this red water, boss, just tell me! An old stock grows branches, and at first there's nothing but a sour bunch of beads hanging down. Time passes, the sun ripens them, they become as sweet as honey, and then they're called grapes. We trample on them; we extract the juice and put it into casks; it ferments on its own, we open it on the feast day of Saint John the Drinker, and it's become wine! It's a miracle! You drink the red juice and, lo and behold, your soul grows big, too big for the old carcass, it challenges God to a fight. Now tell me, boss, how does it happen?'

No doubt, fresh food was something of an obsession in Greece. Diakatos Leonidas had rushed to the pier to buy the fresh catch—the small fish called Gopa—and when he presented the evening meal, he was happy to be nourishing new friends. Cooked in olive oil, lemon, and fresh herbs, the small fish were delicious.

Nor did Doran and Alarice refuse the shots of ouzo offered after dinner by the two Australians they 'd seen on their first visit to the taverna. They, too, seemed to be perfecting integration through familiarity. Patient with the art of travel, they were in no hurry to impress or make something happen. They played mindless card games and idled time away.

DURING DAYS SPENT AT GLYFADA BEACH, visions of distant and exotic places washed over Doran like the metered waves offshore—places like Alexandria and Istanbul. Far away were the tensions of a competitive lifestyle. Instead, he heard the steady and soothing sound of the sea, the call of a bird, a playful voice. Alarice's voice! He casually mentioned to her that he'd been considering resuming his trip and taking the ship for Athens soon.

"I never meant to linger here either," Alarice said. "But considering Gisela's romance with Yanni, I don't know how I might pry her away from Corfu."

"Perhaps we could tour the other islands for a few weeks while Gisela stays here," Doran suggested. "I'll pay the rent through the end of summer."

"But why should you pay the full amount?"

Doran shrugged. "It's nothing, believe me."

"She would probably relish having the place to herself," admitted Alarice. She silently considered Doran's suggestion for a few minutes before asking, "When would you want to leave?"

"A couple of days, I suppose," said Doran.

Alarice nodded. "I will speak to Gisela, and tomorrow

162

we can go to Corfu Town to check schedules."

AT TAVERNA LOYIZA HARA-THEOU, their favorite table was now reserved for them each night. Tonight they drank retsina and waited patiently for a lamb roasting over glowing coals to be cooked to perfection. Chef Stephanos basted the entrée with a mop dipped in olive oil, lemon juice, and homegrown herbs.

Katerina looked especially fierce this evening, and she explained to Doran and Alarice that she was in the midst of a fight with her boyfriend. She clenched her fists as smoked poured out of her ears: "Boom, boom, boom!"

Leonidas played a game called 'Mosquito' with two of his other guests. It was a good-natured game where the unsuspecting newcomers were forced to endure humiliating slaps on the cheek if they were not adroit enough to foil the stinger of the unrelenting mosquito, Leonidas! Everyone in the taverna laughed hysterically at the spectacle, and the obliging Swedish contestants grew more and more red-cheeked by the minute. At game's end they were redeemed by applause.

Not until ten o'clock was the lamb cooked to Stephanos' satisfaction. Portions of the meat were brought to everyone in the taverna, along with roasted potatoes. Before long each guest was eating with his fingers, cajoled and instructed by Leonidas and Stephanos. After the main course, everyone was given baklava and coffee. Leonidas tried to recruit contestants for another round of *Mosquito*, but nobody seemed willing to play. By eleven, most had finished eating and left the restaurant. For those who remained, shots of ouzo mixed with water were offered. Gisela and Yanni wandered into Loyiza Hara-Theou for late night drinks.

By midnight, Gisela and Yanni were playing cards with the two Australians, Brandon Harrison and Matthew Niven. At an adjacent table Doran, Alarice, Leonidas, and Katerina drank ouzo and talked. The Australians certainly realized that traveling friendships were seldom fixed, and changes in focus and locale often came suddenly. But when Katerina learned that Doran and Alarice were planning to sail for Athens the next day, she deplored, "So this is good-bye forever!"

"Not forever," Alarice consoled. "How could we not return? Corfu is part of us now."

"You do not understand," she lamented. "My boyfriend is a beast. I no marry. Tonight I call my mother. She lives on *Kriti*. In two weeks I go there to be with her. This is terrible. I might never see you again!"

"Give us your address," suggested Alarice. "We can write long letters."

"All right. But you must come here tomorrow to say good-bye, yes?"

"Of course we will," they told her.

Their new friend, Diakatos Leonidas, shook their hands and kissed them cheek-to- cheek. "Safe journey!" he wished them and made them promise to visit him when they returned to Corfu.

CHAPTER 17
A NIGHT IN ATHENS

THE LARGE FERRYBOAT, Poseidon, was again docked in its berth, and the white lights, strung mast to mast, reflected on the still dark water. The pier was crowded with sailors and travelers, and porters drove cars and motorbikes into the ship's hold. The ship was not scheduled to sail until eleven-thirty, so Doran, Alarice, Yanni and Gisela walked up Mitropoleos Street and settled in at a sidewalk cafe for a drink together before Doran and Alarice were to board the ship.

"How long will you be gone?" Yanni asked.

Doran smiled at Alarice. "No way to know, Yanni," he said.

Yanni proposed a toast and each raised his glass. "Calm seas and good travels—*Yamas*!"

"*Yamas*!" they echoed as they drank.

At the wharf the sisters hugged and kissed one another good-bye, as Doran and Yanni stood nearby. Then Gisela put her arms around Doran and whispered in his ear, "Take care of my sister, please."

"Don't worry," he told her. "We'll be back before the end of summer."

A single tear formed in Gisela's eye, and her reaction to this departure surprised her somewhat. Alarice had always been a rather distant mystery to her, but here on this foreign pier, in the company of strangers, such an assessment seemed outdated.

Aboard the ferryboat, Doran and Alarice found their sleeping cabin and deposited their luggage before relaxing in the ship's lounge. The ship's horn sounded two times only, then the boat left Corfu Harbor and put out to sea in silence. Some of the passengers stood on deck and watched the lights of the city disappear, while others gathered in the lounge.

"It feels odd to be leaving Gisela behind," Alarice told Doran.

He shrugged and turned up his palms. "As you've said, Gisela is capable of taking care of herself."

"But where Yanni Thromos is concerned, her judgment is still in question. I'm naturally cautious, but Gisela is often overly confident."

"We all move between doubt and confidence," Doran observed.

As they talked and sipped their drinks, Doran became increasingly aware of a demonstrative conversation that was taking place between two men sitting at the next table. The exchange was in German, so of course he did not understand. He looked to Alarice for an explanation. "What is the argument about?" he asked her.

"Their dialect is difficult for me," she related, "but I believe they are debating the ethics of the war in Iraq. The bald one is blaming the Americans for having drawn Saddam Hussein into the conflict."

Doran had no wish to be rude, but their subject was of personal interest to him. He assessed the two men, even as he himself tried not to be noticed. With shaved head and wire-rimmed glasses, the more aggressive of the two leaned forward as he lectured the other. He was round and compact, and the blue veins in his temples began to swell as he made his point. From underneath his black raincoat he withdrew a metal flask and took a long drink between declaratives.

His companion, in contrast, was tall and lean. With flashing black eyes and black curls that cascaded over his shoulders, he was eager to smile as he absorbed each word his friend spoke.

"I beg your pardon," the bald man said to Doran in English. "Normally, I would exhibit better manners, but I began eavesdropping on your conversation only after becoming aware that you were eavesdropping on mine."

Taken by surprise and feeling quite embarrassed, Doran said, "Please, forgive me. My friend speaks German, and she tells me you are talking about *Desert Storm.*"

"You are American?" the stranger said in a thick accent. He continued to stare at Doran over the rim of his glasses.

"Yes, I am."

"Were you personally involved in the war?"

Doran did not answer immediately. Instead, he further appraised the inquisitor. "Not directly," he finally replied.

"And one cannot hide behind an oblique reply," the man stated bluntly.

"I have no need to hide," Doran countered.

"It is my understanding that Americans are proud of this aggression," he imputed.

"There were parades in the streets of New York with brass bands, cheering crowds, and confetti," Doran offered with some sarcasm. "But such displays are common in every culture at war's end."

"If one can truly call this 'Desert Storm' a war..."

Doran sighed deeply. On a nationalistic level he was being severely challenged, though he was not yet checkmated. "I assume you are German," he said to the antagonist.

"My name is Rudolph Grossmund," he said. "But everyone calls me Pablo. You can call me Pablo, too. I am a Czech Jew by birth, but currently I am traveling on an Austrian passport. My friend's name is Jurgen Klimpsch. He comes from Hamburg."

"And I suppose it is safe to presume," Doran postured, "that there is no shortage of automobiles in Germany or Austria..."

"Neither country sent aircraft with high technology to obliterate Baghdad," said Pablo.

"Perhaps not, but that does not exonerate others from the crime of complicity. And maybe that is the worst crime of all," he said with irony. "If Americans are guilty of greed," he continued, "then Europeans are equally guilty!"

"Europe is powerless to subvert the will of the United States," Grossmund declared. "Your citizens continue to pay the taxes that ultimately produce the big guns. American weaponry is sold without conscience to the highest bidder, until, in the end, you are fighting fire with fire. It makes no sense, sir." Again he took out his flask and swallowed more liquor. He winked at his friend Klimpsch, who remained silent because he spoke no English whatsoever.

"How can I speak for the conscience of every American citizen?" Doran appealed.

"Perhaps you are right," said Pablo. "If Americans are short-sighted and dangerous, maybe Austrians and Germans are likewise!" He slapped his palm down on the table, as if to punctuate his conclusion.

Experiencing first eye contact, Doran found himself wishing not to meet Grossmund's glare again. And though their debate was at best presumptuous, he could not deny that Pablo had touched a nerve.

It was two-thirty in the morning when Doran and Alarice left Rudolph Grossmund and Jurgen Klimpsch in the lounge, still drinking. Stepping inside their tiny cabin, they never turned on the light. Each prepared for bed by the pale light of the moon coming through the lone porthole.

Looking out to sea, Alarice watched moonbeams skipping across the waves as Doran slept on the narrow, single bed. She sighed an unresolved sigh, and then lay on her bed without fully undressing. Even though it was late, she could not sleep. In the weak light she could almost detect the curves of Doran's upper back muscles and buttocks. His legs were thick and sturdy from the walking he had done in Europe. And the rocking of the ship did not disturb her equilibrium nearly as much as did the gentle man sleeping on the bed opposite hers.

Alarice caught her own breath as she listened to Doran inhale and exhale in nearly perfect rhythm with the sea's undulation. Without warning, the rocking of the ship seemed to awaken her feminine essence, which Alarice now realized she had, over time, functionally anaesthetized. The pseudo security of her picture-puzzle life in the Netherlands was her symbolic womb; patterns of trade and commerce defined the walls of her prison cell. It was a solitary confinement imposed by her father, and by herself as well. Now she lay aboard a ship bound for Attica, liberated from incessant routines and reprieved for this short interval from crushing boredom. Perhaps Doran was not her knight in shining armor, but their meeting and the level at which their friendship already existed remained a symbol of hope for release.

Doran awoke at first light. Alarice lay on her bunk, asleep and still partially clothed, her lips parted far enough only for a secret. Her wispy bangs covered her forehead, and beneath closed lids her eyes roamed and wandered like ascetics in some foreign desert. No longer satisfied with his solitary disposition, Doran wanted to touch this girl, to brush the stray hairs away from her face, to kiss her on the forehead or cheek. Instead, he dressed and left the compartment.

In the lounge, he found Pablo sitting at the bar. The Austrian sipped coffee from a demitasse and talked with a weary-looking steward.

"I didn't realize you spoke Greek," Doran said.

"I speak seven languages," Pablo informed.

"Very impressive," said Doran. Then he turned to the steward and said, "Coffee, please."

"What work do you do in Austria?" Doran asked.

Pablo stroked his shaved head. "If I am to be truthful with you," he said, "I must tell you that my life in Vienna is finished. *Kaput*! Now, I am on my way to Crete with Jurgen, where I will be captain of my own ship."

"So you are familiar with Greece..."

"I have come to Greece many times. Have you been to Athens before?" Pablo asked.

"No," said Doran.

"Beyond the Acropolis and the Plaka there is little of interest. The city has multiplied twenty times since the end of World War II. Without much concern for aesthetics... The pollution is regrettable. Most days you will find yourself with a sore throat by noon. Unless you climb to the top of one of the eight hills... Then it is more bearable. Unless the breeze is not blowing and the temperature is up... Then you think you will die from dehydration."

"What about the antiquities?" Doran asked.

"Splendid" was all Pablo had to say.

As they drank a second cup of coffee in silence, Doran and Pablo were joined by Alarice. "*Guten Morgen, mein Herr*," she said. She laid her hand gently upon Doran's shoulder. In the suppleness of his body she found immediate acceptance. "Where is Jurgen this morning?" Alarice asked Pablo.

"Still asleep in our cabin," Pablo related. "My voracity exhausts him, and his beauty suffers if he does not sleep enough." Alarice cleared her throat. Doran took her hand as she moved closer to him. "Believe it or not, Jurgen is still quite innocent. Growing up in Hamburg, one might expect otherwise. But he is recently discovering certain tendencies, if you can appreciate what I am saying."

"I believe we understand," Doran told him.

Pablo said, "It is best when there are no misconceptions. Don't you agree?"

"Of course," said Alarice quietly.

Pablo chose to elucidate: "Personally, I have a wide range of experiences. I have traveled my entire life. I first came to Greece when I was twenty-two. Fifteen years ago, the Greeks were not accustomed to travelers, but they embraced me from the start. I embraced them as well. Why I have not chosen to emigrate sooner, I cannot say. One becomes involved in all sorts of intrigues, wouldn't you agree, Doran?"

"An Italian acquaintance assures me that life is full of detours," Doran related.

"Yes, well stated!" Pablo finished his coffee and stood. "May I offer you breakfast in the ship's restaurant?" he said.

"Yes, thank you," said Doran.

Alarice hesitated slightly. "I'm going on deck for a few minutes," she said. "I'll join you shortly."

Alone on the deck of the Poseidon, Alarice walked the length of the port side of the ship. At the stern, she leaned against an iron railing and watched the pastel colors of the Ionian daybreak deepen in hue. Sailing quite near the Greek mainland, she could see the silhouettes of trees and mountains as the sun came up over Attica to the East. As the wind whipped her short hair, she stared absently at the foamy patterns left in the ship's wake. Gulls trailed behind the ferryboat, diving for fish and floating on the warm air current dispelled by the ship's smoke stacks.

She sighed as she conjured up the image of Doran's face. She liked his smile, and she liked his relaxed approach. She liked the way he seemed to ease himself into the waters of debate without making a big splash. So far, they had not tried to move past friendship, but Alarice knew she was falling in love with him.

Again inside, she found Doran and Pablo sitting at a table discussing the questionable stability of ferryboats. Jurgen was now also present, looking dumb and happy. Alarice took a seat beside Doran.

After speaking in Arabic with one of the stewards, Pablo explained that the restaurant would not be open this morning as there were too few passengers to warrant preparing breakfast. He took the liberty of rummaging through cupboards and coolers and found several cans of Canada Dry Tonic.

"Are you sure it's all right?" Doran asked Pablo.

"No problem. The steward and I understand one another," he said cryptically.

The conversation covered many topics, most of which were introduced by Pablo with the clear intent of eliciting some opinion from the American. In some instances Doran was willing to contribute his ideas to the soup that Grossmund was stirring up; on other topics he remained safely uncommitted. Jurgen sat quietly and listened, though he understood only what Pablo chose to translate into German.

Alarice offered few opinions. She did not trust the Austrian. Perhaps it was his obstinate lack of specificity, or the way he controlled his companion by keeping him in the dark. Alarice believed he enjoyed the turmoil he created in others with his intrigues. Or maybe it was that raincoat! It seemed to conceal certain essentials of his identity. All in all, she would have liked to lose the two of them at first convenience. But it was a small ship, and Doran did not seem particularly inclined to shake them off.

"Many of the antiquities in Athens have been stolen or razed," Pablo informed. "Or they have been sandwiched between modern buildings. Fifty years ago the place had declined to a marginally important city. Now, half of all

Greeks live and work there. Though for me the heart of Greece is not Athens, but the villages of Crete. Of course, you must have your own experience. And like each of you, Jurgen wants to walk the streets that Pericles fashioned as much from his civic pride as from stone. He wants to experience first-hand the frenzy of the Athens market, and to see the columns of the Parthenon awash in ten thousand watts of white light. These are images that belong in the psyche of every worldly person, don't you agree, Alarice?"

"Perhaps you would know more about that than I would, Pablo."

His stare was penetrating, unsettling, even unnerving. Grossmund took a long drink from his can of tonic and said to Alarice plaintively, "I doubt there is very much I know that you do not."

When the Poseidon docked at the port of Patras, they were still three hours away from Athens. Along with Pablo Grossmund and Jurgen Klimpsch, they walked into town. There they bought tickets and boarded a bus bound for Athens.

Along the Gulf of Corinth they rode, water on the immediate left and mountains on the right. Old women in long skirts, high-laced shoes, and black head scarves stood by the side of the road offering strings of garlic or bundles of onions for sale. If the Island of Corfu had been their baptism to this country, they now found themselves immersed in a cultural miasma far beyond expectation.

FOLLOWING PABLO GROSSMUND and Jurgen Klimpsch, Doran and Alarice walked up Ermou Street toward the Plaka. This section of Athens was the locale of a rather chaotic bazaar, where every imaginable modern-day gadget and contrivance managed to look out of place. An organ grinder sang 'Never On Sunday' as his monkey collected coins in a tin cup. Street vendors hawked flashy *faux bijoux*, potions for vampire protection, honeycombs and bee-sting poultices, lambs and kids, *haggis*, witnesses, indictments—all manner of orgiastic kitsch. "The Greek language has no word for privacy," Pablo told them. "Perhaps now you can understand why."

Walking shoulder to shoulder with shoppers on the street, they came finally to the Mitropolis Orthodox Church. Turning up Filotheis Street, they intersected with Adrianou Street. Here Doran and Alarice and Jurgen caught their first glimpse of the Acropolis.

Alarice drew a single, startled breath as she beheld the Parthenon for the first time. With marble columns cast against a cloudless sky, the vision seemed to usher one back to an era of mythical extravagance, philosophic reverie, and supreme civic consciousness. She half expected to see Pericles himself walk around the next corner, clad in his white toga and sandals and carrying some architectural design imprinted upon a scroll. With his big feet, Jurgen appeared to be walking on air. Doran, too, was on a high. Attica was a land of broken stones, and he was not unhappy to contribute a few more pebbles to the rubble. He felt vulnerable but alive. And he was certain he was in love with Alarice.

In the Plaka the streets were narrow. Mysterious alleyways spider-webbed off Adrianou Street in every direction. Immersed in the cement jungle, they arrived at a small hotel that Pablo knew from previous visits.

Hotel Adams was surely nothing special, but the rooms were clean and comfortable. Doran and Alarice took a third floor room with a tiny verandah. From the sunny balcony they could watch the activity in the street. Pablo and Jurgen settled in a room down the hallway. All agreed to rest before meeting at four o'clock to have a closer look at the Acropolis.

"I never planned to hook up with Pablo and Jurgen," Doran told Alarice.

She shrugged her shoulders as she sat on the bed. The windows were open and the sun-faded curtains swayed with the gentle breeze outside, but the room was still hot. She blew her bangs off her forehead. "I don't trust Pablo," she said.

"He's probably okay," Doran reassured. "Anyway, we'll be rid of them both in a day or two."

It was past four o'clock when Doran and Alarice and Rudolph Grossmund and Jurgen Klimpsch walked up the road known as the 'Sacred Way', on the west side of Acropolis Hill. They entered the monument through the Buele Gate. Visible from the heights was the entire city and surrounding hills. Once dotted with olive groves and tiny feudal enclaves, Attica's eight hillsides were now covered by a sprawl of concrete development. To the Southwest, the Aegean gleamed in the light of afternoon, and ships could be seen making their way out of Pireus Harbor, heading for open sea.

Up stone steps, past perfect masonry, they came to the small Ionic *Temple of Athina Nike*. In ancient times her wings had been clipped so she could not abandon the city. Perhaps such drastic measures had not been necessary, thought Alarice. Walking over the uneven marble floor of the Propylea, and looking across the hilltop at the columns of the Parthenon from the eastern porch, she could not help being in awe of Hellenic longevity. The grounds were covered with the rubble of twenty-five hundred years. A stonemason's workshop, something vital of the glorious, ancient tradition remained. Despite the ravages of time—wind and rain, plundering, earthquakes, and more recently the *nefos*, Athens' hideous brown cloud of air pollution—the Parthenon's grace continued to abide the city. With dramatic lines and subtle curves, it defined the Golden Age of Greece.

They remained at the ruin until sunset. Below the wall of the citadel, yet not at street level, stood the venerable Odeon of Herodes Atticus, a centuries old, open air theater. Tonight a group of students occupied the stage as they rehearsed a dance for a future performance. Ten musicians clustered against the back wall of the stage and played flutes and bouzoukis, harps and drums. The dancers took their positions as the music began.

Doran, Alarice, Pablo, and Jurgen descended from the upper ring of the amphitheater and took seats about halfway down the bowl. Alarice was entranced by the pageant unfolding on stage, as was Jurgen Klimpsch. Pablo seemed more interested in talking to Doran.

"So, my friend, have you become infected yet by the spirit of Hellas?" he asked.

"I felt it the day I landed on Corfu," said Doran.

"I understand," said Pablo. "As a young man I came to Greece each summer. When the weather began to turn cool, I would return to my distractions in Vienna. But not this time! Now I am captain of my own ship. You understand?"

"I think I do," said Doran.

Pablo slapped him hard on the back and leaned close to Doran's ear. "The world we come from only wants to exploit us," he concluded. "But we cannot allow ourselves to be manipulated, my friend."

By eight-thirty they were eating dinner at the Eden Restaurant off Flessa Street in the Plaka. Since Pablo continued to monopolize Doran's attention, Alarice initiated a conversation with the normally silent Jurgen Klimpsch. Of course her German was excellent, and she was able to learn that he had come to Greece on Pablo's funds to avoid compulsory service in the new German military. Because of his homosexuality, induction frightened him above all else. Even the Neo-Nazis were not as intimidating as the prospect of serving in the army. *"Personliche, meine Philosophie ist Friede. Ich bin Pazifist!"*

After ten o'clock, Adrianou Street was so jammed with people that motor traffic was all but impossible. It was a warm night, and Athens would not sleep for hours. Conversations went on and on: people lingered because tomorrow was uncertain and they did not want to be alone in darkness. Reverie was the logical solution. Loud music poured out of the restaurants and tavernas, and Doran, Alarice, Pablo, and Jurgen milled up and down the street eating ice cream and coconut rolls until it was time for the light show on Acropolis Hill to begin. They walked toward the ancient agora in order to have an unobstructed view of the Parthenon.

At the foot of the citadel, near the ruins of the old marketplace, a sweeping spotlight broke the darkness. The unexpected scent of jasmine made Alarice's blood rush to her head, and she almost faltered. Doran came quickly to her aid, putting his arm around her waist to help her maintain her balance. Perhaps she had drunk too much retsina during dinner, or maybe she felt overwhelmed by the heady atmosphere of the city. The night air in Athens was more intoxicating than any liquor she had ever drunk. Or was it something else? All four sat on the smooth stones strewn throughout the agora to watch the luminary spectacle above.

Even as it grew late, the air remained thick and balmy, but there seemed to be no reason to return to the Hotel Adams just yet. Doran and Alarice lay upon the flat stones, her head resting upon his shoulder, and their fingertips touching lightly. Breathing in unison, they fell asleep where they lay, and their dreams commingled in symbols universally familiar. The last vestige of reticence was finally given up.

Doran stirred first, breaking the spiritual bond. Feeling him move, Alarice opened her eyes, too. She lifted herself on one arm and noticed that Pablo and Jurgen were no longer with them. Now that the lights illuminating the Parthenon were turned off, it was quite dark in the agora. She nudged Doran to take notice of their companions' absence.

"Where do you suppose they went?" he asked.

"Probably back to the hotel," Alarice speculated.

"They might have told us," he said.

177

Alarice began smoothing the creases in her dress. She ran her fingers through her hair and rubbed the sleep from her eyes. They got to their feet, but Doran paused awkwardly. A searching expression came over his face as he began patting himself over his pant pockets.

"What's the problem?" asked Alarice.

"My wallet is missing," he told her with a scowl on his face.

"Are you certain?"

"It's not in my pocket," he confirmed.

"Let's have a look on the ground," she suggested.

They bent down on hands and knees and proceeded to search for Doran's wallet, but they found nothing. The missing billfold, in conjunction with the absence of Pablo and Jurgen, only aroused criminal suspicion.

"Was there much money in the wallet?" Alarice inquired.

"Only a few thousand drachmae," he told her. "I keep most of my funds in my neck safe. Their effort was rather inept."

"I never would have suspected either to be a thief," she said. "But perhaps we should not jump to conclusions. Let's walk back to the hotel and see if they are in their room."

"Somehow I'm not expecting to find them there," Doran said with an irritated look on his face.

At Hotel Adams, Doran banged insistently on Pablo's and Jurgen's door. Receiving no response, he went downstairs to the reception desk. He found the night clerk dozing in front of a hazy TV screen and requested the key to their companions' room. At first the clerk was reluctant to give him the key, but Doran insisted.

Upstairs, they knocked loudly on the door again, but when nobody answered, they unlocked the door and went inside. Turning on the light, Doran determined immediately that their luggage was not in the room. He needed to see no more.

In the privacy of their room, Doran and Alarice began getting ready for bed. He opened the door leading onto the verandah, as Alarice washed her face and brushed her hair in the small bathroom. She felt upset by the theft. "Where do you think they went?" she asked Doran.

"Who cares?" was his response.

"They probably went to the harbor. Maybe we should go after them."

"It's not worth the effort," Doran said.

Alarice came out of the bathroom wearing only her bra and panties. Doran was sitting on the foot of the bed looking tired and defeated. So smoothly, she sat down beside him and began rubbing his neck and shoulders, not deeply but tenderly. She pressed her soft cheek close to his, and her warm breath coaxed him out of concealment. In a moment his hand was on her bare thigh. Her hips moved slightly, and the fine hairs upon her lithe arms rose under his touch. Their lips brushed lightly together, then they kissed fully.

CHAPTER 18
THE CYCLADES

ALARICE AWOKE to the unwelcome disturbance of a couple embroiled in a quarrel just across the street. *He* slammed the door of his Fiat and spat on the ground, and in English *she* called out in utter disgust, "Dimitri, your brain is mush!" The motor of the sports car roared aggressively; the woman clomped inside and slammed the door shut. Secure in her proviso, Alarice stretched and smiled, then nestled closer to her lover and went back to sleep. They did not leave the hotel until after eleven.

On the subway between Monasteraki and Pireus Harbor, they were again on their own—much to their relief. Toward the front of the car on which they were riding, an Arab man stood up and preached loudly for the support of Hezbollah. In the next car an accordion player serenaded riders with happy Greek melodies.

At the dock they booked passage on a ferry leaving for Paros Island at four that afternoon, and the boat bound for the Cyclades left the harbor right on schedule. Once they were away from the Athens metropolis, the veil of haze and smog gave way to intense clear sunshine. The water turned from murky green to a surreal shade of blue. Doran and Alarice were filled with a sense of discovery, as if they were the first adventurers to behold this rare, luminescent beauty. They spent the first hours of the journey on deck. As the sea breeze blew on their faces, and the salty spray made their hair feel stiff and their skins a little sticky, they held hands and imagined what was to come.

The ship docked at the Port of Paroikia, Paros Island's main city, just after ten o'clock. As many as fifty travelers disembarked, and no less than two dozen hotel owners and private room hawkers converged on the newcomers, practically begging each traveler to allow them to show their hospitality. The scene was utter chaos, and within seconds Doran and Alarice became separated.

From across the road a short, bald man dressed in Italian leisure clothes called to Alarice. "*Freulein, brauchen Sie ein Zimmer?*" "Do you need a room?"

"*Haben Sie ein Zimmer frie mit ruhe?*" "Do you have a quiet room to let?" Alarice asked.

He broke into a big smile. "*Ja, ja! Sint Sie allein?*" "Are you alone?"

"*Nein. Mein Man ist auch hier. Er heisst* Doran." "My boyfriend is here, too. His name is Doran."

Alarice called for Doran, and the Greek began calling his name, too. Together they moved through the crowd searching for him. They found him in the clutches of a good-natured hotelkeeper that was trying to drag him away, not understanding that he was separated from his companion. Alarice took Doran by his other arm. "I've found us a room with a charming man," she told him. Alarice's newfound friend was standing beside her, nearly lost at shoulder level.

"*Ich heisse* Fantas Paraskevopoulis," he introduced himself. "*Wilcomen in Paros Insel!*"

"If we don't like his place," Alarice said to Doran, "we

can always look elsewhere."

doran smiled at Fantas, who had not understood a word of their English conversation.

"*Komen!*" he said in his queer German. "*Ich habe ein auto.*"

Twenty minutes later Doran and Alarice were settled in a spacious room at a charming hotel called the Marguerita. Just as their host had promised, the hotel was located away from the noisy port.

Alarice had not anticipated falling in love while on this holiday—especially not with an American from Texas! But there was no denying her feelings now. Doran, on the other hand, had left his country in unspecific rebellion, needing to purge himself of a guilt not easily carried. Alarice seemed to make his doubts bearable with love and undemanding companionship. The newness of cohesion made sleep impossible on these strange pillows of curiosity and discovery. And hopelessly infected by wanderlust, each conjured up strange and interesting faces, unfamiliar customs, and ecstatic encounters. The rest of the night was filled with carefree lovemaking.

Next morning they were out early for a walk by the sea, followed by a hearty breakfast. Interested in exploring the interior and the leeward coastline, they rented a jeep and drove to the fishing village of Naoussa. Here, in a picturesque town of whitewashed buildings, blue shutters, and prolific vines of blooming bougainvillea, they sauntered through the cobbled streets and narrow alleyways. They stopped for a beer at the Labyrinthine Bar on the fishing pier, where baby octopi were hanging in the sun to dry.

Across town, near the Orthodox temple, they came upon some gypsy women—perhaps Albanians, or Bulgarians – who were washing dozens of rugs in the water of Naoussa's only canal. The women wore colorful clothing and gold and silver bracelets. Their young daughters beat the carpets with boards, while the ladies smoked Lord's cigarettes. Seeing Doran and Alarice, the children left their chore to beg for *drachmae*. He fished a few coins from his pocket and divided them among the children.

Next day, they rode the afternoon school bus south ten kilometers to Aliki. There, fields of cornflowers bloomed and the spring-fed Valley of the Butterflies imitated Shangri-La. Thousands of orange and brown Monarchs fluttered in ecstasy, like the eyelashes of Aphrodite flirting with eternal Hellas. Alarice slipped off her shoes and went running into the field. She disappeared in the overgrowth. Fearing he might never see her again, Doran, as well, dove headlong into the unknown.

And each evening the entire population of Paroikia would turn out to wait near the ancient, thatch-roofed windmill for the docking of the seven o'clock ferryboat. It was a matter of supreme curiosity to see who might be coming to town. After cruising up and down the road in front of the seaside tavernas in Fantas's car, Doran and Alarice would have Greek-style coffee with their amiable host at the Countess Hotel, and wait for the horn sounding the ship's arrival. Finally, out of the glowing sunset around the far end of the island, the ship would appear, its hull riding proudly on top of the violet water.

Paros Island was hardly large enough to spend weeks exploring, though it was no less than eleven days before Doran and Alarice said good-bye to Fantas and pulled themselves away to take the hydrofoil to the neighboring Island of Naxos.

THE APPROACH TO THE PORT TOWN of Chora produced feelings of stability within the lovers as they first laid eyes upon the conical summit of Mount Za, the highest, most evident peak in the Cycladic archipelago. Across a land bridge, on the Islet of Palatia, stood the spectacular ruin of the Temple of Dionysus.

Stepping off the boat, the routine was similar to that

which they had experienced landing at Paros. Employing the strategy she had used eleven nights earlier at Paroikia, Alarice took Doran by the arm and led him through the throng of room hawkers. As she suspected, there was a single solicitor at the rear of the crowd, holding back, searching faces. Dressed in black and looking proud and confident, Marsoupa Kontiza Koyka's eyes met Alarice's silent inquiry with affirmation, dignity, and welcome.

At the home of Marsoupa Kontiza Koyka, they were offered a clean, simple room. It was hardly the Ritz, but having traveled in Greece almost two months, Doran and Alarice had come to value authenticity above luxury. They agreed to pay eleven American dollars per night for accommodation.

Their hostess's twelve-year-old son, Alexander, was learning English in school and acted as interpreter for his mother. He told Doran that his father sailed with the merchant marines and was away many months each year. In summertime, he helped his mother run their *dhomatia*. In so doing he honored his father.

"Your English is excellent," Doran complimented him. Then he turned to Alarice, shook his head in chagrin, and said, "I'm embarrassed by my poor language skills."

Alexander blushed. "No, sir, not so good, my English. I do not know many words. I must study more."

Doran patted the boy on the shoulder. "When I get back to America," he said, "I will send you a book, *The Old Man and The Sea*. Do you know the story?"

Alexander looked at him quizzically.

"A novel by the American writer, Hemingway."

"Hemingway?" the boy repeated.

"About a fisherman. I know you will like it. And the English is not difficult."

The boy smiled, looking forward to receiving the gift.

"Naxos is a big island," Alarice offered.

"Naxos is the best!" said Alexander proudly. "It is not like other Cycladic islands. Here we grow things. We raise animals. Of course there are many beautiful beaches, too. But Naxos is not only a tourist island. It is possible to take the bus to the central villages: Filoti, Apollonas, Sagri, Agiassos—all very good! In the villages you will find much history."

"And mythology!" Alarice said.

The boy lectured: "Zeus himself was raised on Naxos. He was worshipped as protector of the flocks."

By day, Doran and Alarice explored the interior of the island. In the main village of Chora, they walked the streets of the Kastro then hiked the length of Saint George Beach. They dined in the tavernas and had iced coffee in Marsoupa Kontiza Koyka's parlor. By day

In the mountain village of Chalkia there was a barber shop. As Doran peered through an open doorway, the barber shaved a sleeping customer in the dark. He shaved the patron in the dark because there were no electric lights: there never had been any. It did not matter. One slip of the razor, Doran surmised, and the all-trusting patron would become part of Chalkia's timeless history. So far the barber's hand had remained steady and true. To Doran, it seemed as if he were able to wield the razor completely by feel. T barbar knew his customers. Each face had a particular contour; each head had distinct cranial ridges and troughs.

Across the road from the Byzantine church of Our Lady of Protothronos, with its domes and chambers, red tile roof and crosses, and underneath a venerable plane tree, stood the only café in Chalkia. The old Greek who owned the cafe was happy to serve Doran and Alarice bottles of Heineken's beer. As they sat at a shaded table, the village tailor, dressed in a mismatched suit, poked his head out of his shop to watch them. Paint peeled off the door jam at the entrance to the tailor's shop. Somewhere out of sight lambs bleated and cocks crowed, as growing thunderheads blocked the sunlight. The grapevines that grew up the wall of the taverna were as gnarled as an old man's arthritic joint. This was *not* the tourist Greece of Paros Island or Corfu. Here milk came in a pail. In Chalkia there was no dentist, and a barn was composed of a pile of rocks hauled one by one for the better part of a century. Spic and Span detergent was a modern convenience.

Eager for conversation, the café owner joined them at their table. "Nothing much happens here in Chalkia," he conceded in understatement. "But on festival days there is much activity in the mountain villages."

"When are the feast days?" Alarice wanted to know.

"For example," he said, "just before Lent is Carnival—and the Ceremony of the Bell-Wearers. Here in the mountain villages, the rites of the ancient Cult of Dionysus are still practiced. These bell-wearers are the young men of the village who wear a garment known as the *abadelli*—a cape with a kind of hood. They hide their faces with muslin scarves to conceal their identity. From braided ropes wrapped round their waist hang rows of bells.

"The bell-wearers run from house to house throughout the village. Climbing upon the roofs of the homes, they create a clamor with their bells. It is also their task to escort an old woman from neighbor to neighbor, collecting eggs in her shopping basket. Of course the eggs symbolize rebirth in nature."

"So you are saying that modern-day, Orthodox religion is practiced in conjunction with the Pagan rituals of the ancients?" Alarice presumed.

"It is so," said the café owner matter-of-factly.

"I mean no disrespect," said Doran, "but throughout much of the world such innocent customs were long ago relegated to superstition."

"The Greeks know this well," explained their tutor. "But we Greeks like our superstition. And we like our food, too!" The café owner laughed. "Greeks are always cooking. You like Greek food?"

"Of course," said Doran. "We like Greek wine, too."

"Ah, the wine!" he proclaimed. "I know a short poem. Let me recite it for you:

'We're making wine
So come and help,
Stand in the vat
And tread the grape.
And if our grapes are trodden
By one as sweet as you,
Then this year's wine will surely be
As sweet as honeydew.'"

The taverna owner slapped his hand down on the table. "What do you think?" he said. "Not exactly Homer, eh?"

"Nearly so," Doran joked.

"You are a funny man, but look! The bus is not coming for at least an hour. How would you like to drink some *raki* with me?"

"What is *raki*?" Alarice asked.

"You don't know about *raki*? *Ohhh... Ahhh...* Could the honor of introducing you to this noble drink possibly fall upon me? Listen! When the treading of the wine grapes is finished, what remains in the vat is never thrown away. It is put into a special jar called the *harani*, and then it is boiled to practically nothing. The end product of the distillation is called *raki*! It is wonderful. You want to try some?"

"Why not?" said Doran.

The Greek danced away to the kitchen, his steps happy and free. *Raki* was his favorite drink. Whenever he drank it he liked to dance the *syrtos* and the *vlacha* to the unlikely accompaniment of bagpipes. *Raki* and dancing! Dancing and *raki*! The foreigners might not understand, but what the hell?

Together they drank *raki* in the shade of the plane tree until the rain came. Then they went inside and the Greek filled their glasses again. Two hours later the bus bound

187

for Filoti arrived, and Doran and Alarice determined that they must leave now, while they were still sober enough to travel. They thanked their raucous host, he waved good-bye as they boarded the bus, and as the bus pulled away, Doran and Alarice watched through a dust covered window as he danced and whirled the steps of the *Nikintres*.

Other than two Hungarian women looking for work as laundresses, Doran and Alarice were the only non-Greeks in Filoti Village. As they passed anonymously through the streets, curtains parted, yet not once did they glimpse the faces behind sheer veils. The village appeared devoid of women, though probably they were inside their houses, cooking or sewing.

Walking up forty-eight well-worn steps to visit the little chapel, they arrived just as the bells began to clang. Nobody in the village seemed to pay much attention. They bought a freshly baked loaf of bread from a bakery next the church. The bakery consisted of a stone oven, a mixing cauldron made of iron, a cooling table, and a couple of centuries' tradition. No signs, no logos: only the most essential tools.

Doran thought to himself: Perhaps Greece is what Earth appears the be in one's dreams—perfect in its imperfection, ruggedly beautiful, eternal, abundant, re-creating itself for its men and women, virtually unaware of the passing centuries. Hellas is earth, air, fire, and water! And this village, like so many others, is waiting at the edge of time. It is waiting for the entrance of Hellas into the modern world. Or perhaps it is waiting for the peace of antiquity...

Back in the town of Chora, Doran and Alarice reached Taverna Renetta for dinner just before a bone-jarring crack of thunder opened the sky. Another flash of lightning turned the mountains a surreal shade of violet, and the rain came down without remorse. The lights inside the taverna flickered, and then faded altogether. No problem! The proprietress sent her boy round the room with lighted candles for each table.

They took their time eating swordfish, rice, and salad. They drank a bottle of Naxos wine, and as Dionysus revealed himself within Doran's spirit, he found himself wanting to buy wine for everyone in the taverna. The Greeks had a word for one's circle of friends: *parea*. Tonight everybody waiting out this storm at Taverna Renetta was Doran's *parea*.

Alarice's now familiar face shone larger than life in the candlelight. The sound of the steady rain slapping the cobblestones outside stirred Doran's sense of longing. After dinner they walked through the drizzle to Marsoupa Kontiza Koyka's *dhomatia* with their arms wrapped round each other's waist, and to the sound of the rain falling on their roof, they made wild love until dawn. Then they slept like children.

DORAN AND ALARICE arrived at Mykonos Harbor as Apollo's chariot gained on the cusp of the aquatic horizon. Not quite ready to relinquish his firm hold upon the day, Apollo ducked behind a billowy cloud, and a brilliant ring appeared around the cloud's perimeter to crown the god's presence. Five picturesque windmills at one side of the crescent-shaped harbor, their white sails still unfurled, set the stage for the drama enacted each day and night at this postcard village. The aggregate of whitewashed houses now glowed pink and purple and pale yellow in the twilight, and fishing boats bobbed gently in the harbor near 'Little Venice', where the water mirrored the last golden rays of sunlight.

Alarice held tightly to Doran's arm as they disembarked from the rocking hydrofoil. There were only twenty passengers coming ashore, so the customary crush was not so pronounced. A blonde, pregnant girl approached Doran and Alarice. She told them she had quiet rooms for rent just up the coast.

"How far from the center of town?" Alarice asked.

"Two kilometers," she answered.

"How much per night?" Doran wanted to know.

"Only four thousand *drachmae*," she told them. "Trust me! It's a nice place. I have twelve rooms, each with a view of the sea. The home belongs to my mother-in-law. Everybody in town knows her as Mama Despena."

What could be easier? They followed the girl to her Renault, and a moment later they were on the road leading up the coast. Scooters roared by a breakneck speed, their drivers risking life and limb by crossing the centerline around curves, but the driver seemed undaunted as the bikers cut in front of her car.

As promised, the room they were shown opened onto a balcony that overlooked the sea. The hostess stood by as Doran tested the bed and Alarice went outside onto the terrace. "Just as I told you," she reaffirmed.

"Terrific!" said Doran.

"When you are settled, come downstairs for coffee with Mama Despena. She likes to meet all her guests."

"Thank you," said Alarice. "We will be there in ten minutes."

Downstairs in the formal living room, Doran and Alarice were introduced to Mama Despena by her daughter-in-law. The old woman shook hands with her two newest guests and invited them to sit in her parlor. The convivial hostess offered coffee and sweets. Mama Despena spoke only broken English, but her smile was endearing. "Mama make coffee?" she said. "Mama make *kadaifi*? You like, yes? Mama make *koukouraki*... And *loukoumi*... Everybody Mama's children!"

On a modern cassette machine, Greek music played softly. Sipping iced Nescafe, Doran focused on the contrite, sorrowful melodies with Oriental features—chromatics and quartertones, grace notes and the nasal quality of the vocal renditions. Bouzoukis and baglamas provided the accompaniment, but it was the swirling nature of the singing that interested him most. "This music is curious," he said to the girl.

"The songs are called *Rembetika* in Greek. I believe their origin is Assyrian or Egyptian—but maybe from Lebanon. A *Rembitis* is a man who once had great sorrow but threw it off. Mama likes these songs because they are nostalgic—when the Greeks were much poorer, but more carefree. But she also likes the Bee Gees," the girl smiled. "*Stayin' alive, Stayin' alive!*" she sang. Mama Despena clapped in time.

"You are obviously not Greek, but you seem to know quite a lot about Greek culture," Alarice observed.

"My name is Kristina Marx. I came to Mykonos from Germany eleven years ago," the girl explained. "I came here on holiday after I graduated from the university. After one summer I returned home. Both my sisters were getting married and settling down to traditional lifestyles, but I was miserable in Germany. The following summer I was back in Greece. I would telephone my mother each week, and she would say to me, 'Kristina, you are not like your sisters; I know I am losing you to that place, and there is nothing I can do to change that.' Of course she was right."

"Then you've not gone back to Germany in ten years?" Doran asked.

"After my marriage to Nikos—I'm sure you'll meet him later—all three of us, Nikos, Mama, and myself, went to Germany for a visit with my family. But it was very difficult for Nikos and Mama."

"So you've felt a natural attraction for Greece from the beginning," Doran presumed.

"Mykonos was quite different ten years ago," she confided. "Not many tourists. And in winter the ships were sporadic. During my first winter all we had to eat was cabbage and bread. No bananas, no fresh vegetables. Not even canned milk. It was difficult—especially after living in Germany where you can get anything. But in my heart there was never a conflict. I felt alive here in a way I never could in Dortmund. Then I met Mama Despena, and because of the increasing number of German tourists coming to Mykonos, she asked me to help her at the *dhomatia*. I was out of money, so the offer came at just the right time. Now, I'm certain she was recruiting me to be her son's wife, not just a caretaker. Of course, Nikos fell instantly in love with me—or maybe it was my blond hair—and, as they say, the rest is history." Kristina gently hugged her tummy, and Mama Despena smiled as she contemplated the arrival of her first grandchild.

"I must admit, I feel a certain empathy with your story," Doran told her. "This is my first visit to Greece, but already I find myself exploring the possibility of a long stay. I keep asking myself: What is it about this place that makes *me* feel so *eternal?*"

Suddenly, Alarice found herself wondering whether it might not be difficult for her to go home to Holland. Until hearing Doran's somewhat surprising admission, it was a question she had not considered. And listening to Kristina's story made her realize just how immersed in Greek society she was beginning to feel.

Kristina struggled to her feet and moved across the room to take down a book from its place on a shelf. Almost comically, she waddled back to her seat on the sofa next to Mama Despena.

"There is a contemporary poet in Greece named Constantine Cavafy," she told her guests. "Nikos introduced me with his poetry about the time we made our trip to Germany. At the time, I was feeling unsteady about my decision to remain in Greece. Cavafy showed me a fresh perspective. Let me read you a few stanzas of his poetry:

> "*When suddenly at midnight you hear*
> *an invisible procession going by*
> *with exquisite music, voices*
> *don't mourn your luck*

that's failing you now,
work gone wrong,
your plans all proving deceptive,
don't mourn them uselessly:
as one long prepared, and full of courage,
say good-bye to her,
the Alexandria that is leaving.
Above all, don't fool yourself,
don't say it was a dream, that your ears deceived you,
don't degrade yourself with empty hopes like these.
As one long prepared, and full of courage,
as is right for you who were given this kind of city,
go firmly to the window
and listen with deep emotion;
but not with the whining pleas of a coward;
listen - your final pleasure - to the voices,
to the exquisite music of that strange procession;
and say good-bye to her,
to the Alexandria you are losing."

Next morning, dressed in shorts, t-shirts, sandals, and floppy hats, Doran and Alarice set out along the coastal road for Mykonos Town. As they approached the harbor, the village spread before them like a brilliant jewel set against the blue infinity of the Aegean. Descending a long flight of stone stairs, they found themselves at a dock where fishing boats were moored. Some of the fishermen were mending nets, while others attended to boat repairs. One swarthy old salt was pounding an octopus against a low wall.

But Mykonos was not so easily defined. Walking so presumptuously up one of the alley-like streets with a hip-swinging gate came a young, Nordic woman in a leopard skin body suit; while just around the corner, in the saving shade of a two-story building, a vendor selling figs and melons and sprigs of verbena off the back of his donkey waited for customers. Next to a small fountain, near the center of an almost impossible-to-find courtyard, a savvy Greek businessman negotiated contracts on a cellular phone. Widows dressed in black carried their shopping baskets from one market to another, while chic ingénues lingered at outdoor cafes, beneath umbrellas advertising Dutch beer.

By day, Mykonos meant going to the beach. Around eleven each morning the fine yellow sands of Paradise and Super Paradise, Elia, or Platos Ialos began collecting sun worshippers. Privileged sybarites with money, pseudo-style, and pampered lives embraced the ritual of a numb morning after a night of hedonistic intensity. The searing Mediterranean sun offered a different kind of delirium, one which devotees occasionally punctuated by a sobering splash in the water. Off came the *sarongs* and *pareos*, for the style here was decidedly *au naturel*.

Together, Doran and Alarice lay on the wide beach, building castles in the sand and watching ships upon the far-off horizon. Alarice was in love. And the thought of returning to Rotterdam—one that she now rarely entertained—held little appeal. Filled with a light so pervasive in the Cyclades, Alarice finally recognized the redundant darkness in which she'd been living. All around were little reminders that life was meant to be enjoyed, not endured. High tension fought stubbornly for its place, but on Mykonos such an internal battle was lost before it ever began.

While Doran would have looked pedestrian in a tuxedo, Alarice could look stunning in the simplest dress. His soft features and relaxed posture always seemed to undermine any attempt made at elegance, while Alarice could put on some costume jewelry and a little make-up and somehow look dressed-up. So they made an unlikely couple as they strolled past the cafés, bars, and boutiques. They watched celebrities and hangers-on, ingénues and castaways, *nouveau riche* and *wannabes*. At Piero's there was a nightly drag show, down the street a Moroccan snake charmer.

The setting sun shone like a huge pink disc through the evening haze as it slipped below the waterline, and Doran and Alarice watched the show of colors from an outdoor table at a restaurant in 'Little Venice'. The fishing boats had returned to the harbor for the night, and the sails had been taken down from the windmills on the hill behind them. Eating squid and drinking *retsina*, they became lost in one another. Shared experience, commonality, touching fingertips and intermingling souls, a sense of escape and irrational freedom, vitality and the as yet unspoken prospect of a shared destiny, a glimpse of antiquity and eternity: all these sensations were instigated and magnified by their surroundings, yet at once turned inward and transformed into a non-verbal language to which only they were attuned.

Doran felt a little restless at Remezzo Discotheque, where the revelers seemed pompous and pretentious. Closing his eyes, he could envision only clothes—no faces. It was hot inside the cavernous room, and the music was earsplitting. Alarice was accustomed to such places; she had gone to *Melkweg* and *Paradiso Club* in Amsterdam when she was a student at Leiden. Doran's taste was usually more refined, nevertheless he found this display of writhing bodies and high priced fashions to be entertaining.

By four o'clock in the morning they were dancing in the stroboscopic glow at Arco Club. Nearly exhausted, they fell time after time into one another's arms. Oh, there were many wet kisses, relinquished inhibitions, the laughter of submission. Might the blaring music never stop? Not until seven the next morning, when the sky was getting light and the orgiastic cycle would begin again.

THE ISLAND OF SANTORINI was altogether different. Borne out of cataclysmic upheaval, this dusky hulk emerged from the deep blue water like a dream out of forbidden remembrance. Located where two of Earth's plates meet, Santorini's precarious identity stood perpetually on the edge of reconstruction. Sailing swiftly past the stunning cliffs and chasms, the luminescent villages on top of the escarpment were reminiscent of snow-capped peaks, but of course they were the homes and shops of the post-Minoan descendants.

At Athinios Harbor the reception was different from other Cycladic islands. An intense-looking mule keeper charged five hundred drachmae for a ride on one of his animals to make the spiraling climb to Thira Town. Doran was an experienced equestrian, but when he tried to assume control, the persnickety mule adamantly refused the reign and took off, headlong up the trail it knew from memory. Looking a bit panic-stricken, Alarice followed directly behind. The mule keeper walked behind *her* mount, his hands holding tightly to the mule's tail as he cursed the animals in Greek for motivation.

"Doran!" Alarice called. "How do I control this animal?"

"Maybe he knows where he's supposed to go. Give yourself over to fate," he advised. "Could be they are taking us to Paradise!"

Once in Thira Town, they walked along a cliffside path to Firostefani. There, a suave and elegant Italian expatriate who lived in a lovely villa offered them a room. The room they were given was quite large and painted white. It had marble floors and arched doorways, and from the private terrace they had an unobstructed view of the volcano, as well as a marvelous perspective from which to watch incoming vessels or admire the fiery sunsets. That night they dined on baked eggplant and Santorini wine. Next morning Doran rented a scooter to take them around the island.

It was intensely bright as they rode the underpowered motor scooter to the Akrotiri digs, one of the pre-eminent archeological sites of the century. Around 1500 BC, a once-in-an-epoch earthquake had totally buried a progressive civilization in ash and pumice. Walking over the ancient city's paved streets, Alarice was enthralled by the advancement of the Minoan society. The homes had been two and three stories tall, with frescoed walls detailing contact with Egypt and various other African cultures. They'd had wood-crafted furniture, fired pottery, and even indoor plumbing!

Much to Doran's surprise, Alarice approached Professor Dumas, who was in charge of the excavation, and asked if she might participate in some small way. "I have no experience in archeological excavations," she told him, "but I'm willing to do almost anything. I'll move dirt, service equipment, or fix lunch—anything!"

"How long are you staying on Santorini?" he asked, apparently impressed by her eagerness and sincerity.

"My time is my own," Alarice said.

"There is no pay," he warned. "These lworkers come here from the university in Athens to volunteer their time."

"I don't care about making money at this," she said.

"Okay. Come here tomorrow," he said. "I will put you to work."

On the far side of the island they discovered Perissa Beach (an eight-kilometer-long stretch of black sand), a dramatic mountainside (on top of which were the Greek and Roman ruins of ancient Thira), and the seaside village of Kamari (so picturesque that one might want never to leave). Sipping cold drinks at a beachside bar, Doran said to Alarice, "Whatever possessed you to ask for a job at Akrotiri?"

"I've been interested in archeology since I was a young girl," she told him. "I've often regretted that I did not pursue my interest when I was at university. But it was never really an option. As I've told you, my course was determined long before I ever went away to Leiden."

"I think it's tragic that people subvert their dreams and

desires," Doran said.

"I agree. At least in principle... But here is an opportunity to indulge my long-felt fantasy to dig up old bones and unearth shards of pre-historic pottery. Why pass up the chance?"

"Why not?" said Doran.

The hot days of August passed with Alarice going off to Akrotiri to work and Doran riding across the island on the rented scooter to Perissa to swim and jog along the expansive black sand beach. Around four o'clock, she would return from the site looking filthy but happy. Brown as cinnamon, Doran would come riding up by six. They would shower together, and then make love as the sciroccos came in from northern Africa. The long white curtains in front of the terrace door blew gently in the breeze, the air coming into the room cooling their torpid bodies.

They arrived at the Oasis Bar in Oia each evening before sunset, and over glasses of a luscious Santorini wine called *Volcano*, they watched the star-like lights of Thira Town coming on. Streaks of violet color in the sky intimated the coming change of season, but for now they continued to bask in the warm currents of late summer.

At Karra's Taverna, they watched happy dancers whirl and writhe to the strains of bouzouki music.

"How is the work going at Akrotiri?" Doran inquired.

"Professor Dumas says we will soon be finished for the season. But it's been wonderful," Alarice related. "Besides meeting you, it's the highlight of my holiday."

She took Doran's hand. In turn, he squeezed hers. Upon this stunning precipice, they each understood that a decision regarding their future together would soon be necessary.

CHAPTER 19
A LOVERS' QUARREL

THE TWO AUSTRALIANS, Matthew Niven and Brandon Harrison, were happy to sip ouzo and play cards during the dinner hour, but after midnight they were ready for Corfu's night life. Glad to have the company of a Greek *kamaki* and a vivacious Dutch girl, they'd invited Yanni and Gisela to meet them at Taverna Loyiza Hara-Theou so the four of them could go dancing at the discos in Ypsos. At one-thirty the party was just gaining momentum at *Disco J'ai Moi!*

Gisela was in an especially festive mood tonight and danced with all three of her escorts. She genuinely liked the two Australians, particularly Brandon Harrison. The attraction, she realized, was frivolous and purely physical. When Brandon looked at her with his dark, warm eyes, she returned the stare. Her expression was filled with innuendo. Of course nothing was going to happen between them. They both knew it was only a harmless game, which made the flirtation all the more fascinating.

After four-thirty, Brandon and Matthew left *J'ai Moi* on

their scooters. The crowd was thinning out now, and Yanni suggested that they ride back to Glyfada. "Okay," Gisela said. "I'm tired anyhow."

They did not talk as they rode across the island on Yanni's motorbike. He gunned the engine to capacity, and Gisela held tightly to his waist so she would not be thrown off the back of the bike as he accelerated.

Once inside the apartment at Glyfada, Yanni broke into a tirade. "How could you do this to me?" he screamed.

"What did I do?"

"You not only expose yourself as a whore, but you humiliate me as well!"

Gisela threw up her arms in amazement. She stormed from one side of the room to the other, looking for some inanimate object she might pick up and hurl at him. "How dare you call me a whore!" she boiled.

"You are a whore! You were so obvious with him that everyone could see your lust."

"You are ridiculous, Yanni! We were just dancing and having a little fun."

"You call it *fun*, I call it degrading."

"I do not accept your stupid jealousy," said Gisela. "You are vain and arrogant. What makes you think you must possess me? If you insist on treating me with such disrespect, get out!"

"You can't throw me out, Gisela," Yanni snorted, "because I'm leaving by my own choice!" He put out his chest like a rooster and slammed the door behind him.

Gisela made herself hot milk on top of the electric stove so she might calm down before trying to sleep.

LIVING BY HERSELF AT THE GLYFADA APARTMENT, Gisela spent every day at the beach swimming, sunbathing, and writing in her journal. Her ill-fated affair with Yanni Thromos was now finished, and she was not inclined to begin a romance with Brandon Harrison even though she found him attractive. She began each day with a leisurely breakfast at Taverna Loyiza Hara Theou. She really liked Leonidas, and a friendship between herself and Katerina seemed to grow. Then, one day in August, Katerina left for her home on Crete. Another void was created in Gisela's Corfu existence. The day-in, day-out beach routine became a little boring, so she sometimes rode the bus to Corfu Town to explore the city and shop.

Searching for the OTE building in Corfu Town, she was directed to a side street off Avenue George Theotokis. Inside, the place was thronged with young travelers needing to make long distance phone calls, so she was forced to take a number and wait her turn for a telephone. Finally her number was called, and she entered the phone booth. She placed a call to the Netherlands, and when the operator answered, Gisela found it odd to hear the sound of her native language. A moment later she was speaking with her father.

"Where are you, Gisela?" he asked her.

"I'm calling from Greece. The Island of Corfu."

"Is your sister there, too?"

"No, Papa. Alarice has gone to Athens."

"Why did you not go with her, Gisela?"

"I preferred to stay here."

"Alarice left you by yourself? Perhaps it would be best for you to come home," her father suggested. "Do you need money? I can send some."

"No, Papa," said Gisela. "I have plenty of money. I told Alarice I would stay here and wait for her to return. There's no need for me to come home now."

"When will your sister return?" he asked.

"We left it open. Not long now, I'm sure."

"Gisela, I never wanted to tell you this sad news on the telephone, but since you are not certain when Alarice will return from Athens, or when you will be coming home, I'm afraid I have no choice."

There was a prolonged silence on the line, each waiting for the other to make some commitment. Finally, Gisela broke the pause. "What's the matter, Papa?"

"Maude is ill," he said somberly.

"What is it? What's wrong with her?"

"Parkinson's Disease," he told her.

She caught her breath as she heard the dire news. Clutching the telephone receiver tightly, she tried to contain her emotions, but a tear came immediately to her eye. Her jaws closed firmly, her lips pursed. "Papa, how serious is it?" she asked.

"It's too soon to know," he told her. "Dr. Voorwinkel has not actually confirmed the diagnosis, but indications are not good. Do you have a way to contact your sister?"

"I have no choice but to wait here until she returns," Gisela told her father.

"The situation is *not* critical," Frederick Van Zyl paraphrased his wife's doctor. "The degeneration can be quite devastating, but people with Parkinson's often live long lives. And of course you have read about fetal tissue transplants, Gisela..."

"How did she take the news?" Gisela asked, choking back a sob.

"You know Maude. She has a long view."

"Papa, I'm so sorry."

"Come home when you can, darling."

Frederick hung up the receiver before Gisela was ready to sign off. She had important questions to ask. She felt the need to intervene. How could Maude have sent both her daughters away while suspecting serious illness? Of course she had wanted only that they have this happy, carefree time together, and come to finally know one another. Gisela hung up the phone, paid her tariff, and walked back to San Rocco Square to catch the afternoon bus back to Glyfada.

AS MODESTOS approached the entryway to the Glyfada apartment, he saw Gisela coming up the path from the shore. He waited at the door for her to arrive.

"I am happy I found you here," he said. They went inside together. "What do you need?" Modestos inquired. "More wine? I bring you more wine. Fresh eggs perhaps? How about spring water? You like spring water, eh?"

"Thank you, Modestos," said Gisela. "You don't need to bring me anything. I buy all my supplies at the market in Corfu Town."

Modestos walked through the French doors onto the terrace to look at the sea. He had always loved this view of Glyfada Beach. Soon he would come here with Sophia and Yanni before the boy went away to school. Gisela followed him outside and they sat at the small table. Searching this familiar sparkling horizon, Modestos said to the girl, "It is not good that you are here alone."

"Why not?" Gisela wanted to know. "I like my privacy."

"That word, *privacy*! I have never understood it. The nearest word we have in the Greek language is *monaxia*, which translates to 'isolation' in English. But what can a person do alone? You die alone. A person must have *parea*, friends! And what about the others? When do you expect Doran and Alarice to return?"

Gisela answered, "It won't be long, I suspect."

"It's not that I want to push you out," Modestos explained. "You are my friends, each and every one! And I want you to stay as long as you like."

"When Doran and Alarice return, I'm certain my sister and I will be going home," Gisela informed. "I've learned that my mother is ill."

Modestos' face immediately expressed his concern. He leaned forward so he could look more directly into Gisela's eyes. "I am very sorry. What is the illness?" he asked.

"Parkinson's Disease," she told him.

"Yes, it is important to be with your family when there is crisis," he consoled.

"Since I spoke with my father, I've been worried senseless," Gisela confided.

"I understand," said Modestos. "But it is useless to worry. There is nothing you can do until you return home. Even then it is in the hands of God."

Gisela touched him lightly on the shoulder. "Thank you for everything you have done for us, Modestos. It is impossible to imagine what Corfu might have been like without you."

He dismissed the compliment out of embarrassment. "I wish your mother a full recovery," Modestos said as he stood up to leave.

CHAPTER 20
INTRUSIONS UPON TIMELESS WAYS

RATHER THAN DRIVE directly across the island to reach Corfu Town, Modestos decided to take the long route around the east side of Kerkyra. At Kanoni, an elevated vantage point revealed a vista of which he was particularly fond. From a cafe located at the pinnacle he could easily see the little church at Valcherne, as well as tiny Mouse Island. He could also see the jet landing strip that had been built just beyond the scenic lagoon where he'd caught fish as a boy.

Over espresso, he stared at the familiar landscape. The sunset had begun to streak the clouds with softer shades of color—magenta and orange, rose and pale yellow—all contrasted by the fading blue backdrop of the Adriatic sky.

Considering the proposed assignment on Cyprus, he could not help contemplating the fact that his father had left his family some forty years before. Aphrodite had never forgiven the husband she never saw again. Modestos allowed that these circumstances were somewhat different, nevertheless he would be forced to leave Sophia behind as he traded his time and expertise to the army in return for Yanni's university tuition. Their family would be scattered on different shores: he at work on Cyprus; Yanni studying in Italy; and Sophia at home on Kerkyra. Certainly Sophia was up to the responsibilities that would be required of her: she was a *drasteria*, a woman of action. And he was confident that his marriage and his family could survive the painful separation, though his heart was aching as he pondered leaving his life on Corfu.

He watched an Olympic jet make its approach, and then heard the roar of its engines as it glided over the lagoon and finally touched down half a kilometer overland. Surely the plane carried more tourists, and as a modern businessman he should have been happy to see them arrive; but for the moment Modestos recalled the simplicity of his boyhood. Such a place was Kerkyra then!

AS MODESTOS walked through the door of his apartment, the phone was ringing. He experienced a moment of *deja-vu*. Picking up the receiver, he was informed by an operator that the call was from Athens.

"Thromos, is that you? This is General Stratiotis."

"*Kalispera*, General."

"I am wondering about your decision, Thromos," he said, coming directly to the point.

"General, I have made up my mind to go to Cyprus," Modestos conveyed.

"I knew you would not let me down, Thromos."

"Relocating poses significant problems," Modestos admitted. "None that I cannot overcome, however."

"Your service will be invaluable, Modestos."

"I hope I do not disappoint you, General. When and where am I to report?"

"One month, if you can have your affairs in order by that time. Phone ahead, and I'll have someone from my staff meet you at Nicosia."

"Very well," said Modestos. "You will hear from me

before September is finished."

Replacing the receiver, Modestos sank into the chair beside the telephone table. The finality of his decision weighed upon him like a giant stone. He took a single, deep breath, held it for a moment, and then exhaled before his stuttering sobs began. He knew he was agreeing to work on Cyprus for all the *right* reasons, still for twenty minutes he could not stem the flow of his tears. He cried over his exile, and for Kerkyra's changing face. Only after total darkness had fallen upon the room did he pull himself together and summon the cognizance to realize that neither Sophia nor Yanni were there to see his desolation.

It was after eight when Sophia arrived home. In the fading light of evening she could see Modestos sitting alone in the parlor. She went immediately to him. Kissing him on the cheek, she tasted the residue of salty tears, now dried upon his skin. Though she made no comment regarding her discovery. "Sorry I'm late," she apologized.

"I am waiting for Yanni," said Modestos. "I am eager to know the results of his entrance exam."

"Then he is not home yet?"

"Not yet."

"Are you hungry?" she asked.

"Not much," he answered uncharacteristically.

Sophia looked at him with concern. "Is something wrong?" she asked. "Are you sick?"

"I am not sick," he said.

"What is it? You're not yourself."

"I have news," he said. "Perhaps this is not such a happy day."

Realizing they had reached the focal point of Modestos' discomfiture, Sophia fell silent. She put her hands upon his shoulder in a show of closeness and support. "Tell me," she said simply.

"Stratiotis called," he related. "I report to him at Nicosia in one month."

In frustration, Sophia bit her thumbnail. Tears welled in her dark eyes. She wanted to show anger but could not. She loved Modestos, and she understood the reason he had accepted the military posting. How would she get through the days ahead? How would she endure the empty nights? Perhaps this was the right time to tell him her secret...

"Ever since you returned from Athens last spring," she said, "I have known this day would come."

"We have both known it was inevitable," Modestos said.

"And I know you don't really want to go..."

"But I must!"

"And Yanni will be away in Italy..."

"It is necessary," said Modestos.

"The idea of being alone terrifies me," Sophia told him. "What will I do?"

"You will have responsibilities," Modestos told her. "You will run the *dhomatia*, and it's become obvious that Aphrodite will be needing more help."

"Well and good," said Sophia. "But I must have more than that. Oh, I know most Greek men are skeptical when their little *nikokyroules* begin talking *feminismos*, but as you say, it's a new world out there."

"What are you trying to tell me?" he asked.

"I have lied to you, Modestos!" she now freely confessed. "I have told you that on Wednesday evenings I go walking for fitness with my women friends along the Esplanade. It is untrue! Instead, for the past ten weeks, I have been to school learning how to operate a computer!"

Modestos was amazed. "A computer? Why?"

"To be part of something that will define the future," she reiterated from her class work. "I graduate next Wednesday evening," she said proudly.

Modestos smiled for the first time that evening. "And let us hope Yanni has fared so well," he said as he embraced her.

APHRODITE THROMOS heard the ticking of her clock as the hour passed eleven, but she did not pull back the bedclothes. She did not take down her hair, nor remove her shoes, nor her knee-high black hose. She did not light her candles, nor pray to the icons of saints. She ate not a morsel and drank not a single cupful of water. Instead, she knelt upon the floor before her chest, handling her weavings, taking inventory of her belongings, putting right years of disarray.

"At last, Constantine Thromos, I shall have the chance to confront you!" she croaked as she fingered the disintegrating, yellowed fabric of her wedding dress. "Unless there is a Hell, and you feed the fire everlasting!"

Moths had long ago devoured the gown's veil, and their progress was well advanced on the remainder of the ancient garment. But the artifacts of youth no longer concerned Aphrodite, and she climbed to her feet in rage and disgust. Moving to the shelf where her photographs were displayed, she took down her favorite picture of Kostas, the one taken just before he'd left home to fight with the Resistance. Holding it to her heaving breast, she called to her dead son.

"Tonight my voice grows thin, my words fly away. My mind is havoc, and my namesake is laughing behind my back. My efforts have turned feeble."

She held the photograph to the light so she might look again upon the face of the son she had favored, but like the sparkle in Aphrodite's eyes, the remembered image was quick to fade, replaced by the likeness of one more immediately familiar.

"What boy is this?" she called. "Yanni, is that you?" She blinked her eyes, hoping for better definition. "What are you doing in your grandmother's chamber at this late hour?"

The grandson's eyes refused to meet her own, nevertheless she knew his features well. She spoke without fear, for she had come to accept visits such as this one.

"Soon Modestos is sending you away. To Italy, of all places! Yanni, you are no older than your uncle was when he left to fight the Nazis. Like Kostas, you are full of shining ideals, and full of recklessness, too. Kostas *never* came home. The loss of a son drove Constantine away, so you never knew your grandfather.

"I will never understand your father. Modestos remains determined to send you away to school. Another son of Greece gone away to distant shores..."

For Aphrodite, Yanni's expression conveyed the innocence of youth, yet she recognized the dark eyes staring back at her to be those of her son, Modestos, as well. In them she saw his hope and ambition; also Sophia's consistency.

"You, Yanni, have become my legacy! Only through you will Constantine's name be carried forward. The poetry of our language anchors our culture! Thromos: it means 'The Way'. It was a name I was proud to accept. Yet for you, Yanni, I am afraid it will become *just* a name, without special meaning.

"So hear your grandmother! It is *I* who bore the Twin Brethren to whom all Dorians pray. Castor and Pollux: one truly immortal; the other gaining life only through the love of his brother. 'Half thy time upon the earth and half within the golden domes of Heaven,' said Zeus. 'One day upon Olympus; the next in Hades! But never together!' Two stars are theirs: the Gemini, the Twins. But which brother truly dwells in Paradise? It is the *modest way* born of *love* and *beauty*."

Aphrodite closed the lid of her trunk, and the garments of her youth turned to dust. The force of emotion nearly took her breath as the gods and goddesses of Olympus whirled round her head.

Golden Aphrodite, the Cyprian who stirs with love all Creation, cannot bend nor ensnare three hearts...

"My son, help your Mother to lie down," she said.

"And, Modestos, know this: From the moment you drew your first breath, I have loved you without hesitation. I have loved you best; it is the legacy of a long life!"

Then came the knocking at her door—this time a gentle rap, not the incessant pounding that had interrupted her dreams and frightened her terribly at first—not the thunderous cacophony of taunting threats, accusations, lies, and vague inferences to which she had reluctantly become accustomed. No longer resisting, and pressing the photograph tightly to her chest, Aphrodite Thromos went heavily to the door and admitted the caller inside.

CHAPTER 21
A LONG JOURNEY'S END

DISEMBARKING AT PIREUS HARBOR after the seven-hour trip from Santorini, both Doran and Alarice were hungry, so they found sanctuary in the familiar darkness of the Eden Restaurant. Doran sipped a glass of soda contemplatively as the pattern Ravel's 'Bolero' wove itself into the fabric of his thoughts. Overhead a four-bladed fan created the false impression of a cooling breeze. "This odyssey of this journey is beginning to make sense to me," he told Alarice. "I'm considering *not* going home."

Alarice was not wholly surprised at this revelation. "Do you have the resources to live independently here in Greece?" she asked.

"My funds are not unlimited," Doran answered honestly. "Eventually I'll have to... Well, I don't know exactly what I might do. Though security is hardly the point of staying here."

Silently, Alarice totaled the sum of the past month's personal experience.

HAVING DECIDED TO FLY BACK TO CORFU rather than spend yet another night aboard a ferryboat, they bought tickets at a travel agency on an Olympic flight leaving Athens at five o'clock the next morning; and instead of renting a hotel room for an abbreviated night's sleep, they had also decided to spend the night waiting at the airport terminal. As darkness fell, they walked to Syntagma Square to catch the bus to Athens Airport.

Sitting on top of a railing in front of a kiosk, Doran watched as hundreds of Athenians went about their business. His eyes followed the frantic traffic—cars and trucks and motorcycles speeding through the roundabout, then down tributaries. Acknowledging feelings of release and discovery, as well as his bond with Alarice, Doran had never felt more alive than at this moment.

He felt grateful to Modestos Thromos of Corfu, for he had given Doran an impression of Greece that would long endure: the importance of fresh food; of having hope; of being cheerful; of preserving history—or of letting it go. For Doran, Modestos was the embodiment of the Greek culture.

Mykonos was something else: pink pelicans scolding sybarites as they nursed hangovers in the cafés at noon. Naxos Island was quaint with its weavings and wines and antiquities; Marsoupa Kontiza Koyka had been so kind and genuine. Traits such as these might be lost, Doran feared. Temptations of the material, electronic world—the digital world!—soon would be knocking upon their door, and the Greeks would *not* resist. And when at last they came to terms with what it was they'd lost, the impending sadness might be so much to bear that Doran wondered whether the Greeks would indeed be able to live with it.

Yesterday morning, on Santorini, he had awakened again to the sounds of roosters crowing, bleating goat kids, and braying donkeys. In truth, he had become quite accustomed to this barnyard serenade—so wild, so ancient. Yet aboard the ship it was all too evident that the Greek children were already addicted to video games. They competed aggressively for position in front of the screen. These children would not become shepherds; they would not care about fresh food in the same way Modestos cared about it. Of course, maybe nobody cared that much!

The wait passed minute by minute, but at 5:00 a.m. they boarded the Olympic flight, and even before the passengers were settled and the seat belts fastened, the pilot took off on the North/South runway. Once airborne, the plane banked and headed out over the Saronic Gulf for the short flight to Corfu.

With Alarice's head resting upon his shoulder, Doran said in a soft voice, "After seeing how happy you were at Akrotiri, it's hard for me to imagine you back in Rotterdam working at your father's business."

"Are you suggesting I stay here with you?"

"Surely our feelings for one another are grounded here," he said.

The plane landed at six-fifteen, but it was ten o'clock before Doran and Alarice arrived at the Glyfada apartment. Even though each had a key, they decided to knock before going inside, as a courtesy to Gisela.

With her hair pinned up and lotion smeared all over her face, Gisela opened the door and was delighted to see Alarice and Doran standing there. "Arissa, thank God you're finally back," she said as she hugged her sister. She hugged Doran as well, careful not to get lotion on his clothes.

"I hope you weren't worried," Alarice said.

"It's not that," said Gisela. "How was your trip?"

"Fantastic!" said Alarice.

"Where did you go?" Gisela wanted to know.

"First we went to Athens," Alarice told her. "After that, we sailed to several islands in the Cyclades. How are things for you here? How is Yanni?" she asked.

"Actually, I've had a peaceful time since you left," Gisela related. "And I'm afraid Yanni is out of the picture."

"What happened?" Doran asked.

"One night we went to the discotheques at Ypsos with Matthew Niven and Brandon Harrison. I'm sure you remember them... Well, we were all pretty drunk... Brandon and I were dancing. Totally innocent, you understand... Well, Yanni couldn't stand the competition, and he began playing a stupid game of jealousy and control. I'm *not* one to be manipulated. Arissa knows that! Anyway, when we came back here to the apartment, he challenged me. I told him to back away, and there was a big fight. At my invitation, he left. I haven't seen him since!"

"That's terrible," said Alarice.

"Not really," said Gisela drolly. She turned and walked back into the bathroom to wipe the lotion off her face and take down her hair.

Doran sat on the daybed. Rubbing tired eyes, he looked round the familiar apartment and realized that if he meant to remain on Corfu—preferably with Alarice, but perhaps by himself—he was going to have to find another place to live.

"You look as though you're getting ready to go somewhere," Alarice called to her sister.

Gisela came out of the bathroom again, for the news she was about to convey was better told face to face. She took a deep breath before she spoke. "Night before last," she related, "Aphrodite Thromos died. The funeral is being held this morning in Puthena Village."

"Poor Modestos," said Doran.

"He came by last night bringing spring water," Gisela said. "That's when I learned about it."

With a look of concern upon her face, Alarice turned to Doran and said, "I know you're exhausted, but we should attend the funeral."

"Yes, of course," said Doran.

"I'll get ready immediately," said Alarice.

"The bus leaves for Puthena in forty-five minutes," Gisela informed them.

FATHER DIMITRIOS stood before the assemblage inside the small, whitewashed church with the bright blue dome and chanted Orthodox verses appropriate to the somber occasion. Aphrodite lay in a linen-lined casket draped with lilies, irises, and baby's breath, and crowned by ten miniature golden domes with lighted candles showing through scarlet portices. Her finest weavings and her collection of pictures were laid round her. The family Thromos—Modestos, Sophia, Yanni, and Tassoula—sat together in the front of the church. The adults wept while Yanni sat stoically with eyes focused straight ahead. Sitting behind the family were Modestos' longtime friends: Giorgos Zervas, Diakatos Leonidas, Panos, the baker, Michalis Delfakis, as well as Mayor Asprouli. Off to one side of the church sat four mourners, because that was the way in Greece of old, and because Aphrodite was of that time. And seated respectfully at the back of the church were three foreigners, lthree *xeni*—a man from America, and two sisters from the Netherlands. Modestos turned to look at these new friends and realized, for better or worse, that the Greeks—his own people—had become strangers unto themselves.

In flowing black robes, Father Dimitrios led the procession through the streets of Puthena Village to the cemetery. The pallbearers followed, then family and friends. They moved quickly and without a word. Those they passed stopped and bowed their heads or crossed themselves before hurrying away.

At graveside, the service was short. Before midday the casket was in the ground and covered with earth. Zervas went to Modestos and repeated his condolence before returning to work at his restaurant. Mayor Asprouli approached Tassoula and offered consolation. Leonidas stood off to the side and talked with Doran and Alarice.

Gisela noticed Yanni standing by himself and went to pay her respects.

"I'm sorry about your grandmother," she said.

"Thank you for coming, Gisela. I'm surprised to see you here. Aphrodite was an old woman. Her life was a full one."

"That may be true," she said, "but you can't help feeling the loss."

He nodded. With his hands in his pockets he turned, somewhat awkwardly, to face her. He knit his brow as he searched for the right words. "I have wanted to apologize to you ever since—"

"Never mind," she stopped him. "I am not angry with you."

"I was a fool."

Gisela nodded her agreement.

"You don't suppose..."

"I will be going home in a couple of days," said Gisela. "My mother is ill. I need to be with her."

"I'm sorry to hear it," he said. "I guess this is a day for being sorry."

"I guess so," she said.

"I failed my exam," he confided to her.

"It's not true!"

"I'm afraid so," he said, eyes lowered.

"It's partially my fault, I suppose," she acknowledged.

"How can I blame you? I chose not to study. I got exactly what I deserved."

"Is your father upset?" she asked.

"I suppose so. Though with Aphrodite's passing he hasn't had a chance to say much about it."

"What are you going to do now?"

"My father has taken a military position on Cyprus," he told her, "so I will stay here to help my mother with the *dhomatia*. I'm going to be serious and study all year long, and next year I *will* pass the entrance exam!"

"You can do it if you try," she said.

"I would like to write to you, Gisela, and tell you how things are going here at Kerkyra."

"I would like that," Gisela said.

"I wanted you to know how I really feel," Yanni said.

"I think I know," she said as she kissed him lightly on the cheek. "Good-bye, Yanni. And good luck to you!"

"Good-bye, Gisela."

Doran went to speak with Modestos, while Alarice wandered off by herself for a quiet moment. Pressing the hand of his friend, Doran offered his sympathy. Sophia patted her husband's shoulder as he spoke to the American. "I am surprised to see you here, Doran. When did you return to Kerkyra?"

"Just this morning," Doran explained. "Alarice and I flew from Athens."

"A sad day for me," said Modestos, full of emotion. "Very sad."

"I've lost both my parents," Doran told him. "It's not easy."

"At least not for those of us left behind," Modestos speculated.

"I'm considering staying here on Corfu over winter," Doran told him.

"The sand is always shifting, eh, my friend?" said Modestos. "Just when you think your foundation is set, cracks begin to appear."

Doran looked curiously at the Greek.

"In two weeks," Modestos continued, "I am leaving for the Island of Cyprus. I never thought I would leave Kerkyra, but my situation demands that I go to Cyprus for two years to work with the army. Imagine... Modestos a soldier again at the age of fifty-one!"

"Sometimes a choice is no choice at all," said Doran.

"What about the women?" Modestos asked.

"I suppose Gisela will be returning home soon. I hope Alarice decides to stay. There is no decision yet."

"I wish you all the best," said Modestos. "In a few days

I will come to see you at Glyfada. Let me know if there is any way I can help you. You are a good friend, and I am at your service."

"Thank you, Modestos. You *are* a good man."

Standing alone underneath the canopy of a plane tree, Alarice found herself profoundly affected by the death of Aphrodite. Though she had never really known the old woman, some unfathomable voice whispered to her that Corfu would never again be the same.

Approaching softly, Sophia brought Alarice out of her meditation by putting her arm around the Dutch girl's waist. "I feel very sad," Alarice told Sophia.

"All children miss their mothers," said Sophia.

Alarice now felt inclined to consider sweeping changes for her future. She tried desperately to balance her long felt commitment to tradition with perspectives that were new and exciting: Here I stand, she thought, among this family of Greeks as they bury their matriarch, and even in this time of grief, their light is intense. I have detested my life in Rotterdam longer than I care to remember. The density of the North, the brown, weathered buildings, the perfect liberalism: it's all too much! Of course it's not Father's fault. He directed me as he thought best. But the monotony is killing me. Do I stay or do I go? I want to stay. I want to...

By late afternoon they were back at the Glyfada apartment. Though Doran was feeling tired, he decided to walk down the beach to Taverna Loyiza Hara-Theou for a drink. He wanted to continue the conversation with Leonidas started at the cemetery.

Alarice, too, was fatigued from two days of travel, followed by a funeral. Still, sleep would not come. Feeling helplessly excited about her recent experience, she told Gisela about their time in Athens with Rudolph 'Pablo' Grossmund and his friend Jurgen Klimpsch. As Gisela listened patiently, Alarice told her about the Valley of the Butterflies on Paros Island, and about the mountain villages of Naxos. She described the compulsive nightlife on Mykonos, and she went on and on about her job at the Akrotiri digs on Santorini. Finally, she confessed to her sister that she was deeply in love with Doran Seeger.

"Arissa, there is something I must tell you," Gisela said as she began stroking her sister's hair.

Sensing gravity in Gisela's voice, Alarice turned to face her. "What is it?" she asked.

"About a week ago I talked to Papa on the telephone. He told me that Mama is very sick."

"What's wrong?" Alarice asked.

"It's Parkinson's Disease," she said. "They don't know how serious yet."

Alarice bit her lower lip in recompense as the events of the spring and summer began to overwhelm her. "Do you think she knew she was ill before she sent us on holiday?" Alarice asked her sister.

"I think she may have suspected it," said Gisela.

"What else did Papa say?" Alarice wanted to know.

"He wants us to come home as soon as possible."

"But how can I leave Doran?" Alarice asked. "And how can I leave this place?"

Alarice shook her head as tears flowed from her eyes.

OVER A GLASS OF WINE at Taverna Loyiza Hara-Theou, Doran pondered his own fate. Back home certain nebulous forces had him right where they wanted him—in a straight jacket, his emotions frozen, talking in clichés, confined within narrow limits. Here in Greece he felt free, though he was not altogether certain he could trust himself to make the most of this new latitude. He recalled the first time he'd seen Alarice Van Zyl at Puthena Beach. Sitting contemplatively upon a giant sunflower, her back turned toward him. Her hair was pinned underneath her big floppy hat. Several mirage-like, Egyptian pyramids floated upon Ionian waters. A solitary island near the horizon... No denying he was in love with her.

Turning to Leonidas, he spoke man to man: "Something tells me *not* to leave Greece—to start all over again—to make Hellas my home. But I don't know..."

"Life is short, Doran," said Leonidas.

"Maybe too short for mistakes," he said.

"Look! Each year hundreds of Greeks leave their homeland for America. Now you tell me you want to emigrate *to* Greece." Leonidas laughed. "I'm sure some would say that you are a crazy man. But if your heart tells you to stay, then who are you to argue? You know the Greeks. They will always help you."

"It's true, isn't it?"

"Drink your wine, Doran. *Yamas*, my friend!"

AS THE SUN WAS GOING DOWN, Alarice found Doran sitting on the beach behind the familiar outcropping of rocks just beyond the *taverna*. He had his sandals off, and the gentle waves were coming just close enough to bathe his feet. Alarice sat beside him and wrapped her arms around her knees. For a time they shared silently the sights and sounds of a place where they had first come to know one another, and fallen in love. They lay on the warm sand and talked in whispers.

"What happens to *us* when the light of Hellas fades from our memories?" she said.

Her words left him breathless. "What are you telling me?"

"It's not you, Doran. Of course you know that. When I think about making a life with you in this magnificent place, I visualize such wonderful possibilities! But while we were away, Gisela talked with my father. We've learned that my mother is seriously ill."

Remembering the confusion surrounding his father's final days, Doran said, "Of course you must go home. What else is there to do?"

Anxious for rapprochement, Alarice conveyed an alternative. "Why not come back to the Netherlands with me? We'll take all the beautiful memories of this summer with us. Rotterdam is a dynamic city; I know you could find work there. We can live in my apartment."

"Or you could return here once everything is resolved…"

Through her tears Alarice saw the evening's first star appear, and no longer able to deny the reality of this impasse, she fervently wished that blind Eros, his arrows dipped in fire, would never leave her heart. Doran's own vision was fading with the light of day.

THEY RESERVED PASSAGE ON DIFFERENT SHIPS, each sailing half an hour apart. Alarice and Gisela were booked on a ferry leaving for Venice at ten that evening. Doran had reserved a cabin aboard the *Espresso Venecia*, bound for the Italian port of Brindisi. His ship was to depart at ten-thirty.

Modestos had promised to drive them to the dock, and he arrived at the Glyfada apartment to pick them up around six o'clock. Driving across the island toward Corfu Town, the ever-engaging host offered a small repast at his city apartment. Surely there was time for one more drink, one last meal together!

"Sophia is not home," Modestos apologized as they entered the apartment. "Tonight she receives her diploma from computer school. This is not a traditional course of study for Greek women, and I am very proud of her. So, please excuse me if the food is not 'important' tonight. And I cannot stay at the dock with you, my friends, because it would make me late for the ceremony. I am sure you understand."

"No problem, Modestos," said Doran.

"Look! Alarice, come with me into the kitchen," said Modestos in his rapid-fire style. "Sophia has left our supper on the stove. I will show you how to operate the burners. And I will bring some wine from the cellar!"

Gatos, the cat, came out of Modestos' bedroom. Gisela

allowed the animal to curl up on her lap. She stroked the cat behind its ears as she looked round the humble surroundings. Not inclined to ponder her own fate, she worried a little about her mother, and felt ill-at-ease for Doran and Alarice.

Left momentarily alone in the dining room, Doran was astounded by the simplicity of Modestos' life - a man who worked sometimes without sleep to try to save enough money to send his less than diligent son, Yanni, to school in Italy. Doran found himself continually touched by Modestos' willingness to share whatever he had - his home, a simple meal of eggplant and potatoes, his free time, his abundant spirit, his love for natural things like a beautiful sunset or a good beach.

Feeling the impact of separation before the fact, Alarice was glad for the diversion of cooking. In less than a week she knew she would be back in Rotterdam, struggling to fulfill expectations, and though it rendered a bittersweet pain, lshe consciously tried to imprint upon her memory as much of the summer's ecstacy as possible.

Modestos returned from the cellar with yet another bottle of Corfu wine. In an almost neurotic flurry of movement, with his attention divided, he was simultaneously slicing a loaf of bread and showing off his television set, on which he received CNN. "Just like Americas, eh?" he said.

Dinner was a ten-minute affair with no clean up. Then it was time to go to the port. Before they were out the door, Modestos loaded their arms with several oranges from his fruit basket, which were meant for breakfast aboard ship next morning.

At the dock they hugged and kissed and promised to write letters at Christmastime. They promised one another that they would return to Kerkyra next summer. But was such a return engagement really possible? Between the delight of newfound friendships and the sorrow of imminent separation, their emotions vacillated without mercy. Already they were old friends—friends of the best kind. The night was black, but the lights from the two ferryboats docked in their berths illuminated their faces. Each searched the face of the other for something not yet recognized, that he or she might squeeze one single drop more from this emotional plethora.

After a final good-bye, Modestos turned to leave. He never looked back, and Doran wondered how many others he had put aboard night ships leaving Kerkyra. Now it was time for the Van Zyl sisters to board their ship, and Gisela put her arms around Doran's neck and hugged him quickly. She whispered a message of affection in his ear, then turned and walked up the pier. But the intensity of the embrace he received from Alarice caught Doran totally off guard, and he found himself swept out to sea and thrown over waves, swallowed by troughs until he was finally washed ashore on that solitary island in her ever so personal fantasy. "No matter what happens," Alarice said, "I will not forget our time together."

Turning away, she ran for the ship, and as Doran watched her climb the iron steps to the deck, he was overcome with a sense of urgency and panic.

Life passes so quickly, he thought, but I am forever grateful for this beacon at Kerkyra. Move quickly, he told himself, before it is too late...

ABOUT THE AUTHOR

David A. Ross was born January 6, 1953 in Chicago, Illinois. He attended William Rainy Harper College for three semesters before dropping out. After being excused from military service on a physical deferment, he moved to a remote area of northern Idaho, where he lived a subsistence lifestyle in a rustic log cabin without plumbing or electricity for more than a year. Returning to Chicago, he worked for Follett Publishers for a short time before relocating to Denver, Colorado. There he taught music for twenty-five years, wrote three unpublished novels, and worked as an associate editor for *Southwest Art Magazine* before moving first to Arizona then to New Mexico.

From 1987 through 2000, he engaged in a series of twelve extended trips to Europe, as well as several to the South Pacific. In 2001, he relocated permanently to Greece where he currently lives with his wife, author Kelly Huddleston, and works as an author, editor and Internet developer. *The Virtual Life of Fizzy Oceans* is his sixth published novel. Also to his credit is *Sacrifice and the Sweet Life*, a collection of short stories and poetry, and *Good Morning Corfu: Living Abroad Against All Odds*, a memoir.